R2

05
005
105

16

08

007
007

007
08

09

2010
2011
2011

MAXWELL'S REUNION

MAXWELL'S
REUNION

M. J. Trow

Hodder & Stoughton

A division of Hodder Headline

The right of M. J. Trow to be identified as the Author
of the Work has been asserted by him in accordance with the
Copyright, Designs and Patents Act 1988.

2 4 6 8 10 9 7 5 3 1

A CIP catalogue record for this book
is available from the British Library.

ISBN 0 340 76778 2

Typeset in Bembo by Hewer Text Ltd, Edinburgh
Printed and bound in Great Britain by
Clays Ltd, St Ives plc

Hodder & Stoughton
A division of Hodder Headline
338 Euston Road
London NW1 3BH

Chapter One

It was the Day of Days, the one they'd all dreamed of for years; the day the Headmaster shook their hands and called them by their Christian names. He who had never touched them before; he who never used a first name when a surname would do. The Great Man had no past, no future. He would not grow old as those who left grew old.

'Peter.' The name reverberated round the quad and echoed in the far cedars, bouncing off the sight screens and skimming the pale blue waters of the pool. To the others, he was Max, or Maxie, according to those strange intimacies that schoolboy hierarchies have. 'Oxford, isn't it?'

'Cambridge, sir,' the boy said, reflecting anew on how on the ball the Great Man was.

'Yes, of course. Philosophy.'

'History, sir.'

'Quite, quite. Anthony – Cambridge?'

'Oxford, sir.' None out of three wasn't bad.

Everyone had looked at Anthony Bingham, most of them not quite sure who he was. To all of them, for the last seven years of their educational apprenticeship, he'd been simply Cret. Short for Cretin. Not that any of them actually knew what a cretin was or how his height measured up.

The Headmaster worked his way down the line of the soon-to-be Old Boys in those purple ties the Upper Sixth habitually wore in their last term; a special privilege bestowed upon them so that the bursar could make even more money out of their parents. The Great Man had left off his gown and looked curiously small in his grey, clerical suit. His eyes still flashed fire but the voice that had been known to shatter glass in the chapel quad was soft and he was gentle. The hand that swung the cane now touched the shoulder. And, horror of horrors, he was human after all.

They'd wandered away after he'd dismissed them, one or two of them glancing back as the Great Man vanished into the shadows. There were sniggers, billowing on the breeze. Someone had once said, when they were all whining new bugs of eleven with their shining morning faces and new satchels, that whenever the Headmaster turned a corner, he was sneaking off for a date with Miss Shrivell, the octagenarian secretary of Halliards School. The boys themselves dreamed of Heaven with Miss Clarke, the Matron's number two. Many was the lad who ran deliberately into a rugger post just to have his head cradled by her.

The little host of leavers reached the seat on the dais over-looking the First Eleven Square, that hallowed turf where not even the Headmaster's dog was allowed to pee. Peter Maxwell ran his finger one last time over the words carved deep into the wood. 'Who spot the verb and stop the ball shall say if England stand or fall.' He'd never known who wrote it, but he could spot the verb with the best of 'em. That was the thing about the Romans – so predictable. They always put their verbs at the end of their sentences. He'd stopped many a ball too, not always in the heroic way of the First Eleven or the First Fifteen. Rugger balls usually stopped him, seconds before the opposing pack bore down in a slaughter of liniment and jockstraps. Cricket balls had magnetic cores designed to catch him in the crotch every time. And as for England standing or falling . . . well, do you really consider those things when you're eighteen, with the world at your feet?

In January, President de Gaulle had refused Britain's entry to the Common Market. 'Ungrateful bastard!' the boys of the Day of Days had agreed with their history master, mindful of what France owed to Britain in the dark days of the 1940s. In May the lads had gone to the pictures to drool over Ursula Andress in a bikini and sheath knife and to discover that Sean Connery's James Bond was shaken, perhaps, but never stirred. David Asheton, sitting next to Maxwell now on the Altar, had a collection of interesting photographs of Christine Keeler in his gym locker and he had written personally to Mandy Rice-Davies, asking for her autograph but hoping for her underwear. At the Brandenburg Gate, President Kennedy, hair blowing in the wind – like the answer, my friend – had told an incredulous crowd that he was a doughnut. Andrew Muir had threatened to hand back his prefect's badge in protest that the new five-pound notes showed Britannia without her helmet. Had his father spent the war years in Catterick for this?

England would stand, of course, Peter mused. And England would be right.

'Maxwell!' The sound of his name brought him back to the here, the now. 'Peter Maxwell, I'm talking to you, for Christ's sake!'

'Sorry, Cret. I was miles away.'

'Are you coming to the party tonight?' Cret was tired of repeating himself. Maxwell was so preoccupied these days.

'Where?'

'Annabel's.'

'Cranton tart!' somebody snorted.

'Don't you think she looks like Mandy Rice-Davies?' John Wensley asked. It was an odd question coming from the Preacher. The others hadn't realized he knew what a girl was.

'That's what I said,' the same somebody countered. And that somebody should know; he was David Asheton, lanky, fair haired, everybody's idea of an arsehole. That was because the girls flocked to him like iron filings to a magnet.

3

'What time?' Maxwell asked.

'Any time you bloody well like, me ol' mucker,' Cret said. 'Annabel will be there, legs open . . .'

'What about her mother?' Richard Alphedge worried about these things.

Asheton dismissed it. 'Nah, too old. Crinkle-cut tits if ever I saw any.'

'When did you see anybody's tits?' Richard asked. It was a fair question. There were those who wondered *exactly* how much mouth and how much trousers pertained in Asheton's case.

'Dickon, Dickon.' Asheton placed a fond arm around the smaller lad's shoulders. 'When you're experienced in the ways of the world . . .'

Andrew Muir burst his bubble. 'She was six at the time.'

'Aye, aye,' they all chorused.

'No, No, Ash was only seven. Be fair. Nothing kinky about our Ash. Not then. He gravitated to sniffing the saddles of little girls' bicycles *much* later!'

'Talking of which . . .' David Asheton became conspiratorial. 'Anyone caught the latest *Titbits?* Absolute corker on page four.'

'You're disgusting, Ash, do you know that?' Muir asked.

Maxwell laughed. 'Worse than that. You're blind!'

And their laughter joined his and rang across the lengthening afternoon shadows that crossed the fields of Halliards. Had they listened to anything other than each other and the beating of their hearts on this Day of Days, they would have heard the single, solemn bell ringing out the hour. Four of the clock and all was well.

'Well?' Quentin asked Maxwell. 'Are you going to do it?'

'Do what?' Maxwell half turned on the Altar seat.

'Chuck your blazer into the pool. We all said we would.'

They all laughed again. 'Yes, we did, didn't we?' Maxwell nodded. 'Well, what the hell. Before that, though . . . Cret. What's it to be?'

'What?'

'Life!' Maxwell shouted, hauling off the old school tie so that the purple silk ran like gossamer through his fingers. 'What'll you do with yours?'

'Simple!' Bingham grinned. 'After a promising start as President of the school's Law Society, I shall become a barrister at twenty, take silk the following year and be a High Court judge by the time I'm twenty-five. Napoleon was a general at twenty-five, you know.'

Maxwell knew. 'And the woolsack?' he asked.

Muir chuckled. 'Leave his mother out of it.'

'How about you, Stenhouse?' Maxwell wanted to know.

'Life?' Muir mused. 'Ah, where would we be without it? I don't know. After university, journalism, I think. After all, winner of the Literary Essay Prize three times in a row isn't exactly chance, is it? I'll be editor of *The Times* by the time I'm twenty four.' Stenhouse always had to go one better than Cret. 'William Pitt was Prime Minister at twenty-four, you know.'

Maxwell knew that too. 'Quent?'

The Captain of Games yawned and squared his shoulders, just to remind them all how broad they were. 'I'll make a mint on the Stock Exchange. Become a bull or a bear or whatever it is and retire as a bloody millionaire. And all at twenty-three! Victor fucking Ludorum yet again!' He smiled broadly, lolling back on the Altar, gazing up at the cloudless blue of the summer sky. 'And not being a sad bastard of a historian, I couldn't tell you anybody who'd arrived by that age.'

Neither, though he was an historian, could Peter Maxwell. 'Alphie, what about you?'

Richard adopted the pose for which he was famous when he'd wowed everybody in the school play the previous year, clutching a rubber asp to his inflated bosom. 'Olivier will ask me to join him at the Old Vic,' he said, 'so I'll probably give RADA a miss. Then it's Hollywood and wall-to-wall Oscars. And I'm not putting any daft age limit on this. Age cannot wither me nor custom stale my infinite variety.'

'Bollocks!' Asheton thumped him on the shoulder. 'Life's been one long bloody act for you, Alphie – you know what I'm talking about. Once a sham, always a sham. To save you the chore of asking me, Maxie, I shall be taking over from Hugh Hefner any day now, with wall-to-wall women as my playthings. Fluffy little bunnies wherever you look.'

'That's it?' Muir asked.

'A lifetime of shagging,' Asheton murmured. 'My dear boy, what finer ambition could there be?'

'What about you, Preacher?' Maxwell asked. No one really knew John Wensley, the quiet one, the one somehow forever in the corner, in the shadows.

Wensley shrugged. 'Whatever comes,' he said, 'I'll go with it.'

'Yes, well . . .' Asheton sighed. 'What about you, Max? What do you want to be when you grow up?'

'Me?' Maxwell was peeling off his blazer, the pocket heavy with pens and the woven gilt of his school badge, the timetable still neatly folded away. 'I don't know, I'll probably be . . .'

'. . . the Head of Sixth Form at a third-rate comprehensive somewhere on the South Coast. I shall be nearly fifty-four, by which time Napoleon Bonaparte was dying from his wallpaper and William Pitt had already shuffled off the mortal coil muttering something about Mrs Bellamy's meat pies.'

'Sir?' Duane looked up at the Great Man from the thankless task in hand.

'Hmm?' Maxwell looked down at the lad. Twelve, psychotic. Serial bed-wetter. Villa supporter. 'Oh, nothing, Duane. Now, tell me, is there any more chewing gum on the underside of that desk?'

'No, sir. Just some writing – about Mr Blenkinsop. I remember him. He was . . .'

'Right you are.' Maxwell also remembered Blenkinsop and cut the lad short. 'And if Mr Malleson tells you to stop chewing again in his class, what will you do?'

Duane had to think about it. 'Stop chewing,' he said.

'Excellent. And what will you not do, Duane?'

'Tell him to fuck off . . . sir!'

'Exactly. That's what they refer to in education today as target setting. Now, we'll keep this little incident to ourselves, shall we? Just you and me and Mr Malleson?'

'Yes, sir.'

'Otherwise it's Mr Diamond, the Headmaster. And you don't want a good letting off from him, do you?'

'Oh, he's an old . . .'

Maxwell's hand was in the air. 'Etonian, Duane? Unlikely, but you'd better leave it there. It's half past four. Ain't you got no 'ome to go to?'

'Yeah,' Duane grumbled, wondering which uncle Mum would be staggering back with tonight. 'See you, Mr Maxwell.'

'Indeed you will.' Maxwell snapped into his Dixon of Dock Green mode, saluting sharply. 'And mind 'ow you go!'

Duane looked up at Peter Maxwell. At least with Malleson you knew what he was talking about . . . well, most of the time. But Maxwell, he was fucking mad, that's what he was. Duane took to the stairs, while the taking was good.

Peter Maxwell strolled back to his office, the one County Hall had wanted to paint turquoise. He had said a polite 'no thank you' to the Deputy Head, who had arrived with a colour swatch; he'd die in a ditch first. He was quite prepared to erect a barricade of children and lob chalk at the decorators if push came to shove. Besides, he already had his wallpaper, those sprawling posters of the silver screen where Rita Hayworth risked lung cancer posing as *Gilda*, Jimmy Stewart was being a nosey neighbour in *Rear Window* and Marlon Brando didn't look too well in *Apocalypse Now*. He put his coffee cup down with the others on the side table and checked tomorrow's lesson plan.

7

Mother of God! – 8F3. Better check the Valium and the body armour. He picked up the phone.

'Nurse,' the familiar voice said.

Maxwell rasped into the receiver, the best Mr Gruntfuttock he'd ever done.

'No, she's not,' came the voice.

'Not what?' Maxwell asked.

'Pregnant. Carly Turnball.'

'I won't have you speaking of my sixth form in that way, Matron,' Maxwell scolded. 'The girl's name is Turn*bull*.'

'Whatever,' the nurse said. 'She's not pregnant.'

'Not the Holy Ghost, then?'

'Not anybody, Max. Just the usual little bit of attention-seeking.'

'Well, thank you, Sylv, that puts half the male population of Leighford's minds at rest, I should think. At least, I've always assumed half the male population of Leighford have minds; for the rest, I'm not so sure. Now, to more pressing matters. Reunions.'

'What?'

'You know, gets-together, geriatric ups of the knee. Assorted chaps of the Old Pals' Battalion who were once joined at the hip contacting each other after a century or so. Ever been to one?'

'You're talking about men, I assume?'

Maxwell was.

'Don't know. Is it a girlie thing particularly? I did go to an old nursing one once. God, it was awful. All of us bitching about the ones who weren't there and feeling really pissed off because Janet Chamberlain *had* caught that orthopaedic surgeon after all and could have bought the rest of us ten times over. Jesus, the knives were out that night.'

'Sylvia Matthews, wash your mouth out!' Maxwell scolded. 'I didn't know you had an envious bone in your body.'

Peter Maxwell really knew very little about Sylvia Matthews' body. There was a time when she had minded about that.

Minded because she'd been in love with him. That was then. Before he'd met Jacquie and she'd met Guy. She still loved him in her way. It was the only way you could love Mad Max.

'Well, I've been invited to one, Count – a reunion, that is. Any thoughts?'

The cat known as Metternich – the Count to the man who paid his vet bills – yawned ostentatiously. He was twelve pounds of black-and-white fur, about as lovable as anthrax with attitude.

'Well, you say that' – Maxwell wagged a finger at him, on the hand that wasn't wrapped around his Southern Comfort – 'but I'm not so sure.' The two of them sat opposite each other in the lounge of 38 Columbine, the master sprawled in an arm-chair, Maxwell on the settee. 'Listen again.' He cleared his throat and read from the letter that had arrived that morning. ' "Dear Maxie, you won't remember me, but that isn't the point. Thirty-five years ago we were the Magnificent Seven riding to do battle against the bandits of Ignorance and Indifference." You know, I never remember old Stenhouse being that poetic, not when we were at school. Oh, he won prizes, of course, but that was because nobody else entered the competition. Sten-house, Count. It was a sort of joke. His name was Muir, you see, so it's Stenhouse Muir, like in the football team over the border. You know . . .' Maxwell caught the animal's cold-killer eyes, the fixed mouth, the motionless whiskers. 'Well, it's all before your time, I expect.' His eyes narrowed. 'Wonder what hap-pened to old Queen of the South?' His mind clicked back to the matter in hand. 'But I digress. Old Stenhouse goes on, "Water under the bridge but now, shock, horror, they're closing the old place down. That's right, Halliards is to be no more. In fact, it's already no more as a school. There are plans afoot to develop it as a conference centre or something similar, so before that happens, I've asked the trustees if we, the Class of '63, can have one last sad wander over the place prior to a first-class piss-up at Graveney Manor." God, I remember the Graveney, Count. I'd fallen head over heels for a girl called Prudence from Cranton, the girls' school down the road. No, don't laugh. I'd have thought you'd go for that – you know, Prudence Kitten? Ooh, of course, that's before your time too, isn't it?'

Metternich yawned again, before curling his leg over his left ear. He did this now and again to remind the old duffer whose territory he shared that he *could* do these things. Some nights, he'd noted, Maxwell couldn't even make the stairs.

'You see, there's something about the halcyon days, Count.' Maxwell tossed Muir's letter aside and lolled back in his armchair, cradling his amber drink. 'Something that says, "Leave them alone. Or perhaps they won't be halcyon any more." Whaddya think? Cranton, eh? God, those were the days.'

Whatever it was that Metternich thought, the great piebald beast wasn't telling, not tonight. It was that hour of cocking tails and pricking whiskers, the hour the rodents rode in the Year of the Rat. He longed for the hunt, with the wind in his nostrils and his eyes pools of murder under the Columbine lamplight. To everything, Metternich knew, there was a season. A time to kill and a time to hunt, a time for every purpose under Heaven. He bounced off the armchair he'd made his own with years of kneading and pirouetted across the carpet to the staircase and the cat-flap, heading for the outer dark.

He hadn't remembered the cedars being so bare. In his day, in the swinging sixties, they'd spread their mighty arms, it seemed to him, across the sky itself, cradling, and protecting. The Altar was still there, in the crisp, pale moon, and he ran his fingers over the words carved into the wood; worn now and crumbling, but he knew what they said – 'Who spot the verb and stop the ball . . .' There was a shiver and something dark ran over the pile of debris that filled the pool. He'd swam in that pool countless times, arcing through the chilled water in the house games days, chlorine burning his nostrils as he came up for air, the cheers deafening as his fingers touched tile at the end of the race. He looked up at the dark silhouette of the buildings, like an old, abandoned film set. The fives courts, still ringing with the thud of ball and the roar of the teams, tumbling over each other. The chapel with its sanctuary candle still glowing and a solitary treble voice intoning the Te Deum, lamenting all the souls who had passed. In Big School he knew, as he knew his tables, the litany of the fallen, the dead of two world wars; he had read them so many times: Archer, R.J., Royal Engineers; Atherton, F.O., Hampshire Regiment; Bannerman, S.L.T., Artists Rifles . . . How often had he run his eyes down the list while the chaplain droned on in a prayer from Michel Quoist, 'Lord, I am a five-pound note . . .'

At the First Eleven Square he stopped, hearing again the faint click of leather on willow, saw the smiling schoolboy faces turn to sneers and applause to contempt. The wind was suddenly chill on the night air, rustling the cedars, creeping through the grass of early hours. He shouldn't be here. But he'd always be here. He hadn't been here for years. And yet he'd never left.

As he reached the edge of the field and heard his footsteps crunch on the gravel, he looked up to the great canopy with its turrets and its bell rope, like a black lance taut on its housings, piercing the moonlit clouds. His days of verb-spotting were over. It was time to stop the ball.

Chapter Two

The weekend starts here. Peter Maxwell strode his narrow world like a colossus, barring the gate to the devious little herberts who consistently tried to sneak through the carpark. What bastard put the Head of Sixth Form on gate duty on a Friday afternoon? Peter Maxwell knew the answer – Bernard Ryan, destined to be a Deputy Head for ever. Maxwell knew. He was biding his time.

'All right if I go through, Max?' A bland, bespectacled face beamed at him above the half-lowered window. It had all the bonhomie of a basilisk.

Maxwell nodded. 'Only because it's you, Headmaster.'

James Diamond, BSc, MEd, was always flustered when his Head of Sixth Form called him Headmaster, and since Maxwell always did call him that, fluster was his usual state.

'Charmless nerk,' Maxwell muttered as the Head's Peugeot snarled out on to the road, only to have to screech to a halt a second later by order of Mrs Silliphant, the lollipop lady, she who had been thrown out of the SS for being too nasty.

Maxwell chuckled. 'Sterling work, Silli. Ah, Gazza. Third Friday running, unless my memory is totally shot to hell.'

'But I'll miss my bus, sir,' Gazza whined, hauling his backpack off his shoulder. He hadn't seen Maxwell lurking by the shrubbery and he'd fancied his chances. He should really have known better.

'Indeed you will,' Maxwell nodded, 'because now you'll have to go all the way round, the way everybody else goes. That's probably an extra three, maybe four minutes. You'll probably miss a couple of buses in that time and have to walk all the way home, like we did in olden times. Life's a learning curve, isn't it?'

Gazza flounced off the way he'd come, longing to swear under his breath, but knowing better. Everybody knew that Mad Max had radar sensors for ears. Dave Bradshaw had called him a bastard once, from three hundred metres. They never saw him again.

The sound of her horn brought Maxwell from his flower-bed and he peered in through the open window. 'Electric windows, Woman Policeman? Whatever next? The vote, perhaps?'

'Sorry I'm late, Max.'

'Not at all.' He hauled his holdall from its hiding place behind the japonica and clambered in. 'Gave me a chance to catch a few miscreants guilty of malfeasance.'

She reached across and kissed him on the cheek. 'You say the most incomprehensible things,' she said.

He looked at her in the Friday afternoon light. Jacquie Carpenter, detective constable. Early thirties, clever, bright, loyal, the only woman in his life. Her auburn hair cascaded over her shoulders and her grey eyes sparkled as he buckled himself in. 'Now, are you sure about this?' he asked again, as he had countless times over the past few days.

She slammed the Ka into gear. 'Am I sure I want to spend my precious weekend with a crowd of boring old farts reminiscing about their pubescent stirrings in the dorm? No, I'm not. Am I sure I want to spend the weekend with you? Yes, I am. Besides, I've got a new frock.'

'Ah, and by spending the weekend . . . you mean . . . ?'

Her smile was like the Giaconda's. 'Let's see how it goes, Max.'

'The letter *did* say spouses welcome,' he reminded her.

'And friends?'

'Ouch!' He pulled his finger away from her frosty aura.

She laughed, patting his leg. 'We'll see how it goes,' she said. 'Fill me in on them.'

'Who?'

'Your old buddies.' Jacquie roared off through Leighford, past knots of Leighford Highenas making their way home, scattering chewing-gum wrappers in their wake and proving every known adage about the youth of today.

'Gemma Hipcrest,' Maxwell murmured, unwrapping his university scarf and settling himself down.

Jacquie frowned. 'I thought you went to a boys' school.'

'I did,' Maxwell said, 'but that doesn't prevent me from seeing Gemma Hipcrest at . . .' He checked his watch. '. . . four-eighteen with a fag cradled in her less than reputable fingers.'

'Max, you're a bastard.'

'True,' the Head of Sixth Form said, 'but a just one, I think you'll find. Rather like Archbishop Temple of nobody's blessed memory but mine. You see, in your capacity, you can arrest the little buggers. All I can do is make their lives hell on a daily basis for the seven years I have them in my clutches from eleven to eighteen. It's just not the same. And the Headmaster's Writ, for what it's worth, covers behaviour to and from school. From the time the little bastards leave their front doors, we teachers are, God help us, *in loco parentis*.' He leaned across to her. 'Oh, you of little Latin,' he chided softly. 'It means "as mad as a parent",' and he winced as she hit him.

They purred north, looking for the Winchester bypass as the rush-hour traffic started to build.

'Well, let's see.' Maxwell slid down in his seat, tilting the shapeless tweed hat over his eyes and folding his arms. 'Of the old gang, the Magnificent Seven, there's Cret Bingham. Always wanted to be a High Court judge. You can imagine the shock I had when there was a Lord Chief Justice of that name a little while ago – no relation, though, as it turned out. I bet Cret was well pissed off – that's a phrase I learned from Gemma Hipcrest, by the way, along with "gagging for it" and "I'd rather eat Mr Holton's shit".'

'Cret?' Jacquie asked, diverting her concentration away from the interchange for long enough to read the Great Man's face.

'Don't ask.' Maxwell sighed. 'They were different days. There was a chap in the Remove who was a Sikh or something. We all called him Woggie. He didn't seem to mind.'

'God, Max, we'd be looking at a roasting from the CRE today.'

'Ah, dear girl, but I'm talking about the good old days, the swinging sixties. Enoch "Rivers of Blood" Powell and the Racists were top of the pops. You weren't even a twinkle in your dear ol' pappy's eye. One could call a spade a spade. Good sound, though, your mum and dad.'

'Hmm?' She fell for it every time.

'The Carpenters. Easy listening.'

She cuffed him round the ear with her gear-changing hand.

'Then there was Quent – George Quentin. He made something of a fortune running the tuck shop. Not to mention Captain of Rugger, Captain of Cricket, Victor Ludorum. No . . .' He leaned across again infuriatingly. 'He wasn't another chum. It means . . .'

'I *know* what it means!' she shrieked, pushing him away.

'Quent swore he'd be a millionaire by the time he was twenty-three.'

'Was he?'

'Don't know.' Maxwell shrugged. 'Come to think of it, I did see him interviewed on the telly a few years back. Dimbleby or Paxman, they're all the same, talking money to the City whizz kids. He was one of them. Grey suit, glass of water, that sort of thing.'

'So he made it, then?'

'All power to his elbow. Then there was Stenhouse, the organizer of this little bashette.'

'Shit, I've missed the turn,' Jacquie muttered. 'Never mind, I'll take the next left.'

'Andrew Muir, aka Stenhouse. Expected to run Fleet Street, press baron *par excellence*, you know the type; Rupert Murdoch by way of Lord Beaverbrook.'

'How did he do?'

'He does a few pieces for the *Mail* from time to time – makes Simon Heffer look like a pinko liberal. Funny thing was, he couldn't string two words together at school. Christ knows how he won those prizes – bit like the Booker really. I ran the magazine.'

'Max, I thought you ran the school.'

Maxwell eased himself upright with the deadly uncoiling motion of a rattler. He lifted his hat brim and narrowed his eyes at her. 'Yes, you'll probably need that,' he said.

'Need what?' she asked, wide-eyed.

'That razor wit. The Magnificent Seven don't take prisoners, if I remember rightly. Oh, and by the way.' He slithered down again, his rattle still, his fangs retracted. 'Watch out for Ash – David Asheton, serial groper. That man could lech for England. I remember one Cranton weekend in particular . . .'

Jacquie shrugged. 'He's probably had the op by now.'

'Doesn't slow you down.' Maxwell flounced, and the two of them laughed together in the warmth of her car, in the warmth of her smile, driving north.

The Graveney once belonged to the Wilkinsons, descendants of that Iron Madman who'd got the army contract for cannon and insisted on being buried in an iron coffin. His descendants still made swords for officers and garden shears and lawnmower blades for hoi polloi, but they'd moved out of the Graveney years ago. It was grander than Maxwell remembered it, a

sweeping nineteenth-century façade with Doric this and Cor-
inthian that, to show how attuned English manufacturers were
in their day were to their classical heritage. It was all but dark as
Jacquie's Ka crunched on the gravel and purred to a halt outside
the main door. Lights twinkled from the chandeliers in the
ballroom.

'What?' Maxwell looked around. 'No flunky?' His knees
ached from the confinement of the journey.

Jacquie got out.

'May I take your bags, sir?' The flunky didn't look too
pleased with Maxwell's question. He'd been blessed with
twenty-twenty hearing.

'Too kind.' Maxwell beamed and the guests made for the
door.

'Do you know.' Maxwell dithered at the entrance. 'I once
spent nearly eight minutes in a revolving door somewhere in
Birmingham. It's really true, your life does flash before you.'

'So you want me to lead?' she asked.

Maxwell nodded. 'Just like a Policeman's Excuse Me,' he
said.

The foyer was dripping with expensive leather and plush
carpets. Half of Sherwood Forest appeared to be growing out of
the floor.

'God, Max,' Jacquie whispered.

'It'll do,' the Great Man muttered, wishing he'd gone for
that threshold pay rise now.

'Can I help you, sir?' a pretty blonde called from the
reception desk.

'Indeed.' Maxwell beamed. 'Peter Maxwell, here for a
knees-up.'

'Ah, yes.' The girl smiled back. 'One of Mr Muir's party.
Would you like to sign the book?'

'Love to,' and he took her pen.

'Mrs Maxwell?' The girl looked at Jacquie.

'No,' she told her. 'Miss Carpenter.'

'Will that be a double room, sir?' the girl asked.

'No,' said Jacquie, perhaps more quickly than she'd intended. 'Two singles, please.'

The girl's eyes flickered for the first time. 'Would that be adjacent?' she asked.

Maxwell leaned on the counter and rested his head on his hand, looking quizzically at Jacquie. 'Please.' She laughed and kicked him hard on the shin.

'Actually,' said Maxwell, straight faced, 'if it's all the same to you, I'd like them side by side.'

'There's a complimentary bottle of champagne in your room, sir,' the girl said, ignoring the remark and handing him a key. 'Second floor, just past the bear. Compliments of Mr Muir. He has asked that all his party meet him in the Baculus Suite at seven for sherry. Will that be all right?'

'I'm sure the sherry will be delightful,' Maxwell said. 'As for the reception, I'll let you know. Does the hotel have a policy on bread-roll fights?' But Jacquie was already leading him away.

'Christ, she didn't say it was a real bear.' Jacquie didn't like walking past it. It was seven feet high on its hind legs, all glass eyes and attitude. Even the moths left it alone.

'The bear and baculus.' Maxwell was still fidgeting with his bow tie. 'That's a ragged staff to you, Policewoman – The crest of the Earls of Warwick. You're in Shakespeare country now, dear heart. *Non Sans Droict*, that sort of thing.'

Jacquie looked adorable in her pale blue evening gown, her red-gold hair swept up and her eyes sparkling along with the chandeliers. Maxwell hadn't worn black tie for years. She saw his face light up as they reached the half-landing that was the entrance to the Baculus Suite.

'Stenhouse Muir!' he roared.

A man in full Highland rig swirled to face the pair. He had a mane of auburn-grey hair and a beard that flashed silver.

19

'Maxie!' The men collided mid-carpet with much back-slapping and hugging. Maxwell grabbed Muir's hand and they strathspeyed the length of the room, guests scuttling aside to let them pass. Muir let out a whoop as they reached the cocktails, twirled round and strathspeyed back again.

'Jacquie.' Maxwell steadied himself as they got back to her. 'I've just given you a lifetime's opportunity to find out what a Scotsman wears under his kilt. And that's hunting Macpherson, unless I miss my guess, you old charlatan. You've about as much right to wear that as Mel Gibson.'

'Madam.' Muir stooped to kiss Jacquie's hand. 'I'll tell you before he does I've never been north of Berwick in my life, but all life's a front, isn't it? Andrew Muir.'

'Jacquie Carpenter.' She smiled.

'Your daughter, Max?' Muir asked. 'Lovely.'

'Aren't you going to introduce us?' A starchy-looking woman had glided to Muir's side. There was something vaguely Scottish about her, overlaid with Home Counties.

'Janet.' Muir placed a tentative hand on her arm as if he were afraid her ice would burn his fingers. 'I'd like you to meet Peter Maxwell, old Hallardian *par excellence*. You've heard me talk of him often.'

'Yes,' Janet Muir said, bored already.

'Charmed.' Maxwell kissed her hand, taking in the expensive cluster on her middle finger.

'This is his daughter, Jacquie.'

The women smiled at each other.

'It's been bloody years.' Muir looked at Maxwell.

'It has that.' Maxwell laughed. 'Any threat of a drink?'

'Dear boy. The straws are this way. Remember that old . . .' And the men disappeared into a small crowd desperately trying to mill.

'I'm not actually his daughter,' Jacquie confided to Janet.

'I'm didn't thank for a moment you were, my dear,' the older woman said. 'I wish I could say I wasn't actually Andrew's wife. Can we get a drink? I think it's going to be one of those weekends.'

'Peter Maxwell!' The name was roared above the chatter.

'It can't be. Cret!'

'Er . . .'

'Oh, sorry . . . er . . . Anthony.'

Anthony Bingham gripped Maxwell's hand. He loomed larger than Maxwell remembered and the hair was on its way out. The pin-stripe had gone out years ago. 'Yes, I'm not sure "Cret" cuts much mustard in the Inner Temple.' The judge looked at him and offered his verdict. 'The years have not been kind.'

'Bitch!' Maxwell took up the champagne flute a passing tray afforded him. 'Still place-dropping, I notice. Inner Temple, eh? Good address.'

'You?'

'Thirty eight, Columbine Avenue, Leighford. Know it?'

'Leighford? South Coast somewhere, isn't it?'

'Somewhere.' Maxwell nodded.

'Anthony was just telling me, Max' – Muir joined them, Scotch in hand – 'how he was saying to the Lord Chancellor only the other day . . .'

Maxwell caught Muir's raised eyebrow and buried his nose in his champagne flute. 'Ash!' He caught sight of the old lecher on the landing as he turned. David Asheton, the bastard, hadn't changed at all. He looked as if he'd just thrown his blazer in the swimming pool. 'Jesus!' Maxwell faltered a little as he crossed the floor. On the bastard's arm was the most gorgeous girl he'd ever seen, with long black hair and eyes to drown in. They sparkled like the gems that circled her neck and tumbled on to her breasts, loosely held in place by an exquisite white gown.

'Maxie!' Asheton threw his arms around the Head of Sixth Form. 'You old fox. It's been centuries!' And they stood there, slapping each other's backs like idiots.

'Who is this ravishing creature?' Maxwell asked. 'If you tell me it's Mrs Asheton, I'm going to kill you.'

'Veronica, I'd like you to meet Peter Maxwell, historian, wit, raconteur. He used to be something of a film buff way back when.'

'Still am, dear boy.' Maxwell beamed. 'Paul Getty's always ringing up to borrow the odd vid.' He shot a glance in Bingham's direction. 'Veronica' – he kissed her hand – 'the pleasure's all mine.'

She purred at him.

'The gang's all here,' Maxwell said, 'or at least some of them. Jacquie.' He waved her over. Policewoman Carpenter was between a rock and a hard place. It had taken her all of ten seconds to discover that Janet Muir was a prize bitch and she wasn't sorry to be called away. On the other hand, she felt, as any woman would, the poor relation standing alongside Veronica.

Maxwell introduced them. 'Jacquie Carpenter, my ol' mucker David Asheton and . . . Veronica.'

Jacquie smiled and raised her glass to them. 'Come on, Veronica,' she said. 'I'll get you a drink while the boys reminisce.' And Veronica slid her hand along Asheton's sleeve before undulating across the room in Jacquie's wake.

'Not Mrs Asheton the First, I assume,' Maxwell muttered to his oppo.

'Not Mrs Asheton at all,' Asheton muttered back. 'Sex on a stick, Max, I assure you. No, Mrs Asheton the First is a raddled old bitch with a drink problem. The last time I saw her she was living in Slough with a struck-off doctor. He had the same problem. Mrs Asheton the Second . . .'

'I don't have *all* night, Ash!' Maxwell laughed.

'So be it.' Asheton beamed. 'Now that's rather a little cracker you've got with you.'

'Oh, no you don't!' Maxwell warned him. 'You're not pinching my girl again!'

'You bastard!' Asheton slapped him playfully round the head. 'I wish!'

'I remember Cranton, '62,' Maxwell told him.

The smile left Asheton's face. 'I thought we agreed we'd never bring that up.'

'And I won't,' Maxwell said. 'Not until the *News of the World* makes me an offer I just can't resist. Drinky?'

'I'd kill for one,' Asheton said. 'My God, and "pat, he comes".'

'Who's Pat?' Maxwell asked, turning as Asheton did to the new arrival on the stairs. 'It's not Sir Richard Alphedge, the great actor?'

'Ah, takes one to know one, Max!' Alphedge's vowels were even more rounded, his tone stentorious and cocktail-shaking. He too had lost most of his hair. He gripped Maxwell's hand and kissed him on both cheeks.

'Gone French since we last met, Alphie?' Maxwell asked.

'Gone queer,' Asheton grunted, and promptly got the same treatment. 'Dickon, how the hell are you?'

'Well, well.' Alphedge beamed at them both. 'Sad day, eh?'

'Hmm?' Asheton asked.

'Halliards going under the bulldozer or whatever.'

'Oh, yes,' Asheton said. 'Tragic, tragic.'

'Oh, I'd like you to meet Cissie.'

Maxwell half expected to find a slim juvenile lead on the actor's arm, knowing what he did about actors, but instead found a rather buxom lady in multicoloured silks.

'Cissie.' Maxwell kissed her hand. 'Wait a minute . . .'

'Yes,' she sighed. 'I did it in that *Morse* episode where there's all that kerfuffle at Lonsdale College.'

'And we'll sign the autographs later,' Alphedge said, leading her away. 'Never work with children or actresses, Maxie,' he muttered. 'Especially when one's actress wife is more famous than oneself. Is there a bar?'

A gong sounded from nowhere and a rather menacing-looking maître d' announced that dinner was served. The Old Boys found their scattered partners and ambled towards the dining room.

'Spotted dick, I hope,' Alphedge shouted.

'Haven't you had that seen to yet?' Asheton called back.

Jacquie's eyes rolled skyward and Maxwell patted her arm. 'When we get to the school song,' he whispered, 'just la-la-la it.' He winked at her. 'You'll be all right.'

She almost stumbled at the sight that met them in the lobby. A tall man stood there, with a long Barbour coat and a broad-brimmed hat, dripping with the rain he'd brought in from the blustery night. He looked like Clint Eastwood.

'Good God,' Maxwell said. 'Preacher?'

The tall man swept off his hat. 'Peter Maxwell.' He bowed low. When he straightened, there was a white collar at his throat.

'Oh God.' Maxwell hesitated. 'You really are a preacher, then?'

'Church of God's Children,' the tall man said.

'Yes, well, we're all God's chillun.' Alphedge, behind Maxwell, lapsed into his Al Jolson, waving his hands in the air.

'Richard!' Cissie scolded. There was something about the tall man's eyes that told her he had no sense of humour.

'Jacquie.' Maxwell was looking at those eyes too. 'I'd like you to meet John Wensley . . . er . . . the Reverend John Wensley.' And Wensley solemnly shook her hand.

The grandfather clock they kept in the foyer for old time's sake had long since struck one. Peter Maxwell's left shoe lay at a rakish angle on Jacquie Carpenter's bedroom carpet; his right snuggled against her bathroom radiator. His jacket hung non-chalantly on her chair and his body was sprawled on her bed.

'So,' he said, smiling at her. 'You survived the first round.'

She smiled back. 'It could have been worse,' she said, easing off her earrings.

'Undeniably,' Maxwell acknowledged. 'Quent could have been there.'

'Isn't he coming?'

'Stenhouse told me he'd replied and seemed very keen. I expect something came up on the Dow Jones or whatever and he had to turn into Gordon Gekko for the night. I dare say he'll show up tomorrow, red braces and all.'

'What's the itinerary?'

'Well, you may or may not be pleased to know that it's an all-chaps morning. We're going to a funeral, or a wake, or both. We're going to say our farewells to an old school. Stenhouse has wangled the keys out of the caretaker. You wouldn't want to be there – to see grown men cry.'

'I've got hair to wash,' she said, kicking off a shoe and letting the blood flow back to her heels.

'Or there's the sauna. I hear the Graveney does an excellent colonic irrigation.'

She threw something at him.

'I remember doing that in geography in the Upper Fourths,' he told her. 'The colonic irrigation of the Nile Delta. Got an A- for my map from old Bloxham just before we got him on to his war stories. Never did another stroke of geography.'

'One of the Few, was he?'

'Wrong war, my dear. He got dysentery at Harfleur before marching on to Agincourt.'

Jacquie gave him an old-fashioned look. You never knew with Peter Maxwell. She kicked off her other shoe, to join the first near the bed. She sat in front of the mirror at the dressing table and let her hair cascade over her shoulders.

'Time for the mud pack and cucumbers,' she said, looking at him.

Maxwell smiled and finished his Southern Comfort. 'A nod's as good as a wink to a blind horse,' he said, and dragged himself off the bed. 'You know' – he bent down and kissed the top of her head – 'I was the luckiest man there tonight.'

'Oh?' She arched an eyebrow at him, watching his face in the mirror. 'I should have thought you'd have given that distinction to David.'

'Ash?' He frowned. 'Oh, you mean Veronica?' He thought about it for a moment. 'Nah,' he decided. 'Airhead.' He lifted her gently by the shoulders and turned her round. 'I like my women to understand what I'm talking about,' he said.

'Your women?' She widened her eyes. 'And anyway, I don't understand; not always.'

'Nearly always is good enough.' He laughed. 'I asked Veronica to pass me the salt at one point and she had to reach for a dictionary.'

They heard the grandfather clock strike two, distant, as though in a dream. 'That'll be me away,' Maxwell said, retrieving his shoes and his tie, before finding his jacket.

She stopped him. 'I'm only next door, Max,' she said, and she kissed him, a deep kiss, long and close. He held her at arm's length. 'What a coincidence,' he said. 'So am I.'

The dead man hung at the end of the rope, creaking slowly on its taut housings. One shoe had dropped with a thud, echoing through the empty hallway and the dark, dead corridor beyond. His hands dangled at his side, the fingers hooked as he'd fought for breath, a little away from his body, as though balancing as he walked on air. His head was at an odd angle with the knot of the noose behind his left ear, his eyes bulging in the darkness, trying to see through the night gloom. His tongue protruded obscenely through the clenched teeth and the peeled-back lips, his final gesture to the world.

Ahead of him the wrought iron of the first landing glowed eerily in the fitful moon. After the rain, a scattering of clouds sailed past the tall oriel window with its coat of arms and its school motto. No school song now; no rousing chorus roared until the rafters rang, but the slow, swinging creak of the rope and the moan of the wind on the lonely stair.

Chapter Three

The dew was still heavy on the ground as six of the Magnificent Seven wandered the grounds they all knew so well. Maxwell had left Jacquie sleeping, grabbed some orange juice and coffee in the Graveney's breakfast room and piled into Cret Bingham's Galaxy.

'Tom Wilkinson was killed there,' Richard Alphedge remembered on their way over. 'Back there, on that bend. Some stupid bastard in a juggernaut. Do you remember, Max?'

'I remember hearing about it in chapel the next day.' Maxwell nodded. 'You could have heard a pin drop. The HM was steady.'

'The HM?' Bingham called from the driving seat. 'Heart of stone, that man. You don't get tears from granite. My God, look at that.'

They had. Beyond the wild privet, tipped silver in the fading frost, the sweep of Halliards hung like a ghost in the morning. The Galaxy snarled through the open wrought-iron gates, the gilded arms peeling now in the autumn weather, in the twilight of their years. To the left, the concrete block that was the science lab, new in the Seven's time, its walls corroded and grey. To the right, the bulk of the chapel and the Old School beyond. Matthew Arnold would have been at home here.

'Parking under the limes, Anthony?' Maxwell clicked his tongue. 'Old Gregson'll get you.'

'Old Gregson!' Muir laughed. 'Now there's a name I'd forgotten. Groundsman extraordinaire.' Their minds raced back to the surly old sod they all swore had been drummed out of the Cheka for excessive inhumanity.

'And bastard by appointment to Her Majesty the Queen.' Asheton chuckled. 'It *was* you who turned the hose on the First Eleven Square, wasn't it, Max?'

Maxwell drew himself up to his full height. 'That is a gross calumny, sir, and you will withdraw it.'

'Not very good at withdrawing, old Ash.' Muir grunted and laughed as the blond man cuffed him round the ear.

Then an odd silence fell as the Galaxy crunched to a halt on the gravel, each man alone with his thoughts. The Preacher was out first, gazing up at the school chapel with its Gothic crosses and its stained glass. Somebody had put the Head of Classics' bike up on that roof once, a miracle of engineering, ingenuity and schoolboy pluck. Alphedge took in the fives court wall and the workshops beyond, looking oddly derelict and silent, like a concentration camp. He remembered the stage with its worn, scarred surface and that indefinable smell in the wings, born of greasepaint and first-night nerves.

'Do they still do woodwork and stuff in school, Max?' he asked.

Maxwell gave him a faraway look. 'When I looked last,' he said, 'it was called Design Technology – or was it Craft, Design Technology? You can't give the little darlings a hammer or they'll bash their thumbs and sue the county.'

'Or kill each other.' Muir slammed the door behind him.

'Ah, yes.' Maxwell nodded. 'I teach Peter Sutcliffe Appreciation classes every Thursday.'

'Thursday!' Alphedge dashed on to the dewy grass. 'I remember Thursday. CCF!' And he broke into a brisk march, swinging his left arm while his right held his rifle butt at the carry. He sang out the monotonous notes of the parade ground.

'God, yes,' Bingham groaned. 'That bloody bugle. Weren't you something in the CCF, Max?'

Maxwell nodded. 'Company deserter.'

'That's right.' Muir clicked his fingers. 'Didn't you ask Captain Bashford if you could form a cavalry arm?'

'And didn't he cane you to within an inch of your life for impudence?' Asheton joined in.

'Yes on both counts,' Maxwell confessed.

'Bingham laughed. 'Mad as a bloody snake.'

'Oh, God. Look at that.' They followed Alphedge's finger to what was once the pool. The cold blue water had gone now, as had the roars of the house-mad crowd, cheering home the swimmers. The rectangle, with its peeling pale blue plaster, was full of debris, brick, glass and timber.

'You know what that is, don't you?' Bingham asked.

'The cricket pavilion.'

They turned to look at the Preacher. It was the first time Wensley had spoken that morning.

'God, he's right.' Instinctively, their eyes came up to the distant line of cedars looming in the grey of the morning. It had stood there, by the far hedge, where Asheton made small talk with the stragglers from Cranton, the girls' school down the road, who were going through the motions of cross-country; where Bingham had thrown up most of the smoke from his first cigarette; where Quentin had rammed home the hundred that took the Public Schools' Cup from Rugby that year.

'God, it's like a grave,' Bingham said. 'I'm not sure I can face going inside.'

'Yes, you can,' Maxwell told him. 'It's why we came. Why we all came. Stenhouse, got the key?'

Muir had. They crossed the grass in front of the old Tuck Shop, padlocked now, but with most of its windows gone. How many iced buns, Maxwell wondered, how many packets of hamburger-flavoured crisps had disappeared down his ravenous maw before the world had invented E numbers and cholesterol? Then their

29

shoes were clicking on the flagstones where the local town crier had stood all those years ago, looking a prat in his stockings and tricorn hat, to grant them their half-day holiday in honour of something or other that everybody had forgotten; probably it was International Doo-Dah Day. They wandered into the darkness of the cloisters, where dog-eared papers still flapped on their rusty drawing pins. Maxwell tried to read the faded notices. The Shakespeare Society was to meet on Wednesday. There was house cricket practice on the West Field. The orchestra was to meet for rehearsals in Gatehouse Lodge at four-fifteen.

'Sorry, Preacher,' Muir called back to the tall man at the back of the meandering line. 'I don't have a key to the chapel.'

Wensley glanced to his right and ran his finger lightly over the carved oak of the doors.

'Didn't you sing falsetto in the choir, Dickon?' Asheton asked Alphedge.

'Only until gravity and nature combined to lower my testicles, dear boy. And anyway, it's called treble. I, of course, had perfect pitch.'

'"A perfect pitch and a blinding light,"' Maxwell misquoted, but Newbolt's poem was lost on these scholars of yesteryear. Muir's key grated in the side-door lock. They stood, the six, staring down the long corridor ahead, the massive water pipes dark with dust.

'I'm sorry there's no light,' Muir said. 'All the power in the place was switched off last month.' They had to rely on the gleam from the high windows overhead.

'Jesus,' Asheton moaned. 'It's as cold as a witch's tit in here,' and he watched his breath smoke out.

They heard their footfalls echo as they ambled past the cream-painted walls and the silent classrooms with their half-frosted windows. Somehow, impossibly over the years, the old indefinable smell was still there.

'In Latin lessons—' Muir's voice was dark brown – 'no one can hear you scream.'

They all remembered the rows of ancient photos that once lined these walls. Faces long dead had stared back at them beneath tasselled, gold-laced caps and above striped jerseys. The First Eleven, the First Fifteen, Boxing Team A and Boxing Team B. The fives teams had been there and the Rowing Eight, proud and haughty and sure of themselves and their world. Then had come the Great War and the names of those who perished were gilded in the locked sanctums of the chapel. Bastard, E.F.L., Featherstonehaugh, B.F., Golighty, A.J.S., all lying together in foreign mud to prove there was a corner of a field that was forever Halliards.

'The bell!' Alphedge shouted. 'I used to ring it when I was a prefect. Race you for it!' And he shot off down the corridor, leaving the others in his wake.

'Not bad for an out-of-work luvvie,' Bingham commented, 'that turn of speed.'

Alphedge had spun on his heel in a pool of light at the bottom of the central staircase. In profile to the others, his jaw had dropped and his fists had clenched. To the Preacher, it seemed that the hairs on the back of his neck were standing on end.

'Oh, my God.'

Asheton laughed. 'Don't tell me. They've carpeted Big School.'

But Alphedge wasn't looking at Big School. He had his back to it, as they all knew, as Asheton should have known. One by one they reached him, and one by one they saw what he had seen. The body of a man twirled in the updraught, a half a twist to the left, another to the right, like some demented Newton's cradle in Hannibal Lecter's study.

'Who is it?' It was Bingham who gave voice to the question rising to all their throats.

'It's Quentin.' The Preacher saw it first, mounting the worn stone of the steps so that he was on the dead man's level.

Bingham moved for the rope, lashed around the banisters.

'Don't touch it!' Maxwell shouted. And they all looked at him.

'For Christ's sake, Max,' Asheton screamed at him. 'We must. That's Quent up there – George Quentin. We can't leave him like that.'

Maxwell grabbed Bingham's arm, staring steadily into his eyes. 'We can and we must,' he said.

'He's right,' Bingham echoed, looking up at the bell rope creaking on its housings. 'Old Harry will hold him till the police arrive.'

The Preacher's eyes were closed now and his lips were moving silently in prayer.

'Yes,' said Alphedge. 'We must call the police.'

But nobody moved. Nobody except George Quentin at the end of his tether.

'Anybody got a mobile?' Maxwell asked.

Asheton shook himself free of the moment and flicked his from his pocket. '999?' he asked them.

Maxwell shook his head. 'No, there's one nearer than that.'

The frost had gone by the time they took George Quentin's body away. A line of blue-and-white tape fluttered across the open gateway and men in white hoods and galoshes tiptoed their way across the gravel to waiting vehicles.

'Max.' His head came up at the sound of Jacquie's voice. 'Max, are you all right?'

He eased himself up off the fallen lime that lay sawn and trimmed at the end of the avenue of trees. 'I'm fine.' He held her hand briefly, sensing a figure at his elbow.

'Max, this is DI Thomas, Warwickshire CID. Peter Maxwell.'

Thomas nodded. He was the wrong side of forty-eight, Maxwell guessed, and could probably have given David Jason a run for the most slovenly clothed detective around. 'You

found the body?' He also sounded like something out of *The Grimleys*.

'One of several who did,' Maxwell told him. Thomas looked at Jacquie.

'The others are back at the Graveney,' she told him. 'I checked it with your DS Vernon.'

'Can we get one thing straight, Ms Carpenter?' Thomas said. 'As far as I am concerned, you are a civilian. You have no more jurisdiction here than any other member of the public, and anyway, in my patch, detective constables don't conduct enquiries; detective inspectors do. Clear?'

Maxwell's mouth opened, but it was Jacquie who spoke. 'Perfectly,' she said, and shepherded Maxwell away. She got him to her car without too much of a scene and bundled him inside.

'One of nature's gentlefolk, I presume?' Maxwell hauled off his shapeless tweed cap, and fumbled for his seat belt.

'I *have* met more co-operative colleagues.' Jacquie slammed her door and kicked the engine into life. 'The Graveney?'

'That depends,' Maxwell said.

'On what?'

He turned to face her. 'On whether George Quentin took his own life or whether he was murdered.'

Jacquie chewed her lip. 'Do you want my best guess?'

'I'd settle for that,' Maxwell said.

She looked into the steady, brown eyes. 'I'd guess it was murder, Max.'

He nodded slowly and mechanically pulled the seat belt around him. 'Not the Graveney, then,' he said. 'Let's drive. Directions are on me.'

Maxwell hadn't been to the Badger's Ease at Charlecote since he was a carefree young undergraduate with fluff on his chin and a Cambridge scarf around his neck. He still had the scarf, of course, but in those days, shortly after they'd invented the

wheel, and only let 7.3 per cent of the population's youth into universities, he'd been a driver and had coughed up to the Badger's main doors in his dad's Triumph Herald. He was young. He was carefree. He was broke.

A lot of water. A lot of bridges. A lot of sighs. Maxwell was a teacher now and still broke. The Badger's had had a face-lift and it was busy. They'd added a carvery on a wing that rolled to the west and a pétanque piste beyond that. A giant orange elephant formed a slide for the kiddies, and the little dears even had their own menu that boasted Dinosaur Dips and Brontosaurus Bites. In Maxwell's day ancient biddies who had won the vote came staggering in for a Danish or, throwing caution to the winds, a French fancy. Now, most soul-destroying of all, the place was called Zak's. No explanation was given.

'Tell me again.' Maxwell's pickled onion bounced wilfully off his plate and rolled under somebody else's table. No matter – it would be back in the jar by evening.

'It wouldn't have been a painless death, Max.' Jacquie was pushing her coleslaw around her plate. 'He'd been hit over the head, I don't know how many times, on the landing at the top of the first flight of stairs. There was blood . . .'

An old crone, whose hearing was the healthiest thing about her, looked up sharply at a nearby table, her dentures parting company with their neighbouring gums. Jacquie's head leaned closer to Maxwell's. He looked tired. For the first time since she had known him, nearly six years, he looked old.

'Hit from behind.' Maxwell was musing, picturing it in his mind, trying to make sense of it.

'Probably,' she said. 'We don't know.'

'It would have to be,' he told her. 'Quent was the best of us. Captain of the First Eleven. Victor Ludorum three times. House Captain, of course.'

She looked at him. It was like something out of that depressing play she'd done at school – *Journey's End*. They didn't have houses at Jacquie's comprehensive, still less captains

of things. And as for Victor Ludorum, Maxwell might as well have been talking about Victor Meldrew. Come to think of it, he was dead too.

'That was a long time ago, Max,' she said softly. 'People slow down. Reflexes . . .'

He flipped a beer-mat into the air with the back of his finger and caught it in the same hand.

She laughed. 'How did you do that?'

'Reflexes.' Maxwell smiled for the first time that morning. 'It was a party piece of ours, the Magnificent Seven. We could all do it. Used to bore everybody to death, girlfriends and barmen alike. But Quent could do it with both hands, simultaneously.'

She looked at him. 'It *was* a long time ago,' she said softly.

'You're right.' He sighed, leaning back in his chair, and pushed the uneaten ploughman's away from him.

'Everything all right, sir?' the child waitress asked, sweeping past buried in trays.

'Delicious, thank you.' Maxwell was still looking at Jacquie. Then his eyes swivelled to the girl, chancing, dancing, backing and advancing on her way to the kitchen. 'Year Eleven,' he said. 'Mum doesn't want her to have this Saturday job, because it might bugger up her GCSEs. *She* does, though – it'll be a useful cop-out if she does. And anyway, she might pick up the makings of a GNVQ Retail Management qualification. By the way, her name is Jade, her favourite band is Westlife and her boyfriend's called Lee.'

'Max.' Jacquie frowned. 'Do you *know* all this?'

'Of course not.' He smiled at her. 'It's the educated guess of someone who's been around kids for ever.' Then he was serious again. 'And I've been around corpses too, Jacquie. Remember how we met?'

She did. When both of them were trying to find out who killed one of Maxwell's Own, one of his sixth form at Leighford High. He'd been around nearly as many corpses as she had.

'So, Quent was still alive when somebody put a rope around his neck?'

She nodded. 'It's my guess he'd have been too weak to resist after the hammering he took.'

'Why the rope?'

'What?'

'Why the rope? Why not finish the job with whatever blunt instrument we're talking about? What blunt instrument are we talking about, by the way?'

Jacquie shrugged. 'Sorry, Max. That's forensic. You heard DI Thomas's attitude. I won't get a smell at that.'

'Where's dear old Jim Astley when you need him?'

There was nothing dear about Jim Astley, except perhaps his hourly rate; although 'old' was fair enough. But he was the pathologist-cum-police surgeon on Maxwell's own turf, far to the south. Not for him the Midlands, which were sodden and unkind.

'This Thomas.' Maxwell was running a finger round the rim of his lager glass. 'Did he give you a hard time?'

'Let's say he didn't appreciate outside help,' she said.

'So he'd appreciate mine even less.'

She nodded. 'When did the DS say he wanted a statement?'

Maxwell checked his watch. 'They're coming to the hotel at six. I thought they might want us at the station.'

'Not yet.' Jacquie was shaking her head. 'They'll try you on friendly turf first. There'll be two of them, plainclothes, discreet.'

'Softly, softly, eh?'

Her eyes flickered. 'Something like that. What can you tell me about him, Max?'

Maxwell sat back in his chair. 'Quent?' He shook his head, swilling what was left of the lager at the bottom of the glass. 'Christ knows. When asked to decline the verb "to be" in a French lesson, he began "I be, you be, he be . . ."'

Jacquie couldn't help but laugh. Neither could Maxwell.

'That's when I first became aware of him. We called him "Hebe" for a while. That was the Lower Fourths. We were eleven, still wearing short trousers. 'Course, I had the knees for

it.' And he slapped them both, just to make sure they were still there. 'That would have been around 1956. People were ripping up cinemas as they rocked around the clock and the Hungarians told the Russkies they were tired of being pushed around. Wars and rumours of wars, Jacquie; nothing changes.'

'What kind of man was he?'

Maxwell shook his head slowly. 'That's just the point,' he said, throwing his hands in the air. 'I haven't the faintest idea. Oh, I can tell you what sort of *boy* he was – sporty and funny and brave. But I hadn't seen George Quentin – until today – for thirty-seven years. Not in the flesh. All the clocks stopped in '63, Jacquie. As far as this lot goes, when I threw my blazer into that damned swimming pool, time stood still.'

She reached across and held his hand. 'Have I told you how sorry I am?' she asked.

He held hers. 'I know.' He nodded. 'I know. Come on. We've got some years to roll back.'

'Max . . .'

He held up his hand. ' "It's not your business," ' he said. ' "It's all a long time ago. There's nothing you can do. Leave it to the professionals." Is that what you were going to say?'

She smiled in spite of herself, arching an eyebrow at the same time. 'As a matter of fact' – she leaned towards him – 'I was going to say "Be careful out there". *Hill Street Blues*, remember?'

Peter Maxwell did. 'Careful?' He threw his head back and laughed. 'Careful is my middle name.' He looked at his watch. 'Let's see if we can track down Jade and pay the bill. Last one back at the Graveney's a suspect.'

The Graveney had thoughtfully set aside the under-manager's office for interviews. 'There'll be two of them,' Jacquie had said, and she was right. DS Vernon was there, mid-thirties perhaps, thick black hair, a London Scottish set to his nose. Maxwell had met him, of course, at Halliards when the squad cars rolled in, all

flashing blue lights like something out of *The Bill*. The one he hadn't met was the DCI.

'Nadine Tyler.' She had a powerful grip for a woman. 'It's Mr Maxwell, isn't it?'

'Peter Maxwell.' The Head of Sixth Form smiled.

'Do sit down.' DCI Tyler was tall, statuesque even, well aware that she was a woman in a man's job and that she had just crashed through the glass ceiling. Well aware too that the resultant shards had embedded themselves in the backs of some of her male colleagues, who were bitter, touchy, resentful.

Maxwell looked at her across the desk. She was playing the body language game well. He was in a low chair; she in a high swivel. The light was behind her so that sometimes, depending on her angle to the late afternoon sun, she looked like the winged devil out of *The Exorcist*, with beams from Hell at her elbows.

'You realize this is not a formal interview,' she said in what Maxwell took to be a cultured Wolverhampton accent, if that wasn't a contradiction in terms. 'Just a little chat?'

'Of course.' He nodded.

'But equally, you won't mind if DS Vernon takes a few notes?'

'Of course not.' Maxwell smiled at the man with his notebook on his knee across the office.

'Tell me about yourself,' Nadine Tyler said, leaning back in the chair. There were no rings on her fingers, no jewellery round her neck. The eyes were hard and grey, flinty in the afternoon light.

'Well . . .' Maxwell cradled his left knee in locked hands, as relaxed as she was. 'Let's see. I'm an eligible bachelor. I live in Leighford with my cat and collection of model soldiers. Oh, and I've been teaching for nearly four hundred years.'

Vernon, Maxwell could see, had written nothing down, but Nadine Tyler was smiling. 'What do you teach?' she asked.

'Children.' Maxwell smiled back, wondering just how much

rope she'd give him. 'History,' he said. 'I'm Head of Sixth Form.'

'Nice job?' she asked.

'Nicest in the school.' He shrugged. 'Nicer than yours, I'd wager.'

Nadine Tyler laughed. When she did the years seemed to fall away and Maxwell was looking at a girl again. 'Let's stay with you.' She leaned forward, her hands clasped quietly on the under-manager's desk. 'Obviously you and George Quentin go back a long way?'

'Oh, yes.' Maxwell nodded, resisting the urge to echo her posturally. 'I've known George for years, boy and boy. I suppose you'd say we were inseparable.'

'Were?'

'Chief Inspector,' Maxwell felt obliged to confess, 'I haven't seen George Quentin since 1963, not in the flesh.'

'In the flesh?'

'I caught him on the telly once, some chat show on City stockbrokering. I was just flicking through the channels, like you do, and there he was.'

'Tell me about the others.'

'Others?'

'Richard Alphedge.' She wasn't reading from any notes; she was staring straight at Maxwell.

'I don't really think . . .'

'Mr Maxwell.' The smile had gone and the eyes were cold and hard. 'You do realize that I'm conducting a murder en-quiry?'

'Yes.' He unlocked his fingers and shifted his position. Time for the serious stuff now.

'And that I need to *know*.'

'And that we are all suspects,' Maxwell added.

She nodded. 'That too,' she said. 'That's one thing that's not very nice about my job, Mr Maxwell; you start to suspect everybody, all the time. Is that woman *really* collecting for Help

the Aged? Is that bloke *really* a Scout leader? Where did a dropout like that get a Ferrari? It just goes with the territory.'

'And you'll be talking to the others?'

'Oh, yes.' She nodded. 'Depend on it. Alphedge.'

'Alphie is an actor; to be precise, an actor's actor. He doesn't do much any more, I understand. Bad agent, one performance, who knows? I remember he was St Joan in *St Joan* when we were in the Upper Fifths – diabolical. Some of us wanted to burn him for real. I understand his wife gets all the parts.'

'You mean, he's a kept man?'

Maxwell laughed. 'I didn't say that,' he said. 'Looking at the biceps on Mrs Alphedge, I'm not sure I dare. Chief Inspector' – he shuffled forward a little in his chair – 'can I ask you something?'

She raised her hands in the air and lolled back on the pale blue of the swivel.

'How did George Quentin die?'

The DCI thought for a moment. 'You're familiar with the cliché "I'll ask the questions, if you don't mind"?'

'Oh, yes.' Maxwell nodded. 'Jack Frost, Adam Dalgleish, even Jane Tennyson, they all say it.'

'Yes,' she said coldly. 'But this is real, isn't it? Your friend is dead.'

'Yes,' Maxwell said flatly. 'Yes, he is.'

'What about Bingham?' she asked.

'Cret? Um . . . Anthony? On your side, isn't he? Judge and all?'

The DCI shook her head. 'Don't you believe it,' she grunted. 'As a profession, lawyers are second only to journalists as prize bastards.'

'Ah.' Maxwell sensed a twinge of pique there.

'Have you seen Bingham recently?'

'Until yesterday, no. Again, not since we all left school.'

'Tell me, Mr Maxwell.' Nadine Tyler got up from behind the desk and sauntered to the far window, watching weekend

guests coming and going in the carpark outside. 'The seven of you . . . were you some sort of club, a gang?'

'What, you mean the Famous Five meet the Lords of Flatbush? No, not really. Oh, I suppose we hung around together. In the sixth form we were going to form a group, except that none of us could really play anything, and only Alphie could sing and we realized that Ash was only in it for the groupies. Then we had this ludicrous schoolboy plan to spend the night at Borley rectory, the most haunted house in England . . .'

'Yet you didn't keep up your friendship. Why was that?'

Maxwell shrugged. 'Why indeed?' He sighed. 'It happens. We none of us ended up at the same college. Cret . . . er, Anthony, went to Balliol, Oxford; Alphie to RADA. Stenhouse was with me at Cambridge, Peterhouse in fact, but he broke his leg skiing in his first Christmas vac and had to miss the rest of the year; we never got back together after that.'

'And Quentin?'

'LSE, I'm afraid.' Maxwell screwed up his face in mock disgust. 'We didn't talk about it. The LSE in those days was one up from borstal. Asheton went to Durham, although somebody told me years ago, he'd got a girl pregnant and threw it all up.'

'And Wensley?'

'Ah.' Maxwell raised both eyebrows. 'There you have me. The Preacher was always a little, shall we say, different? One of us, yet not, if you know what I mean. He was due to go, I think, to King's, London, to read theology. But there again, he often talked about living in Tibet and getting in touch with his inner self, so God knows. He seems to be ordained now.'

'Indeed.' The DCI turned to him. 'But there's nothing really about this weekend that is as it seems, is there, Mr Maxwell?'

Chapter Four

'Am I interrupting?' Anthony Bingham's head peered round Maxwell's door. The coat and scarf of the day had gone and the judge wore a jumper and cravat.

'Not at all,' said the Head of Sixth Form. 'I wondered who'd be first.'

'First?' Bingham was in the room, the door still ajar. 'Are you playing some sort of game, Max?'

'It's all a game, Ant . . . Look, I'm sorry, but inappropriate as it is, I feel I've still got to call you Cret. Can you live with that?'

'In comparison with what many a felon who has come up before me calls me, I'm sure I've got off lightly.' He closed the door. 'Any threat of you breaking open your minibar?'

Maxwell smiled and dragged himself off the bed. 'Looks like Scotch or Scotch,' he said, rummaging among the miniature bottles in the wallside cabinet.

'Fine.' Bingham threw himself down on Maxwell's settee. 'You've talked to the filth, of course?'

'The . . .'

'Police, Max. It's underworld jargon.'

'Yes.' Maxwell nodded. 'I have heard the term. I'm just a little surprised to hear *you* use it, Cret.'

'Never forget, Maxie, my boy.' Bingham took the proffered glass. 'Today's judge is yesterday's lawyer. When I took defence

43

cases I despised the boys in blue because they planted evidence in people's pockets. When I became a prosecutor, I despised them because they didn't. Either way, a dead loss. Who did you have?'

'A woman,' Maxwell told him. 'A DCI Tyler.'

'Ah, yes, Nadine. Hard-nosed bitch, I'd say. Here's to the return of capital punishment,' and he drained his glass. 'I dare say Ash will be in her knickers by nightfall. Didn't see you at dinner.'

'No. Jacquie and I ate out. Had lunch out, too, as a matter of fact.'

'Right. Rather a little cracker, that piece of yours.' The judge's eyes swivelled in all directions. 'I don't see any smalls, those little tokens of domestic bliss.'

'Jacquie has her own room.'

'Oh, really?' Bingham raised an eyebrow. 'I don't remember you being such a prude, Max. Remember Cranton, '62?' and he chuckled. 'Don't tell me Mrs Maxwell thinks you're on some sort of teaching conference?'

'There is no Mrs Maxwell, Cret.' He smiled. There had been, of course; not that Cret knew. She lay under the flowers now with her little Jenny, two girls with the bluest eyes in the world. He could still smell their warm, soft skin cradled in his arms on countless picnics, still hear their tinkling laughter down the years. He couldn't hear the scream of tyres or the rip of metal as their car bounced on tarmac and their lives ebbed away. A bend too tight. A road too wet. A police car too single minded in the chase. Those were the noises of the night. And he heard them then.

'So, what did they ask?' Bingham prompted.

'About you, and Stenhouse and Ash and the Preacher. All of you. And me, of course.'

'Did you have your solicitor present?'

'Of course not.' Maxwell chuckled. 'I haven't got a bloody solicitor. No doubt you'd have advised me to.'

'No doubt I would, but I didn't get the chance. What time did this Gorgon interview you?'

'Er . . . let's see. About four, I think. Why?'

'Divide and conquer.' Bingham nodded. 'It's the oldest trick in the book. What did she say? "Casual chat"? "Just a few queries"? "We'll take formal statements later"?'

'Something like that.' Maxwell nodded. 'Look, Cret, do you want to tell me what this is all about?'

'Sure.' Bingham shrugged. 'It's not a secret. At school, what happened? After we'd found the body, I mean?'

'Er . . . I called Jacquie.'

'Then?'

'She arrived, gave the scene the once-over and called the local law.'

'Right. She had to, of course. No choice there. Then what?'

'Said local law turned up. All Hell was let loose.'

'We were shepherded away,' Bingham recounted. 'Spotty youth with terminal keenness took our details and then what?'

'We were told we'd be interviewed at four.'

'Wrong personal pronoun, Maxie,' Bingham corrected him. '*You* were told that. I was told now, please. Consequently, I spent a very long two and a half hours in Leamington nick.'

'Two and a half hours?' Maxwell sat back on his bed again. 'Cret, do you know something the rest of us don't?'

'I am a High Court judge, Maxie. I know a *lot* the rest of you don't. I got DI Thomas, by the way, a misogynist who could misog for England. It's just his bad luck he's got a woman boss. Takes it out on suspects.'

'Is that what you are?' Maxwell asked.

'It's what we all are, Max,' Bingham said. 'Didn't Wonderwoman tell you that?'

'I believe she hinted.' Maxwell nodded. 'So you had the tape recorder, the whole works. And no solicitor.'

Bingham sighed. 'When you're a High Court judge, Maxie, you don't need one. You'd have had a tape recorder too.'

'No,' Maxwell said. 'I told you, it was just a casual chat.'

'You'd have had a tape recorder,' Bingham replied. 'There was a sergeant, yes, taking notes?'

'That's right.'

'Take many, did he?'

'Well, no, actually, now I come to think of it.'

Bingham nodded, smug and sure of himself. 'That's because he had a mini-cassette player in his pocket. Oh, it's not legal, of course, but it's there to record every word. Some talentless shite of a WPC will be on that already, analysing your inflexion, reading bollocks into your tone. Christ knows what they'll make of the Preacher.'

'Have they seen him yet?'

'Wensley? Yep.' Bingham nodded. 'Half two. Now there *is* a weirdo.'

'He's a friend of ours, Cret,' Maxwell reminded him.

'Is he, Max?' the judge asked, suddenly sitting forward. 'Are any of us friends any more? We haven't seen each other in thirty years. And did we really know each other back then? Stenhouse with his permanent sniff; remember that? We used to work him over on a regular basis. Ash was always sniffing too, wasn't he? Around the girls from Cranton or the younger dinner ladies. We didn't give it a second thought. What is he now, some reptilian old pervert? Alphie – couldn't act the skin off a rice pudding, could he? Remember he came to us late, from Uppingham or somewhere. George, dear old George . . . Victor Lubloodydorum. Remember how we hated him, all of us?'

'Did we?' Maxwell frowned.

'Of course we did – the Preacher most of all. What's this bloody Internet sect he's into?'

'I don't know,' Maxwell said. 'It's funny all this. We've got so much to catch up on, this weekend, but with Quent dead, well, it's as though we can't. It's the only topic of conversation, like a giant rock we can't see through and can't get round. What do the others say?'

Bingham stood up, finding a surface for his empty glass. 'I haven't seen the others, Max,' he said. 'I came to you first.'

'Over dinner?'

Bingham shrugged. 'Over dinner we made small talk with the ladies and whinged about Blair's government. Nobody mentioned Quent, Max; nobody at all.'

And he opened Maxwell's door. For a moment, he stood framed against the dim light of the corridor beyond. Then he turned. 'I'd lock this, Max,' he said slowly. 'You know as well as I do, it was one of us.'

It was a little after twelve when someone knocked softly on Maxwell's door. 'It's not locked,' he called.

'Mine is.' Andrew Muir was in his dressing gown and slippers, a towel around his neck. 'Janet insists on it. Have you got a minute, Max?'

'Always,' Maxwell said. 'If you want to raid my bar, it's Scotch or Scotch.'

'That'll do me,' the journalist said. 'Tangle o' the Isles. In fact, I'd settle for boot polish about now. God, what a day!' and he threw himself down on the settee. 'That daughter of yours in bed?'

'Stenhouse.' Maxwell poured for them both. 'I feel I have to tell you she's not my daughter.'

'Not? Oh, Christ.' Muir slapped his forehead. 'I'm sorry, Max. Getting a bit long in the tooth for that sort of thing myself. You old dog, eh? Still, I should watch her around Ash. You know what he's like.'

'Oh, yes.' Maxwell sat on the edge of the bed.

There was a silence; something neither of them had ever known at Halliards. 'Did Bingham come to see you earlier?'

Maxwell nodded. 'He did. Advised me to lock my door.'

'Me too,' Muir said. 'I wouldn't have, of course, but for Janet.'

'You said,' Maxwell reminded him. 'Janet is a bit windy about this?'

'Well, you know what women are.' Muir leaned back, cradling his glass. 'Still, it's a bit of a facer.'

'What did the police ask you?' Maxwell wanted to know.

'Everything, really. I had that surly bastard, Thomas. You?'

'Nadine Tyler.'

'Ah, yes. Ash had her.'

'In the biblical sense?' Maxwell asked.

Muir laughed. 'Wouldn't be surprised. Thomas seemed very interested in you.'

'Really?' Maxwell sipped his Scotch. 'How very flattering.'

'Max, I don't know how to put this, but I got the impression you were in the frame.'

'Indeed?' Maxwell nodded. 'Should I make a bolt for the door, do you think, or slash my wrists?'

'Be serious, Max.' Muir started to pace. It wasn't a good sign. 'He kept asking things like did you and Quent get on at Halliards. Were you jealous of him as Victor Ludorum and Captain of Games and so on.'

'I seem to remember winning a place to . . . where was it now? . . . Cambridge. While he scraped in to LSE. No offence to the pinko liberal egalitarians at UCAS, of course.'

'I told him all that, Max,' Muir explained. 'I'm not sure he bought it. Jesus, Max, I just feel so guilty.'

'You do?'

'Well, this whole thing is my fault, isn't it? I mean, the weekend, the reunion – it was my idea. I just thought we couldn't let Halliards go under the bulldozer without one last get-together. What a bloody auld lang syne this has turned out to be.'

Maxwell was alongside him, clapping a hand on his shoulder. 'Look, Stenhouse, you weren't to know, all right? There's some maniac out there who had it in for Quent. He happened to choose this weekend, that's all. It isn't down to you.'

Muir looked at him through eyes unconvinced, afraid.

thing, you know, bowled over by the show and so on. Had his wife with him.'

'Wife?' Maxwell frowned.

'Is that so odd?' Alphedge asked. 'I've got mine with me.'

'No, of course not. It's just that nobody mentioned a wife, not the police, not anybody.'

'Why should they?' Alphedge asked. 'You wouldn't expect her to be twirling up there with him, would you? God, Max, you don't think she did it?'

'I really don't know, Alphie,' Maxwell said. He'd been around men at breaking point before. He'd seen it. In the corridors that led to the chalkface, the subterranean caverns crawling with kids, he'd seen the pale faces, the shaking hands, heard the hysterical laughter. He'd counted the paces across the staffroom floor and noted the twitching of the eyes.

'It's all right, Alphie.' Maxwell reached out and gripped Alphedge's arm. 'Everything will be all right,' and he nodded to Cissie to get the man back to bed.

She smiled and helped her husband up, twirling him round. Alphedge was still muttering, 'Got to do something, Max. Must do something,' as Cissie helped him through the door. In the corridor, she turned and kissed Maxwell on the cheek, mouthing 'thank you' in the silence of the early hours.

He watched them go, then checked his watch. He needed a drink and the bar didn't close until two. He grabbed his key and made for the stairs.

'It's a quarter to three,' David Asheton crooned, watching the hanging tankards through the distortion of his glass. 'Well, ten to two, anyway . . . Max, thank Christ. I hate drinking alone.'

'I thought I'd have to.' Maxwell perched on the high stool next to him.

'Not while there's a bar open. Mine host!' Asheton thumped the counter. 'My old friend will have a . . . what?'

'Southern Comfort, barman, please, and have a little one yourself.'

The barman had rather less humanity than the bloke who kept Ray Milland company in *The Lost Weekend*, and he was a million years younger. He'd lost the will to live by half past twelve and the dark circles under his eyes said it all. 'No, thank you, sir,' was the sum of his repartee.

'Ash?'

'Hair of the dog.' Asheton waggled the empty glass at the man. 'But it's my round, Maxie.'

'You're pissed,' Maxwell said, fumbling in his pocket for his wallet.

'As a fart,' Asheton conceded. 'Don't tell me you've left that lovely little thing Jacquie alone in a great big bed?'

'I fear I have,' Maxwell nodded. 'Veronica?'

'The time of the month.' Asheton sighed. 'Ah,' and he accepted the brandy gratefully. 'Max, your health,' and they clashed glasses. 'And here's to the bastard who killed dear old Quent. May he rot in Hell.'

'I'll drink to that.' Maxwell did. 'I gather you had DCI Tyler.'

Asheton sniggered and winked at his old oppo. 'She was gagging for it by the time the interview ended,' he confided to Maxwell, the barman and any other lizard still lounging at that hour of the morning.

'What did she ask you?'

'Oh, inconsequential stuff, mostly,' Asheton said. 'They're going through the motions, Max. They know who did it.'

'They do?' Maxwell was all ears.

'Of course. The Preacher.'

'The Preacher?'

'Is there a fucking echo in here?' Asheton slurred. 'Of course it's the Preacher. "Behold, a dark horse. And his name that sat on him was Death." Oh, come on, Maxie.' Asheton reached across and shook the man's knee. 'You remember Wensley, what a social misfit he was, what a bloody pariah. None of us could work out what he was doing at Halliards, remember? He just didn't fit in. Christ knows how he got to be one of the Seven.'

Maxwell shrugged. 'We were sorry for him, I suppose.'

'You were,' Asheton grunted. 'Personally, I couldn't abide the bastard. What possessed Stenhouse to invite him? It's all bollocks.'

'Formal statements tomorrow, apparently.' Maxwell drained his glass.

'Not before midday, I hope,' Asheton said. 'I don't do the Sunday morning thing. Besides, it'll all be over by then. The Preacher will have cracked.'

'Will he, Ash?' Maxwell slapped the man's shoulder, and winked at him. 'I wonder. You get your beauty sleep now,' and he was gone.

There was no reply at the Preacher's door. Maxwell knocked once, twice, waited in the silence of the Sunday morning. Nothing. The man slept the sleep of the just. Or was it the dead? For a moment a shiver darkened Peter Maxwell's soul, a step on his grave. He looked right. Nothing. Left. Nothing again. There was a desolation about hotels in the watching hours. The building was full of people, but the people were silent, missing. Even Asheton had stumbled off up the stairs, footsteps padding erratically along the carpets; and the barman had washed his last glass and had slid down the metal grille with a crash.

Only the soft lights burned. The old building groaned, stirring in its own sleep, lost in its own memories, melting with the years in the still of an autumn night. He knocked on another door and a face he knew, a face he loved, appeared on the other side of it.

'It's late,' he said.

'That's my line.' She laughed and pulled him inside, wrapping her arms around him and holding him close.

'It's cold,' he told her, 'out there.'

She took him to the bed and knelt on it. 'It's warm in here,' she said. He kissed her soft, wet mouth and breathed in the tent of her hair which covered his face. 'I'm afraid, Jacquie,' he whispered.

She frowned, holding him at arm's length. 'No, you're not,' she said. 'You're Mad Max. A thousand children go in awe of you every day and a thousand children love you. They'd walk through fire for you, Max.'

He laughed. 'What am I, some bloody Pied Piper?'

'You call the tune,' she said.

'Have you been reading my lines again?' he asked her, arching an eyebrow.

'Why have you come, Max?' she asked, holding his face in both hands.

'I couldn't sleep,' he told her.

She closed her eyes and sighed. 'Why have you come?' she asked again. And her eyes wandered to the pillow to her right.

Maxwell's did too. 'You haven't been asleep,' he said.

'How do you know?' she asked. 'I've got my nightie on.'

Maxwell couldn't miss that. Her breasts jutted under the silk and her hips swelled as she moved to the carpet, looking up at him. 'There's no dent in the pillow,' he said.

She laughed and clapped. 'We'll make a detective of you yet.'

'And. . . .' He got off the bed. 'This is the real clincher. No teeth in the jar.'

She squealed and threw the pillow at him. 'You bastard!'

'I came to talk, Jacquie.' He was serious again. The wit, the wag, the raconteur, the teller of tall tales was a little boy lost on a sea of blood.

She knew his moods, felt his pain. 'It hurts, doesn't it?' She nodded.

'Like Hell,' he said. 'But I don't know why.'

'Yes, you do, Max.' She held both his hands. 'Because it

wasn't just George Quentin hanging there, was it? It was your childhood, your school. For a lot of us, schooldays are the worst of our lives. We hate them; can't wait to leave. But for you, for every old Halliardian, I expect, it was a way of life. That life's been snuffed out. *That's* what hurts. Come on, I'll make us both a cup of cocoa and we'll talk about tomorrow.'

'Tomorrow?'

'Tomorrow,' she said, 'is one day nearer to catching the bastard who's killed your childhood.'

He stood where the pavilion had stood all those years ago. Far away, beyond the hedge and the broad sweep of the playing fields, Halliards looked grim and black against the lightening pearl of the sky. Dawn streaked flat and purple to the east. He knew the police tape still fluttered in the grounds, could see the fitful moon gilding the helmet plate of the copper patrolling the grounds. He strained to hear the man's boots crunching on the gravel. He'd done it; what he'd set out to do. And in the end, it had been so easy, so laughably bloody easy.

He walked away into the morning.

Chapter Five

'George Quentin,' the man in the green mask said. 'Male Caucasian, approximately fifty. Well nourished. Good muscle tone.' He swung away in his swivel chair and slid the length of the mortuary table. 'But I expect you already know most of that, Inspector.'

Ben Thomas did. He hated Sunday mornings. He hated them most of all when he was sitting in a morgue that was colder than a penguin's arsehole with a dead man for company. 'Cut to the chase, Rajiv. Shouldn't you be in church?'

Rajiv raised an eyebrow and hooked his mask under his chin. Ben Thomas was a racist bastard. There was no doubt about that. But, unlovely as he was, he had a way of getting away with it, a way he'd learned as an insider with Warwickshire CID. You loved him or you hated him. Come to think of it, Rajiv Nagapon hated him.

'Hanging, then.' Thomas lounged against the cold white of the wall tiles.

'Not exactly.' Nagapon turned to his computer and hammered the keys with his stubby fingers. 'Let's deal with the superficial injuries first. He has a compound fracture of the skull. Somebody struck him three, possibly four times on the back of the head. There are radial cracks from the point of impact on the parietal region . . . want to take a look?'

Thomas didn't. He would die rather than admit he was uncomfortable around corpses. He had his back to the dead man and that was how he wanted it to stay. 'Weapon?' he asked.

'A club. Or at least something heavy and wooden. There were fibres matted in the hair. I am having them tested as we speak.'

'That would be on the landing.' Thomas was remembering the murder site, the flight of stone steps at Halliards and the blankness of the oriel window that looked down on to the place where Quentin's blood was found. 'We think he was facing away from the window, standing on the landing overlooking the hall below. He'd have been looking at the statue of the school's founder, in the niche opposite the front doors.'

'That would work.' Nagapon nodded, swivelling his chair along the counter to check something. 'Here.' He fitted an X-ray into place and flicked on the white light. 'Parietal view of Quentin's skull. See the point of impact?'

Thomas did.

'And the radial cracks?'

Again, yes.

'He pitched forward, hitting his mouth on something . . .'

'The balustrade.' Thomas was fitting it all into place. He remembered the brass railings worn smooth by countless school-boy hands.

'He loosened two teeth and, of course, there is much bleeding from the lips and gums.'

'Then he went down?'

'On his right side. There is some minor bruising to the shoulder as it hit the floor.'

'Stone,' Thomas murmured, 'unyielding.' He had knelt on those flags, worn and slightly uneven. Even now he remembered the cold.

'And here.' Nagapon flicked up a second X-ray. 'A crush fracture of the right orbit. He was lying on his front, with his face turned to the left when the last one, perhaps two, blows were delivered. As you see, the point of impact has slipped sideways.'

'We found blood on the stairs,' Thomas told him. 'SOCO counted sixteen drops.'

'From the murder weapon.' Nagapon nodded, glancing across to the white, dead soles of George Quentin, waxy in the glare of the neon lights. 'He took it away with him.'

'You think it's a he?'

Nagapon shrugged. 'I have no way of knowing that,' he said. 'It depends on the weapon used, the frenzy of the attack.'

'What happened then?' Thomas asked. 'The hanging.'

'This is where strength would have come in, from the scene-of-crime report I have read.'

Thomas nodded. 'He would have had to have been lifted nearly three feet on to the balustrade with the rope around the neck. Gravity would have done the rest.'

'But not very well.' Nagapon got out of his chair for the first time and crossed to the corpse. He lifted the finger of the left hand. 'The nails have changed colour,' he said, and he let the hand fall. 'The tongue protrudes from the teeth, the lips and ears are blue. There is a light froth of blood around the nostrils. The right hand' – he reached across George Quentin's lifeless form with the Y-shaped incision yet to be sewn up – 'is still clenched in spasm. The man was still alive when his killer put the rope around his neck. He may even perhaps have been conscious.'

'Jesus,' Thomas whispered, shaking his head. 'Can you give me a time of death?'

'When was he found?' Nagapon asked.

'Mid-morning, yesterday.'

'SOCO says the murder site was cold.'

'An empty school,' Thomas confirmed. 'About as warm as this place.'

Nagapon didn't smile. He didn't share the gallows humour of his calling or of the police. He was a professional. And death was nothing to smile about. 'He's almost free from rigor now,' he said, tilting the shattered head with the sawn-off cranium and feeling the jaw muscles soft under his gloved fingers. 'My guess, and that is all it is at present, is that he died about two a.m.'

'The early hours of Saturday.' Thomas was tracing it back. 'Right.'

'There's little more I can tell you, Inspector.' Nagapon pinged off his gloves. 'You have the rope that hanged him. The knot was to the left?'

Thomas nodded. He still felt cold at the memory of the man dangling there in the half-light, his hands like talons, his eyes bulging under the dark matted blood of the hair. Memories like that never go away. You bury them for your family, your mates, if you've got any who aren't coppers, but the night terrors bring them back, screaming through dreams without end.

'Thirty minutes?' Thomas frowned, working it all out, assessing the time it would have taken to strike, haul the man into position and perhaps wait until he died. 'So, if that's the case, the attack could have happened at – what? – one-forty, possibly a little earlier.'

Nagapon glanced at the clock, taking a little leaf from the good inspector's book of black humour. 'If you will excuse me, Mr Thomas, I think I hear the muezzin calling me to prayer. Which way is Mecca?'

'Now we are six,' Maxwell murmured, looking around the room. Stenhouse Muir's original plan for this Sunday was lunch at the Graveney, followed by a quick round on the hotel's golf course. As it was, the old gang were sitting in a police waiting-room, waiting for the police.

Asheton was the first to respond, sitting opposite Maxwell, frowning. 'Is this what this is?' he asked. 'Some bloody replay of *Ten Little Niggers*?'

'Indians, please.' Muir wagged a finger at him.

'Native Americans, if we're going down that road.' Alphedge smirked. 'PC is as PC does.'

'Where did they take the ladies?' Bingham asked.

'Some WPC whisked them upstairs,' Alphedge told him.

'Divide and conquer.' Bingham nodded. 'They'll get Thomas. We'll get Tyler.'

'Sexy policeperson, repulsive policeperson?' Maxwell asked.

'Something like that,' Bingham said.

The clock on the wall said ten to twelve. A pale sun was streaming in through the slats of the blinds, the trees of the carpark silhouetted like ghosts on the blankness of the wall, shifting in the morning breeze.

'What do you know about this, Stenhouse?' Asheton asked.

The mock Scotsman looked at him. 'What's that supposed to mean?'

'Well, this whole thing,' Asheton said. 'This reunion nonsense. It was your bloody idea.'

'So, what are you saying?' Muir was leaning forward in his chair, facing his man down. 'That Quentin's death is *my* fault?' He knew Asheton was only putting into words what he'd said to himself a thousand times in the last twenty-four hours.

'You had the key,' Asheton said. 'Who else could it have been?'

'Look, come on, boys.' Alphedge was on his feet, ever the mediator, the go-between.

Then they were all shouting at once, except the Preacher, who sat beneath the clock, his face motionless, his eyes closed. He looked like a Norman Rockwell painting.

The door flew open and a burly copper stood there in a blue jumper with sergeant's chevrons glittering silver on his shoulder. 'Mr Maxwell?'

'Yes.' Maxwell was glad of the moment. The six were falling apart. It was *The Usual Suspects* and only one of them knew who Kaiser Sose was.

'The DCI would like a word. Can I get the rest of you gentlemen a cup of tea?'

Maxwell grabbed a baguette to keep body and soul together. He sat in the lounge of the Graveney, sunk in the leatherette of a massive armchair. He was on his second Southern Comfort when the man he wanted to talk to strode through the lobby.

'Preacher?'

John Wensley turned and half smiled. 'Hello, Max,' he said.

Maxwell crossed to him. 'Can I get you a drink?' he asked.

'I'll have an iced tea,' Wensley said.

Maxwell raised an enquiring eyebrow to the girl at the bar. This was likely to tax her NVQ training to the limits, but she bustled away to do her very best. Maxwell wasn't to know that she came of stiff-upper-lip stock and her great-granny had worked in the NAAFI when they bombed Coventry.

'I haven't really had a chance for a chat.' Maxwell ushered his man to the little circle of chairs. 'How the hell are you?' As he said it, his focus inevitably settled on the man's dog-collar, but he was in for a penny by this time and a tactical withdrawal would only make matters worse. 'What did the police ask you?'

'What did they ask you?' John Wensley had been a careful boy. Now he was a careful man.

'My whereabouts on what they predictably call the night in question.'

'What did you tell them?'

'The truth.'

'Which was?'

Maxwell leaned back in the snug of his chair, crossing his legs. 'I was in my room, number forty-six, on the first floor.'

'Asleep?'

'No.' Maxwell was prepared to play along for the moment, but it would be the Preacher's turn next. 'I read until about one,

one-fifteen. Some tosh, before you ask, on the death of Chris-topher Marlowe.'

'Interesting man.' Wensley nodded. 'An atheist.'

'It's at times like these I thank God I'm one.' Maxwell beamed. The joke died in the ether.

Wensley's tea arrived and he called the girl back. 'What's this?' he asked her, holding up the sweet in the saucer.

'That's your free chocolate augmentation,' she said.

'I don't want it,' he told her. 'Take it away.'

She looked embarrassed, but Maxwell saved the day. 'Waste not, want not,' he said, and snatched it expertly from Wensley's fingers. 'Thank you, my dear. Delicious.'

'So you're a teacher, Max?' Wensley stirred the cubes with the long, elegant spoon.

'For my sins,' Maxwell said. 'But don't change the subject, Preacher. What did the police ask you?'

'It sounds very similar,' Wensley said, leaning back and cross-ing his legs too. 'They wanted to know my movements on Friday night, particularly the early hours of Saturday morning.'

'What about your movements last night?' Maxwell asked him, slowly rolling the cut glass between his fingers.

'Last night?' Wensley frowned.

'I came a-calling,' Maxwell told him. 'It was late. About half twelve. You were probably asleep.'

'No,' said Wensley. 'I wasn't there. What did you want?'

'To make some sense of all this, John.' Maxwell couldn't remember when he'd used the man's name before. It didn't sound right.

Wensley nodded. 'That's what we'd all like to do,' he said. 'But it won't happen without God's grace.'

'Ah, yes.' Maxwell had known this moment would come. 'Tell me about this church of yours.'

'My church?' Wensley looked at him. 'It's not mine, Max, it's for all of us. Anyone who wants to come in. The door's always open.'

'Where were you last night?' Maxwell was suddenly aware of how cold the lobby was and how still. The hubbub from the dining room had stopped, as though every punter in there had paused, Yorkshire-laden fork inches from their mouths, to hear the Preacher's answer.

'Wandering, Max,' Wensley said as he sipped his tea. 'It's what I do.'

Goodbyes had been difficult. Muir and Asheton weren't speaking. Their respective women had followed suit, Janet Muir all too keen to loathe Veronica on account of the woman's age and looks alone. Both Alphie and his wife had hugged Maxwell, in the way that luvvies do, and this bonhomie had extended to Jacquie, who was still wiping off Cissie's lipstick as she drove for the Graveney's gates.

The Preacher hadn't been there as the others settled their bills in reception. Maxwell imagined he was wandering again. They'd all promised Maxwell they'd see him again, all swapped addresses and phone numbers. When it came to e-mails, Maxwell gave up. His old oppos appeared to have embraced the twenty-first century. He was almost as aghast at this as at the death of George Quentin. The stone-faced Bingham implied that when they met again it might be across a court of law; there were testing times ahead. Maxwell suddenly had a mental picture of how fatuous the man must look in his wig.

'I'm sorry, Jacquie.' Maxwell was looking at her as they inched their way through the traffic on Warwick's High Street, the Tudor timbers of the Lord Leycester Hospital looking surreal in the afternoon sun, like a film set waiting for Joseph Fiennes.

'Max,' she scolded him, slapping his leg. 'Even in my professional capacity, I don't think for a moment any of this is down to you.'

'At the very least,' he said, 'it was something of a busman's holiday for you.'

'I'm the one who's sorry, Max. Halliards won't be the same again, will it?'

He shook his head. 'We all thought we were coming to witness the death of a school, and what we actually saw was the death of a scholar. How was DI Thomas?'

'Once he'd got over whatever chip he's carrying on his shoulder, he was all right. What's this DCI like?'

'Tyler?' Maxwell let his head loll back on the rest. 'Not a suitable job for a woman, is it, Jacquie?' he asked her.

'Any more than it is at my level, you mean. God, Max, you're a dinosaur. I love you dearly, but . . .'

'Ah, yes.' Maxwell laughed. 'The cruelty of that word "but," eh? DCI Tyler is . . . what's the word? Predatory.'

'Insecure,' Jacquie said.

'Ah.' Maxwell smiled. 'A woman's point of view. You mean she's got a lot of living up to to do?'

'Something like that,' Jacquie said. 'When she started in the job, there'd have been the name-calling, the sexual innuendo, the sending her on endless trips upstairs so the blokes could have a butcher's up her skirt.'

'Just like school,' Maxwell muttered. 'Did you know Josie Fancut in Year Ten wears pink knickers?'

'No.' Jacquie bridled in mock horror. 'And I don't think you should, either.'

'If I had the time, dear girl,' he said, folding his arms and closing his eyes, 'I'd fill you in on the complex socio-erotic nature of teenage girls and their relationships with male teachers. On second thoughts, you'd probably arrest me.'

'What are you going to do, Max?' she asked him.

He didn't open his eyes. 'There's a little-known passage in Genesis,' he said. 'And on the eighth day, the Lord rested, decided he was still pretty bushed, so he made half-term that man may be exceeding glad and rejoice in his name, saying, "Yea, God is good and we shall gather and give thanks for the breather and the lie-in." That great event happens next week.'

She laughed her tinkling laugh. 'You old hypocrite,' she said. 'And anyway, I didn't ask when you were going to do it, I asked what you were going to do.'

Maxwell opened his eyes and sat up. 'What are our options, Jacquie?' he asked. 'Quent's murder, I mean. Passing maniac?'

Her eyes flickered across to him, leaving the traffic for as long as she dared. 'Motiveless murder, you mean?'

'It happens, doesn't it?'

'Oh, yes.' She nodded. 'And with increasing frequency. Some poor bastard is found by a battery of psychologists and psychiatrists to be deranged. He serves time in a secure unit, drugged to the eyeballs, whereupon a different battery of psychologists and psychiatrists decides he's fine now and releases him into the community. Except, he's not fine. He's a danger to himself and others.'

'And he kills George Quentin?'

Jacquie was shaking her head. 'If George Quentin died in a street, and if nothing had been taken from the body, I'd say yes, that's definitely a scenario worth considering. As it is, no. Unless, of course, your maniac wandered into Halliards School late on Friday night and bumped into him.'

'All right.' Maxwell was eliminating possibilities. 'Theft.'

'Well,' Jacquie said, raising a casual middle finger to a white van driver who had just cut her up. 'Now I know what it feels like to be on the outside of a case. We don't know, do we, if Quentin was robbed?'

'No, we don't,' Maxwell agreed. 'None of us touched the body. I've no idea if Quentin's wallet was on him or not.'

'Had he checked into the hotel?'

'No,' Maxwell told her. 'That I was able to verify. His name isn't in the signing-in book, he hadn't paid for the room, and no one had seen him on the hotel premises.'

'No one?' In Jacquie's profession, it paid to be sure.

'No one I spoke to,' Maxwell qualified. 'None of the six.'

'Theft is a possibility,' Jacquie went on, mechanically going through the motions of driving south along the M40. 'Let's suppose Quentin disturbed a burglar.'

'Were there any signs of that?'

'None that I could see,' Jacquie said. 'Of course, Halliards is a big building. How many doors are there?'

'Christ knows.' Maxwell shrugged. 'There were parts of the place I never went into in my seven years there. I'd stick my neck out and guess at six entrances on the ground floor; that's apart from windows, of course. Stenhouse used a key.'

'On the Saturday?'

Maxwell nodded. 'When we found Quent. We went in by the chapel cloisters.'

'Where did he get it?'

'Stenhouse? I've no idea. Presumably off the property developers. Unless, of course, he'd had it all along, ever since we left school. That wouldn't surprise me.'

'Is that likely?' Jacquie asked. 'After all these years?'

Maxwell hadn't considered it to be, but now, he wasn't so sure.

'All right,' he said, 'let's go with the burglary theory for a moment. Let's assume that somebody in a striped T-shirt and mask gets into the school by some means we didn't have a chance to find. There he is, filling his bag marked "swag" with . . . what? What's to steal?'

'What was there?' Jacquie had only had time to check the entrance hall, corridor and Big School before the local force had arrived. The rest of the place was a closed book to her.

'Bugger all, as far as I know. The school itself closed last year, according to Stenhouse, and they were about to turn it into a conference centre, knocking walls down, putting in Jacuzzis, whatever. I know from my own dear experience what our light-fingered friends go for in school attacks is computers, music centres. There's no money in books and, anyway, Jo Scuzzball can't read.'

'All the hardware had gone from Halliards, then?' Jacquie asked.

'My dear girl.' Maxwell spread his arms as far as safety allowed. 'We'd only just finished writing on slates the year before I left. I don't think Halliards was ever at the cutting edge of technology. Anyway, we're missing the point.'

'Which is? Oh, sorry.' Jacquie thumped Maxwell's knee with a particularly cavalier gear change.

'Which is, what was Quent doing at Halliards the night he died? Did I go there? No. I went to the Graveney, as per Stenhouse's invitation. And that's three miles away as *Corvus corone* flies. If Quent received the same invitation, and presumably he did, why not do likewise?'

'Which brings us back to one of you,' Jacquie said.

'Thanks, light o' my life.' Maxwell frowned.

'All right, one of *them*,' Jacquie corrected herself. 'Can you live with that, Max?'

'That's not the point, Jacquie,' he told her. 'The point is, George Quentin couldn't.'

In the beginning, there were open fields on the high ground above Leighford, within a walk of the sea. The little village that one of William of Normandy's clerks had noted in the Domesday Book as having eight ploughs in demesne in the vill of Aelfric in the Confessor's time had grown a tad by the time the bulldozers moved in and they built Leighford High School. They skimped, of course, dreaming of a secondary modern of a mere three hundred pupils where the hewers of coal and drawers of water would learn the rudiments of the arts their ancestors had followed since the Conqueror's time, plus a bit of readin', ritin' and 'rithmetic. Since then, the great Comprehensive Revolution had followed, whereby everybody from the Prime Minister to the groundsman had come to believe that Jack was as good as his master and the great leveller, the National Curriculum, had produced generations that couldn't read or write or do arithmetic and had long since forgotten how to hew coal or draw water.

Peter Maxwell had stood out against all that. During all his years in teaching he had railed against those no-hopers who split their infinitives like matchsticks and ended sentences with prepositions. So much for his colleagues; some of the kids were just as bad.

That Monday morning, Maxwell once more bestrode the narrow world of Leighford High like a colossus. 'Morning, Matilda,' he bellowed at the hapless librarian, not in fact of that name, who stood dithering next to a computer screen. He held up her copy of the *Grauniad*. 'Encouraging leftist twaddle again, librarian mine? I must have a word with the Thought Police about you.'

The woman's frozen smile said it all. She'd never been able to cope with Mad Max. As if on cue, the Prefect of the Thought Police swept through the library on one of his rare forays. When you're a head teacher, with degrees in education and biology, books are an alien concept to you.

'Performance management, Mr Maxwell.' James Diamond, BSc, MEd, was always formal with his staff in open-plan areas of the school. Lest there should be a child lurking.

'Wash your mouth out, Headmaster!' Maxwell was appalled.

'Seriously, Max.' Diamond was more relaxed once he'd satisfied himself that there were no students in sight. 'I need your input on this. You're a senior teacher – bound to be a mentor.'

'Oh, bound to be,' Maxwell agreed. 'I'll get straight on it, right after 9C4 have done their "I can tie my shoelaces" lesson.'

'Max.' Diamond was a boring fart, it had to be said. He looked Maxwell in the eye through the curve of his gold-rimmed glasses and straightened his Marks and Spencer tie. 'Do you have to be so flippant?'

Maxwell stared back at the man. 'About performance management? Indubitably, Headmaster. But about the serious business of education, never. Can I have Friday off?'

'What? Why?'

'A friend of mine died at the weekend. Friday's the funeral.'

'Oh, Max, I'm sorry. Er . . . yes, of course. See Tom about cover, will you? Um. A friend, you say?'

'That's right.'

'Well, how good a friend?'

'An old friend,' Maxwell insisted. Unlike the headmaster, Maxwell had a choice.

'Well, you see, unless it's family, I shall have to ask you to lose a day's pay.'

Maxwell beamed at the petty bureaucracy of the man. 'Consider it lost, Headmaster,' he said.

He made his way across the quad past children without number trudging to their first lesson. Patiently, he placed one or two mavericks on the right side of the corridor as he swept through H Block. Then he was up the stairs and into the staffroom. 'Bugger and poo!' was Maxwell's usual expletive when he saw yet another memo in his pigeonhole. Today was no exception.

'Morning, Max.' Sally Greenhow, the tall blonde who was number two in Special Needs, hurtled past him, carrying the usual bundle of rap sheets for a case conference.

'Morning, light of my darkness,' but he wasn't looking at her. The memo in his hand said there'd been a phone call, at eight-thirty that morning. More, it was a message on the school answerphone. 'Shit!' and he was gone, hurtling down the corridor, notices on walls fluttering in his wake.

'Thingee!' He came down like a wolf on the fold into reception, firing his deadly stare at the hapless girl on the switchboard, whose name was no more Thingee than the librarian was Matilda. 'You've got a message for me?'

'Yes, Mr Maxwell.' She turned to the incomprehensible machine to her left and pushed buttons. There was a ping and a whirr, followed by an electronic whine, all the noises of the twenty-first century.

'Max, it's Anthony Bingham. Look, I'm sorry to leave a

message like this, especially at work. I tried your home number, but you'd clearly left. I need to see you. Urgently. I'm coming to Leighford this afternoon. I'll be at yours by . . . five-thirty.'

And the line went dead.

'Is everything all right, Mr Maxwell?' Thingee noticed that Maxwell had gone a funny colour.

He looked down at the girl with the headset. 'I hope so, Thingee,' he said. 'I'll let you know.'

Chapter Six

Five-thirty of the clock came and went, as it tends to do at least twice a day. Peter Maxwell had abandoned the curry he'd intended for Monday night – bad Korma – and promised himself pie and chips at his local later. Except now it was later and he was still waiting. He took one last look at the naked street outside 38 Columbine, the tarmac orange under the streetlamp. Then he climbed the stairs to his Inner Sanctum.

They stretched out before him under the lamplight, the riders of Lord Cardigan's Light Brigade, immaculately recreated by the Head of Sixth Form in all their fifty-four millimetre splendour. Cardigan himself sat with Lord Lucan, the plastic brother-in-law he hated, listening to an exasperated Captain Nolan pointing down the Valley of Death. Beyond this knot of officers, the men of the 13th Light Dragoons were still smoking their pipes, their plastic stomachs still rumbling from a lack of breakfast. Maxwell had been lovingly collecting these models for years. They were his weakness, his indulgence; they and Southern Comfort. Oh, and Metternich, the cat.

He threw himself down on the swivel chair and switched on his modelling lamp. He caught his own reflection in the skylight as he patted the jaunty Crimean forage cap into place on his forehead. Then he went to work. Captain Soames Gambier Jenyns lay on his back on a sheet of newspaper. Beside him, his bay charger, Moses, champed the plastic grass. Maxwell put the man into the saddle, lining up the stirrup irons and checking the length of the rein.

'A cigar, I think, Count, don't you? Someone with names like Soames Gambier would be smoking a cigar as he reasoned why, don't you think?'

He didn't glance up. He knew the great black-and-white beast was watching him from his perch on the linen basket that housed only God knew what, ears flat, tail idly lashing. The darkness of the mid-October evening all but complete, it would soon be time for the hunt.

'Mind you . . .' Maxwell whittled the tiny piece of plastic with his craft knife and stuck it expertly to the man's lips. 'The good captain hadn't been well, Count. He was at Scutari in September, before Ms Nightingale got there, of course. A touch of gutrot, I shouldn't wonder. Christ, Cret!' and he threw the good captain down, scraping back his chair and pacing the attic room. 'Where the hell are you?'

No one could measure the hell where Anthony Bingham was. His mortal remains could be measured easily enough. They'd been found the next morning, a little after six-thirty, by a jogger pounding up the gentle gradient on Ryker Hill. His arm had been sticking out from under an upturned sofa the colour of mud through which the rusty springs poked. The jogger hadn't seen clearly in the half-light, which is why he'd stumbled over the hand. Then he crouched to feel it. He would never be quite the same again.

By the time Henry Hall arrived, it was already mid-morning and the blue-and-white tape and knot of constables kept the morbidly curious back. Geeks in anoraks huddled in the rain and the first of the paparazzi were sheltering under the trees, keeping their cameras and their powder dry, waiting for developments. Hall's arrival galvanized them into action.

'What can you tell us, Chief Inspector? Any clues as to the victim's identity? Got a motive yet?'

Hall didn't break his stride. 'Later,' he growled at them. That was when he'd know anything; when he might, God forbid, have need of them. All he knew so far was that a man was dead.

Henry Hall was a bland bastard, fortysomething, fast track, as inscrutable as Maxwell's cat, but without the attitude.

'Guv.' The burly DS in the parka nodded at him.

'What have we got, Graham?' Hall crouched by the settee, pulled back now to reveal its secret.

'Male Caucasian, guv.' Graham Rackham was prepared to go only so far. 'Mid-fifties. There's a lot of muck where the back of his head used to be.'

'Where's Astley?'

Dr James Astley, the police surgeon, was slithering down the slope ahead, the only one of them, in his white plastic outfit, not getting wet. 'Sorry,' he called. 'Having a pee. Bloody bracken's thick up that way. Are you well, Henry?'

Astley was the wrong side of fifty-five, solid rather than overweight, core hair rather than balding, a middle-aged man in a hurry.

'I was,' Hall told him, 'before I got this call. What can you tell me, Jim?'

'Sergeant.' Astley cocked his oddly garbed head to one side. 'Feet.'

'Oh, sorry, Doc.' Rackham stepped backward.

Astley looked at the SOCO boys going about their business, measuring, photographing, weighing and collecting the evidence. 'I don't know how much good that little lot'll do. It's like the night before Agincourt around here. I've never seen so many footprints and this bloody rain isn't helping.'

It wasn't, and Hall knew that Jim Astley was right. Ryker Hill, with its woodland path that wound through the ferns and the silver birch, had blossomed in recent years. Discarded tissues and condoms dripping off the bracken told the tale that this was

75

a lovers' trysting place, for spotty sixth-formers with nowhere else to go and ageing roués with their bits on the side. The piles of doggie poo through which Hall and Astley had just waded spoke volumes for the incidence of canine exercising. Then there were the pony-trekkers and the joggers and the ramblers and the twitchers, all the flotsam that used the countryside. And every single one of them would be a suspect.

'Your best shot, then?' Hall said to Astley.

The doctor crouched, as well as his sciatica would allow, and pointed with his pen. 'He didn't die here, I'd lay money on that.' And Hall knew that Astley didn't make *that* offer every day. 'See?' He pointed to the flattened bracken that led to the path. 'That's been recently done, I'd say by dragging the body across.'

Hall looked down to the road that lay half hidden below them. 'Someone could have brought a vehicle up so far. That would mean the body need only be carried a hundred yards or so.'

'And the sofa was too good a chance to pass up.'

'Not the best hiding place.' Hall looked around. There were other items of furniture too – a broken bar stool, a soaking mattress, an elderly kettle. Incomprehensibly, but inevitably, a rusting supermarket trolley. 'It's quite exposed.'

'Thankfully' – Astley straightened up with a grunt, grateful to change position for a while – 'that's not my province. John Doe here was clobbered from behind, probably three or four times. Until I get him on the slab, I can't tell you with what.'

'Any ID, Graham?' Hall asked the sergeant.

'Nothing, guv.' Rackham shook his head. 'But the suit is Savile Row. Everything about him reeks of money.'

'Let me do the rounds, Jim,' Hall said, and crossed to the police van where a shaken jogger sat on the tailgate, his hands around a flask of tea. Somebody had put a blanket around his shoulders.

'Jacquie.' Hall nodded at the plainclothes policewoman standing with him, the rain soaking through her anorak despite its promise of proof.

'Morning, sir. This is Mr Beddoes. He found the body.'

'Mr Beddoes.' Hall didn't smile. He could see that the man was still shaking, the rainwater dripping off his nose into his tea. 'Are you all right?'

' 'Course I'm not all right,' the jogger blurted. 'I've been here for three bloody hours. I found the bloody body. Of course I'm not all right.'

'DC Carpenter.' Hall motioned Jacquie aside. 'Didn't you tell him he could go home?'

'Of course, guv,' Jacquie said. 'He said he'd rather not. Wanted to help.'

Hall glanced back at him. 'What are we looking at? Delayed shock?'

'I'd say so,' was Jacquie's verdict.

'Don't give him the option, then,' Hall said. 'The last thing we want is another death on our hands, from pneumonia. Bad enough with John Doe.'

'Anthony Bingham, sir.'

'What?' Henry Hall blinked at the girl through the rain-lashed blankness of his glasses.

'I didn't say anything to DS Rackham because I wasn't sure at first. Now I am.'

'Is he local?'

'No, sir.'

'Jacquie, what's going on?'

Jacquie didn't like Henry Hall's office. She'd been on the carpet in here once too often for that. And it had always been because of Max; her relationship with him. It was again now.

'So, let me get all this straight.' the Chief Inspector sat across the desk from her, leaning back in the chair, his jacket gone, his hands behind his head. 'You met this Bingham last Friday at a reunion in Warwickshire.'

'That's right, guv.'

'And he's a judge?'

'In the High Court.'

'Yes, that's right.' Hall nodded. 'I've heard of him. One of the no-nonsense school. Not exactly a copper's friend, but a sound officer of the law, I believe. I'd not have recognized him in the bracken this morning, not from the odd photo I've seen. He's a crony of the Lord Chief Justice.' He focused on Jacquie again – the honest grey eyes, the firm mouth and cheeks. 'And there was a murder?'

'An old school-friend of his, George Quentin. He was found hanging from the bell rope of the old school. He'd been battered over the head beforehand.'

'Warwickshire CID on it?' Hall asked.

'Yes, sir, a DCI Tyler.'

'You met?'

'Briefly.'

'Thorough sort of bloke?'

'Woman.'

'Really?' It wasn't often anyone saw Henry Hall smile. He regarded it as a weakness. 'Well, well, well.'

Jacquie didn't want to plumb the depths of meaning in any of those wells. She knew the question that was coming next. 'And you were there, at this reunion. Why?'

'I was with a friend, sir,' Jacquie said.

Hall paused. If Jacquie knew the question, he knew the answer. 'Does this friend have a name?'

'Peter Maxwell.' She cleared her throat in the vague hope that he wouldn't hear.

'Well, well, well.' Hall unlocked his fingers and reached for the phone. 'Get me a car. And put a call through to DCI Tyler at . . .'

'Leamington, sir.'

'Leamington CID. If she's available, I'll take it on my mobile.'

And he was on his feet. So was Jacquie. 'Sir, I . . .'

'Haven't you got some reports to write up?' he asked her.

'The Fridge' did some of them; Mad Max did most. UCAS reports, that is, those gems of truth-economy that got generations of hopefuls into universities. As he wrote the platitudes, as his nimble pen hurtled across the page prior to work by Thingee Three, the lady in the office who had to decipher his scribble for the necessary word-processing, he comforted himself thinking that the world's greats would never have got to university at all. Einstein was still having trouble speaking, wasn't he, at seventeen? And Shakespeare was quite capable of spelling the same word three different ways in the same sentence; rejections aplenty there.

'The Fridge', Mrs Maitland, was Assistant Head of Sixth Form, a huge apparition in the virginal colour that had prompted the late, great Wilkie Collins to rush into print with his first crime novel. Not that Helen Maitland was remotely the criminal type – a fact that the policemen facing her that Tuesday afternoon quickly took on board.

'I'm afraid he's teaching, Chief Inspector,' Helen had said, UCAS form in one hand and a coffee mug in the other. 'Is it urgent?'

'A little.' Henry Hall put away his warrant card and stood motionless in the corridor outside the Head of Sixth Form's offices. Unlike other year heads at Leighford High, the Heads of Sixth had an office each. This was simply, explained Maxwell, because an ego the size of his needed its own space.

'Well, I'll lead the way, then, shall I?' and she waddled along passageways without number. Posters told the detectives that Leighford High were putting on *Grease* in December. Judging from the chewing-gum wrappers that littered the floor, the entire school seemed to be method actors getting into character.

There was a wail from H4 as the two arrived. Helen Maitland tapped on the glass and went in.

'There, t-h-e-r-e, Ian, has nothing whatever to do with their, t-h-e-i-r. They don't even sound the same, man. I've been telling you that since Year Seven. Be assured that when this lesson is over, I shall be straight on the phone to that nice Ms. Morris to insist that elocution be placed on the National Curriculum forthwith. Only in your case, of course, it'll be pronounced – and spelt, no doubt – electrocution. Mrs Maitland?' He spun to face her as she hovered at the door.

'Sorry, Mr Maxwell, there are two people to see you.' Helen Maitland didn't use the 'p' word. She knew 11 B2 of old. One whiff of scandal and it would be all over the school and town by desk-shut time. 'I'll hang on here, hold their hands. What are you doing?'

'Usual old crap.' Maxwell sighed. 'Hitler's foreign policy. Anschluss followed by Munich and the Polish corridor.'

There were jeers from the motley crew of psychopaths and jailbirds that were 11 B 2. 'I'll just teach them some biology, shall I?' Helen Maitland offered.

'Whatever,' Maxwell said. 'I'm not sure they'll notice the difference.' And he was in the corridor. 'Mr Hall, this is a not altogether looked-for surprise. Have I parked my bike some-where illegal?'

'This is DS Rackham, Mr Maxwell.' The sergeant flashed his warrant card. 'Is there somewhere we can talk?'

'My office,' Maxwell said, and led them back the way they'd come. 'Can I get you anything?' he asked as he closed the door. 'Tea? Coffee? Signed photograph of the Secretary of State for Education?'

Both men shook their heads. 'This isn't a social call, I'm afraid,' Hall said.

Oh dear, thought Maxwell, clichés already and it's only Tuesday.

Hall sat in the proffered chair, Maxwell behind his desk, Rackham standing with his back to a pile of poo newly delivered from that very Secretary of State for Education of whom Maxwell had just spoken; that was usually Maxwell's position. The Chief Inspector opened the batting. 'How well do you know a Mr Anthony Wayland Bingham?'

'Cret?' Maxwell frowned. 'I knew him very well.'

'In the past tense, sir?' Rackham asked. Maxwell looked him up and down – a man bucking for promotion if ever there was one.

'I mean I knew him well in the past,' the Head of Sixth Form explained. 'Now we are what you might call acquaintances. Has anything happened?'

'Happened, sir?' Hall threw at him. 'Why would you think that?'

Maxwell looked at Hall. The two men went a way back, ever since the murder at the Red House. Then it had been one of Maxwell's own sixth form and he had taken it up close and personally. Hall knew he was about to again. 'Because,' Maxwell told him, 'I was due to meet him last night and he never turned up.'

'What time was this?'

'Five-thirty. Unless she's erased it, Thingee in the office can let you hear the answerphone message he left.'

Rackham was writing things down.

'And what time was that?'

'The phone call? I don't know. Mid-afternoon? You'd have to ask Thingee. Messages aren't always relayed very quickly. It was nearly three weeks before I knew Mafeking had been relieved.'

No one was laughing – least of all Peter Maxwell. 'Are you going to tell me what this is all about, Mr Hall?' he asked.

Hall looked at Rackham and nodded. The sergeant took up

the tale. 'The body of Mr Anthony Wayland Bingham was found by a jogger early this morning. Needless to say, we have reason to suspect foul play.'

'Jesus!' Maxwell sat back in his chair. 'Then there were five,' he said.

'Where were you, sir,' Rackham felt obliged to ask, 'around nine or ten last night?'

'That was the time of death?' Maxwell asked.

Hall leaped in. That was typical of Maxwell – give the man a criminal inch and he'd go the whole green mile. 'Could you answer the question please, Mr Maxwell?'

Maxwell shrugged. 'At home,' he said.

'Alone?'

'Yes,' Maxwell told him. 'Apart from the cat, of course.' He held back the obvious Macaulay Culkin joke, lest it gave offence.

'Ah.' Rackham grinned. 'Not very reliable witnesses, are they, cats?'

Maxwell fixed the man with his cutest smile. 'Mine isn't, Sergeant. He's never forgiven me for cutting his nads off – not that I did it personally, of course. But that probably makes it worse, in his eyes, don't you think? Coward that I am, I get a hit-man in a white coat to do it.'

'You're unusually flippant, Mr Maxwell.' Hall frowned. 'We tell you a friend of yours is dead and you're joking about your cat.'

Maxwell's smile had gone. 'Perhaps it's just my way of coping,' he said. 'Where was the body found?'

Hall nodded at Rackham. 'Ryker Hill,' the sergeant said. 'On the edge of Tottingleigh Woods. Know it, sir?'

Maxwell nodded. 'Like the back of my hand,' he said. 'I often walk there – along, I should think, with half the population of Leighford.'

'When did you see Mr Bingham last?' Hall wanted to know.

'Let me see.' Maxwell was scanning the plaster board ceiling for an answer. 'It would be . . . er . . . Sunday afternoon. We'd all been to the nick . . . Oh, God.'

'Yes, Mr Maxwell,' Hall said quietly. 'We know about Mr Quentin.'

'Jacquie. Of course,' Maxwell said.

'Your friends are popping off in all directions, aren't they, sir?' Rackham chirped. Maxwell didn't care for his bonhomie.

'There's probably only one direction,' Maxwell murmured. 'I just can't see it yet.'

'I'd like you to make a statement, Mr Maxwell,' Hall told him. 'To cover your relationship with Mr Bingham. Would you be prepared to do that?'

'Of course.' Maxwell nodded. 'Anything I can do.'

Hall was on his feet. So was Rackham. The interview with the vampire was over. 'There is one thing you can do,' Hall said as he looked his man squarely in the face. 'You can do us all a favour and stay away from Jacquie Carpenter. In a professional sense, I mean.'

Staying away from Jacquie Carpenter was the last thing on Peter Maxwell's mind. Over the months of knowing her, he, the crusty old bachelor whom half the kids thought to be gay, had fallen in love. He didn't think he would again, could again, not after Paula. But Paula lay in a cemetery far, far away, with her daughter by her side and Maxwell's ring on her finger. There was lichen on her headstone now and Maxwell hadn't the heart to brush it off. He went back from time to time when the solitude and the silence seemed too much to bear. Just to hear the wind in the trees. Just to hear her voice.

But now it was different. Paula was still there, in his heart, where she'd always be, but she'd moved across. And the girl with grey eyes was there too.

'I'm not allowed to talk to you, apparently.' He was sitting on his settee that night, his feet up on the coffee table. The cat,

Metternich, yawned. Why, oh why did he persist in talking with that plastic thing in his hand? The one that made those terrifying noises occasionally?

'Max . . .' Jacquie's disembodied voice sounded distant, tired.

'So I'll make it easy,' he went on, 'in case, in this free country of ours, they tap our phones.'

'Max, we don't do that. At least, not routinely . . .'

'Jacquie' – he let his head loll back – 'I've dropped you in it enough in the past.'

'Look, Max,' she said. 'I won't bullshit you. Hall has come the heavy on this one. I know he's been equivocal in the past, but that was then. I am not to discuss the case. He knows you're involved.'

'Too right I am,' Maxwell agreed.

'No, I mean, involved – as a suspect.'

'A suspect?'

'You rang Bingham's chambers.'

'How did you know?' Maxwell asked.

'The Met have checked for us, logged his calls. The one timed at nine-thirty this morning was from Leighford High School.'

'Don't hang around, you blokes, do you?'

'So why didn't you tell Hall you'd rung?'

'It slipped my mind,' Max told her.

'Yeah, and I'm Joan of Arc. Why didn't you tell him, Max?' She sounded concerned.

'I needed, in the American phrase, to cut a little slack. I'm going for this one myself.'

'You can't, Max, not now.'

'Why not? You didn't seem too opposed at the weekend.'

'That was then,' she said, and her voice had changed, grown louder. 'Now is now. It's my patch and I'm part of the case. You'll do what you have to do, you always have, but you'll do it without me.'

The line went dead. He didn't see her switch on the answerphone immediately she hung up. He didn't hear her fight back the tears. But he knew Jacquie and knew she had done both those things.

Peter Maxwell looked at the pile of sixth-form essays taunting him from across the room. He picked up the first then threw the whole pile into the corner. Metternich knew the signs. Even before the drinks cupboard door had opened and the clink of Southern Comfort on glass hit his ears, Metternich was, in the American phrase, out of there.

'Your views then, Donald?' Jim Astley sat in his swivel chair, playing patience on his laboratory computer.

'Rather fond of his port, I'd say,' Donald called from the cadaver across the morgue. 'A cardiac waiting for an arrest.'

'Quite.' Astley sighed. 'Come on, come on. Where's the bloody Jack of Hearts? I was rather hoping for a squint at the cause of death, though.'

'Oh,' Donald chirped. 'Blows to the back of the head. I count three.'

'Well done, Donald,' Astley patronized. 'Coming on like a pathologist. What do you make the time of death?'

Donald was a large young man who had a history of glandular trouble and KFC abuse. He bent down with difficulty and fished out the fallen chart he knew to have landed a moment ago in the area where logic told him he ought to have some feet. 'Er . . . approximately nine, nine-thirty Monday night.'

'Monday.' Astley was dabbing at his mouse with a ferocity unusual in a middle-aged man.

Donald waddled across to the wall calendar. 'That's right,' he confirmed.

This was the first time Dr Astley had given him free rein on a murder victim and it had gone to his head a little. On the other hand, he had seen Mickey Mouse in *The Sorcerer's Apprentice* and didn't want to make any mistakes; especially with the sorcerer only feet from him.

'Weapon?' Astley was keeping an eye on the clock counter. Didn't time fly when you were enjoying yourself?

'Heavy blunt instrument.' Donald nodded, his face creased in effort, his glasses sliding down his ski-jump nose. 'Wooden.'

'Type of wood?'

'Oh, come on, Doc.' Donald's composure had cracked, but he found himself looking into the deadly twin barrels that were Jim Astley's blue eyes.

'I mean, I don't know,' the Apprentice said, limply.

'Then I suggest you find out. Third shelf up. Red cover. It'll give you a chemical breakdown of any British tree type and not a few American and African hardwoods. Made a slide yet?'

'Er . . . not while we've been chatting, no.'

A pinging sound proclaimed Astley's success on the computer screen. 'Do I want to play again?' he growled at the PC. 'What do you think this is? A game?' He slid back in his swivel chair. 'Prepare a slide, Donald, from the fibres you dug out of the hair. Henry Hall is a patient man, but he'll want some answers. Seems like they had a similar killing in the Midlands and I think we're in some sort of race.'

David Williams, Chief Reporter on the *Mail*, went to town on Anthony Wayland Bingham in Thursday's edition. A double-page spread showed the great man, bewigged like a spaniel, staring arrogantly from his perch on the Queen's Bench. 'What price justice?' Williams asked, and the Lord Chief of that rare commodity was quoted as saying how black the day was for England. The editorial, elsewhere, howled its protest too. If His Lordship was the victim of some vengeance killing, what was the country coming to? Who was safe?

'Who judged the judge?' the *Sun* wanted to know, before it got down to the nitty-gritty of Kirsty's breast measurements on page three. On his way back from the Tesco's run, Maxwell had paused to scan the lot. He read the tabloids as they stood and took the others home. He was starting to get funny looks from the security staff. He pedalled in the gathering dusk over the flyover, the dynamo of his bike, White Surrey, humming like the bees' wings that were his legs. His old college scarf flapped around him and his hat was rammed low on his head as he whistled round the corner into Columbine and wheeled his faithful boneshaker to bed in the outhouse.

Tomorrow was Friday, the day he'd get off; the day he'd told James Diamond he had a funeral to go to. That wasn't strictly true, of course. He had no idea when they'd bury George Quentin. But now he had two funerals to go to, two murders to solve. And he wouldn't start with Quentin. He'd start with Ryker Hill.

The rain of the last two days had gone and a frost had coated West Sussex in the early hours of Friday morning. Maxwell wheeled Surrey off the road and leaned it against the dull silver of a tree trunk. The mud tracks were iron hard this morning and a pale sun was doing its damnedest to burn off the hoar of the morning. He tramped the crisp bracken, crunching it underfoot, ducking under the frozen ribbon that was the police tape. 'Do not cross', but he'd crossed it, the Rubicon that marked the resting place of Cret Bingham.

He heard a dog bark in the distance, somewhere high in the woods. The road was – what? – a hundred yards away, two? He couldn't be exactly sure where the body had been found. Anything from the site would have gone. But he'd passed this way recently, only last week, after the Staff Meeting without End during which James Diamond – 'Legs' to Maxwell, in honour of the Chicago gangster of the same name – had worried along with his colleagues about the likelihood of an impending Ofsted examination. He hadn't cared for the apathy of his staff;

still less the curiously loud muttered response from his Head of Sixth Form – 'More a case of Off-fuck, I think.' He'd never forgiven Maxwell for burning the effigy of Chris Woodhead, the outgoing director of Ofsted, in the school skip that time. Maxwell had vehemently denied it, of course, but, as Diamond reasoned with his deputies, who else could it have been?

Maxwell remembered he'd seen an old settee lying by the path, just to the right of where he stood now. There was a kettle somewhere, handle rusted, spout gone; a supermarket trolley. Possibly, if he looked hard enough on the conveyor belt of other people's leavings, a cuddly toy! It always annoyed him how people came to lovely woodland glades to dump their rubbish. It's a beautiful spot; watch some bastard spoil it.

Someone had spoiled it now, all right. Spoiled it for ever. Mad Max looked up at the silver birch branches, naked against the sky. He was looking for the bastard now. And he wouldn't be spoiling anything else.

Chapter Seven

It was noon by the sun — or would have been could Maxwell have seen it through the gathering cloud — by the time he'd reached King's Bench Walk. Typical of the eminent jurist Anthony Bingham had become, before the company broke up at the Graveney, he had left the others his office address only.

Maxwell was suitably impressed by the opulence of the man's chambers. A wiry-looking clerk with the air of a pompous Boston terrier opened the large, black-painted door.

'My name is Peter Maxwell; I was a close friend of Anthony Bingham.'

'Yes?' The Boston terrier apparently couldn't see the connection.

'I wondered if I might have a moment with his colleagues?'

'I have no information about the funeral,' the clerk said. 'Perhaps you can call back?'

Maxwell's foot was surprisingly fast against the already closing door. 'Well, I could.' He smiled. 'But of course, if I did that, it would almost certainly be with a camera crew and sound team. Do you think Anthony's learned colleagues would mind being pestered by the media? I've got Jeremy Paxman lined up . . .'

And the door mysteriously swung open again. He was shown into a vestibule the size of Leighford High's gym. 'Wait here,' the Boston terrier snapped. 'Spy' cartoons of judges great and terrible looked benignly down at Maxwell. The kindly Mr Justice Stephens, madder than a snake and related to Virginia Woolf; the amiable Mr Justice Humphreys, who christened his son Christmas; the appalling Lord Chief Justice, Rayner Goddard, prone, it was said, to needing a spare pair of trousers each time he passed a death sentence. They all made Mr Justice Bingham look quite ordinary.

'Mr Maxwell?' A large man in a black coat and pin-striped trousers emerged from the secrecy of an oak door. He held out his hand. 'I'm Philip Massendon.'

Maxwell took the outstretched hand. He knew the face. Massendon had been at the centre of a cash-for-questions row some years ago and he had maintained his innocence loudly to any newspaper within earshot. He looked larger in real life.

'Look,' Massendon said, 'I'm due at the House – or at least I was half an hour ago. Does it take you out of your way?'

'Not at all,' Maxwell said. 'It's good of you to see me.'

Massendon was handed a metal box by the clerk, who also helped him haul on a coat that represented a year's wages for Peter Maxwell. At the kerb outside, under the limes that lined King's Bench, a sleek black car waited.

'Get back to the Lord Chief,' Massendon called to his clerk. 'Tell him I can do Thursday, but the Mannering business is taking longer than expected.'

'Very good, sir.' And the black door closed.

A chauffeur held the passenger door open and the judge clambered in. 'One door closes, another opens,' he muttered. 'Scotch, Maxwell?'

Maxwell declined. He sat opposite Massendon, with his back to the engine as the chauffeur seat-belted up and made for the Strand. The judge poured himself a stiff one from the limo's bar and pulled a pained face as it hit his tonsils. 'The doctor says if I have many more of these I shall be facing another kind of judge altogether.' He pointed skyward. 'That great colleague in the sky. What's the story on Anthony?'

'I was hoping you'd tell me,' Maxwell said.

Massendon sized the man up for the first time. He didn't look like paparazzi, though he'd hinted to the clerk he was. 'You'll forgive me,' the judge said, 'if I ask you to declare your interest.'

'He was an old school-friend,' said Maxwell. 'I hadn't seen him in years until last weekend. We had a reunion.'

'Oh, yes. Where did Anthony go?'

'Halliards.'

'That's right.' Massendon rinsed his teeth with Scotch again. 'I'm a Wykehamist myself. Bit of a blow, this.' He leaned forward and tapped the glass. The chauffeur's intercom clicked on. 'Jenkins, are you armed?'

'Thirty-eight, sir,' the voice crackled back.

Massendon caught Maxwell's enquiring look. 'High Court judges have minders, anyway,' he explained. 'People like Jenkins are primarily drivers, but they are also trained in various martial disciplines. The Lord Chancellor is insisting since Bingham that they carry guns too. I should have had you frisked, really, but I just can't get used to all this.'

Maxwell held open his coat. 'I'm not packing,' he drawled in his best Clint Eastwood.

Massendon nodded. 'Glad to hear it. So how can I help? On Anthony, I mean.'

'He was on his way to see me,' Maxwell explained.

'Was he, now?'

'The police have been here, I assume.'

'The Met have asked their usual penetrating questions, yes. None of us could be of much assistance, really.'

'You know there was another murder at Halliards?'

Massendon did. 'Thanks to the fourth estate,' he said, and tapped on the window again. 'Get through here, Jenkins, or we'll never get there.' The limo lurched to the left without signalling and Massendon beamed to a motorcycle officer who would have obligingly felt the collar of any ordinary mortal offending in that way. 'No, the odd thing was, Anthony said nothing about it. Come to think of it, he was rather tight lipped last Monday.'

'You saw him . . . at what time of day?'

'Luncheon. We dined at the Garrick. His shout. He was out of sorts. I made some comment and he bit my head off. Not like Anthony. He was normally quite a balanced sort of chap. Ah, here we are.'

The limo had purred down a side entrance to the Mother of Parliaments, past security men without number and coppers in uniform, and Jenkins switched off the ignition. Massendon looked at Maxwell in the dim light of the subterranean garage. 'Airey Neave died back there.' He jerked his head out of the rear window. 'The IRA got him. We're none of us safe, Mr Maxwell. Not me; not you. Anthony had stumbled on to something. I told the boys in blue that.'

'What?' Maxwell needed to know. 'What had he stumbled on to?' This was an emergency; prepositions at the end of sentences could go to the Devil.

Massendon clicked open his door and Jenkins was outside, glancing right and left with his hand inside his jacket. 'Judges have enormous case loads, Mr Maxwell. Anthony's death may be connected with any of them. And before you ask, that's classified. Let the Met do their job, will you? They've been doing it for some time now. Jenkins, get Mr Maxwell out of here, would you? He doesn't have a pass and you know how paranoid this lot are.'

'Mr Massendon.' Maxwell was out of the car and alongside his man. 'Anthony Bingham wasn't just a friend of mine; he was on his way to see me when he died. I feel . . . well, responsible.'

'No, no, my dear fellow, never feel that. God, if we all felt responsible for what happened around us, we'd none of us get through a single day.' And he turned to go. Then he turned back, staring steadily into Maxwell's dark eyes, into Maxwell's soul. Thank God, Maxwell thought, he couldn't pop his black cap on any more. 'Look,' Massendon said, '*I* can't help you – ethics of chambers and all that – but I know a woman who can. She's been unkindly described as the Temple bicycle by her critics – and believe me they are legion; but she just *may* be able to shed some light. Her name is Anne. Jenkins, take Mr Maxwell to the Mews, will you? Call for me at four. Surely to God even the Lord Chancellor will have finished by then.'

It didn't take Jenkins long to lose Maxwell altogether. He knew this was Chelsea, but after Tite Street, with its still-Wildean frontage to the river, the limo had snarled through a rabbit-warren until it halted outside an unobtrusive house in a cobbled mews.

'No doubt you can catch a cab from here.' Jenkins had spoken for the first time and he and the limo were gone.

Maxwell rang the bell and a disembodied voice answered. 'Yes?'

'My name is Maxwell.' He spoke to the grilled box near the latch. 'Mr Justice Massendon sent me.'

There was a pause and Maxwell saw the nets shiver in an upstairs window. A click and a whirr followed and he was inside. The hallway was tasteful, plushly carpeted and professionally papered. An elegant woman was walking down the stairs to meet him.

'Anne?' he asked, sweeping off his tweed hat.

'I'm Anne Dickinson,' she said. 'Mr . . . ?'

'Maxwell.' He held out a hand. She didn't take it. 'I'm . . .'

'A fraud.' She'd already turned on her heel. 'And a graduate of Jesus College, Cambridge.'

Maxwell was taken aback. 'You know your collegiate scarves,' he said with admiration.

'And my old school ties.' She ushered him into a deceptively large first-floor lounge and turned to face him. 'In my line I meet quite a few. That's Old Halliardians.'

He applauded. 'Very good. And your line is . . . ? Not wig-and gown-making, surely?'

Anne Dickinson threw herself down on the settee. She was still an attractive woman, with brass-blond hair, although the years were threatening to catch up with her. 'You know what my line is or you wouldn't be here. Does Philip owe you a favour?'

'Philip?'

'Philip Massendon. You said he sent you.'

'He did. But I was hoping it was you who could do a favour for me.'

She looked him up and down, then lit a cigarette and offered him a chair. 'I'm not sure you can afford me, Mr Maxwell,' she said. 'I don't come cheap. For less than a k, I don't come at all.'

Maxwell cut to the chase. 'Anthony Bingham.'

Anne Dickinson sat upright, stubbing the cigarette out in a Wedgwood ashtray. 'I don't like where this is going,' she said.

'Ms Dickinson.' Maxwell unwrapped the scarf from around his neck, and sat back in her armchair. 'I'm an old friend of Anthony's, from way back. You noticed the tie.'

'So?'

'So, the man is dead.'

'Yes.' Her mouth was hard as she said it. 'Yes, I know.'

'He was on his way to see me when he died. They found his body a mile or so from my home.'

'I don't see . . .'

'Philip Massendon thought you might be able to help.'

'Did he, now?'

'Was he wrong?' Maxwell searched the woman's face. Her eyes were triangular, which to the Chinese denotes ambition, but there was a sensuousness around the mouth. It was probably the association of ideas, but she reminded him of Christine Keeler, friend of KGB generals and British war ministers, who had snatched the headlines in Maxwell's last year at school.

'What do you want to know?'

'Anything,' Maxwell told her. 'Everything. I hadn't seen Anthony for thirty-seven years until last weekend – that's a helluva gap to fill.'

She lit another cigarette with an expertise born of years of neurotic socializing. 'I first met Tony, what, ten years ago? His marriage was on the skids and he needed solace. That's what I do, Mr Maxwell.' She blew smoke rings expertly towards the ceiling. 'Solace. Philip calls it solaciting, but it's not very funny and I don't need comments like that.'

'You and Philip don't get on?' Maxwell asked.

'I was his mistress for a little over eighteen months. Then I met Tony.'

'I see.' Maxwell's eyes were being opened. 'So Tony . . . Anthony . . . rather took Massendon's place, did he?'

'Undeniably,' Anne Dickinson said. 'What was particularly galling for Philip was that Tony was a far better lover. We used to joke about it, Tony and I – Philip's little endowment. I'm afraid he didn't see the joke.'

'Were you still having a relationship with Anthony?'

'Good Lord, no. Oh, I suppose we were together for about two years. He found preferment and I found Lincoln's Inn. That's the way the legal cookie crumbles.'

'When did you see Anthony last?'

'Heavens, I don't know. Oh, he still called round for the odd bit of solace now and again; you know, when the affairs of state became too much, he'd renew ours. He was always very considerate, however . . .'

'Can you remember precisely?' Maxwell asked. 'Can I pin you down?'

She looked at him through half-lidded, sultry eyes. 'I'm not sure you could.' She smiled. 'September. Over a month ago. He popped round one lunch-time; a Thursday, I believe.'

'For solace?'

'Yes, but I gave him lunch too.'

95

'Did he seem his usual self?'

'Oh yes.'

'Tell me, Ms Dickinson, was Anthony in the habit of confiding in you, his thoughts, feelings and so on?'

She shrugged. 'Sometimes.'

'Do you remember anything that Thursday? Something that was bothering him?'

She smiled. 'He had his mouth full for part of the time,' she said. 'But no, nothing in particular. The usual whinges about chambers – what arseholes they all were. But that's *de rigueur* among lawyers, Mr Maxwell. They all hate each other.'

'Someone hated Anthony Bingham enough to want to kill him,' Maxwell reminded her. 'Do you have an address?'

'I thought you were a friend of his,' she said.

'So I was, but that was a long time ago. I've lost it.'

'Denbigh Street, Pimlico. Number eighteen.' She blew smoke down her nose. 'Now, was there anything else? I'm expecting someone.'

Maxwell took in the tight pedal-pushers, the skimpy top pulled taut across the nipples, and didn't doubt it for a moment.

'It's been quite a blow, Mr Maxwell.' The lady in the crisp white apron bustled in with the tray.

'I'm sure it has, Mrs Daniels.' Maxwell took the cup she held out to him.

'Now.' Mrs Daniels sat down on the chair, looking wistfully at the photograph of the bewigged judge on the table. 'Where were we?'

'Monday,' Maxwell reminded her. For a moment the impact of the jasmine tea unsettled him, then he recovered.

'Of course. I prepared Mr Bingham's breakfast as usual. Bligh was due to call at nine-thirty.'

'Bligh?' Maxwell sniffed a naval connection.

'Mr Bingham's driver. Justices of the High Court always have drivers, Mr Maxwell.'

'So I understand,' Maxwell said. 'Tell me, was there anything . . . odd about Anthony that morning?'

'Well, not at first,' Mrs Daniels said. 'Then he had the phone call. I told the police about it.'

'Phone call?' Maxwell frowned. 'What time was this?'

'Um . . . about nine o'clock, I think.'

'Who was it?'

'I don't know. A woman certainly.'

'How do you know?'

'I took the call, Mr Maxwell. Justices of the High Court do not take calls themselves, you know. It could be a cold sell. What would Mr Bingham do with double glazing or life insurance . . . ? Oh dear.'

'Did she give a name?' Maxwell asked.

'Who?'

'The lady caller.'

'Not at first. She said it was personal, but I told her I couldn't accept an anonymous call; I had to have a name. She told me she was Joanna Smith, but she refused to tell me what she wanted. I took the call in the drawing room, but when Mr Bingham picked it up he transferred the call to the study. There were raised voices.'

'You didn't . . . er . . . ?' Maxwell glanced at the phone.

'Listen to the conversation? Mr Maxwell, please. It has been my privilege to be housekeeper to Mr Bingham now for nearly eight years. I do *not* listen to other people's telephone conversations and I do not peep through keyholes.'

'Forgive me, Mrs Daniels, but the telephone call could explain a great deal about Anthony's death. What happened afterwards?'

'Mr Bingham was clearly agitated. He kept looking at his watch and never got round to finishing his breakfast. He told me to contact his chambers and cancel his day's engagements. Luckily he wasn't due in court until Wednesday.'

'And then he left?'

'Yes. He asked me to throw a few things into an overnight bag and when Bligh arrived, he told him to take the day off.'

'And he didn't tell either of you where he was going?'

'Only that he had someone to see, urgently.'

'That was probably me. He must have guessed I wouldn't be at home and probably remembered where I worked. Mrs Daniels, this Joanna Smith; did you know her? Had you heard the name before?'

'No, Mr Maxwell.' The housekeeper shook her head. 'The police took away Mr Bingham's phone book and diaries, but it was a withheld number. Well, that's standard in the legal profession, of course. Even Justices come into contact with some extraordinarily low life.'

'Who did you speak to?' Maxwell asked. 'From the police, I mean.'

'There was a DCI Wentworth, from the Met; I've met him before on official business at the court. The other was a woman, not local.'

'DCI Tyler?' Maxwell asked.

'That's right. Rather a deep type, I thought. Didn't give much away.'

'No, indeed.' Maxwell sighed. 'They never do.'

The carpets in Sussex Gardens hadn't got any less lurid since Maxwell's student days. He'd met a girl from the LSE (but he was the forgiving type) and they'd spent a night of torrid lovemaking together in one of those idyllic little love-nests behind Paddington Station. The B & Bs always had a quaint fifties air about them, as though they ought to be lived in by the first generation of Jamaicans to step off the boat, or dodgy young Cambridge spies with names like Burgess and Maclean.

The same smell had hit Maxwell that had hit him all those years ago; old sausages and cheap perfume.

'How much?' His jaw dropped slightly on being told the tariff for the night. He seemed to remember it had done much the same back in '65, with the beehived Stephanie on his arm, clinging like a limpet to his beatnik jumper. He wasn't sure this was the same hotel, but the landlady looked at him just as suspiciously now as her mother may have done all those years before.

'Mr *and Mrs* Maxwell, is it?' the old crone had asked, scanning the students' fingers for signs of rings. 'Sure it isn't Smith?'

'By yourself, are you?' the slightly newer crone had asked, looking for luggage and marking him down secretly as a paedophile. 'We don't have no Net facilities 'ere.'

'Good, good.' Maxwell beamed. 'I'm all surfed out; suffering from a surfeit, you might say.'

Clearly that was the last thing the old crone would say, and she wandered off to do whatever it is proprietresses of cheap hotels do.

That night, Maxwell rang Jacquie.

'It's good to talk.' It was the best Bob Hoskins she'd heard in a while.

'Max, where are you?' she asked.

'The Ritz.' Maxwell sprawled on the bed. 'I've just thrashed Mr Al Fayed at backgammon and I take over his yacht and the corner shop in Knightsbridge tomorrow morning.'

She laughed. 'Seriously, Max.'

'Seriously, I'm in bed-sit, dropoutsville in search of the bastard who killed Cret Bingham. Sussex Gardens, to be precise.'

'Max. . . .'

But he interrupted. 'Now, no lectures, Jacquie. Some teachers go fishing over half-term, some paint the parlour. There's even an ugly rumour, which I can't believe, that some of them prepare lessons for next week. Me? I solve crimes. How about you?'

'You know,' she told him firmly, 'I can't help.'

'I know.' He sighed. 'And I didn't call to put you on the spot. I miss you, that's all. What's that old song Sir Cliff used to sing? "Miss You Nights"? "And the warm wind that embraced me just as surely kissed your face." Not quite Byron. But not bad.'

'Oh, Max.'

They looked, both of them, into the middle distance and saw each other's faces.

'Willow,' she said.

'What?'

'The fibres found embedded in Anthony Bingham's skull and hair; the pieces of wood. They were willow.'

'Willow!' Maxwell was sitting up. 'What about George Quentin?'

'Max,' she said softly, 'I've just broken every rule in the book telling you what I have. George Quentin is somebody else's patch, remember? I'm just a passer-by up there.'

'Nadine Tyler's working with the Met,' Maxwell told her, 'on Cret's case.'

'Of course she is. It'll be a three-pronged attack, Max. That's how it works these days. We don't call the Yard in any more. They're just as likely to call us. Quentin died in Warwickshire – that makes it the local CID's business. Bingham died in Leigh-ford – that's our pigeon. But they both lived in the smoke, hence the Met. Actually, there's a further complication there.'

'Oh?'

'According to what we have, George Quentin was in business in the City. That means the City force. My guv'nor's driving up tomorrow.'

'Saturday?'

'Vandeleur Negus are opening up specially for him.'

'Are they, now? Time?'

'Uh-huh, Max. Love may be blind, but this little neck of mine only sticks out so far.'

★ ★ ★

He wisely stuck to toast for breakfast. And kept the dubious-looking coffee to one cup. Then he was gone, taking out a second mortgage to hire a cab to convey him eastward. The Old Lady beamed at him as the black vehicle growled along Threadneedle Street. He swung left into Bartholomew Lane and left again along Throgmorton Street. He toyed with tipping the cabbie, then remembered he hadn't gone for the £2,000 threshold payment and thought better of it.

The offices of Vandeleur Negus put the 'o' into opulence. They soared to the leaden sky of a City Saturday while the pigeons flapped across those air-conditioning pipes that Prince Charles so publicly hated. An electronic door slid open and a security man the size of the Tower stood there.

'Detective Chief Inspector Hall.' Maxwell flashed his NUT card. 'West Sussex CID.'

'Mr Vandeleur's expecting you,' the Tower said. 'I'll take you up.'

Maxwell was already suffering from oxygen deprivation by the time the lift shuddered to a halt.

'Keith Vandeleur.' A snowy-haired cadaver of a man was rising from his massive seat beside a huge mahogany desk. Behind him, a picture window gave a better view than the London Eye. It was like Hitler's playroom at the Berghof.

'Henry Hall,' Maxwell lied, taking the man's outstretched hand. 'It's good of you to give up your Saturday.'

'I didn't expect you till eleven,' Vandeleur said, obligingly giving Maxwell a timeframe by which he needed to be out of there.

'Sorry about that.' Maxwell took the indicated leather chair. 'Got quite a bit on.'

'George Quentin,' Vandeleur said. 'Hell of a player. Er . . . no Roger Bacon?'

The only Roger Bacon Peter Maxwell knew was a monk who'd discovered gunpowder. And he'd been dead for seven hundred years.

'Bacon?' He chanced his arm.

'DCI, City force. I understood you'd both be here.'

'Ah, sorry.' Maxwell smiled, in an 'I know a lot of Bacons' sort of way. 'Roger was called elsewhere last night. I'll have to brief him later. Tell me about George Quentin.'

'Good golfer was George,' Vandeleur remembered, clasping his hands across his scrawny linen-shirted chest. 'That's what I liked about him. A ruthless bastard after my own heart.'

'It's who was after his heart I'm concerned with, Mr Vandeleur.'

'Quite. Rum business. Was it you I spoke to on the phone yesterday?'

'Er . . . no, that would be my sergeant. Sergeant Rackham.'

'Ah, right. So, am I correct in this? He was hanged?'

Maxwell nodded. 'I can't tell you too much, of course.'

'No, of course not.'

'When did you see him last?'

'George? Er . . . Friday. Week yesterday, that is. He was quite excited. Had this old school reunion. Personally, I couldn't imagine anything worse. I hated my old school. Even tried in my amateur way to burn the place down. Oh!' Vandeleur laughed. 'Shouldn't really be telling *you* about all this, should I?'

Maxwell laughed with him. 'One case at a time.'

'Yes, there was some nonsense about a joke,' Vandeleur remembered.

'A joke?'

'Yes. I was having coffee with George and he said he'd had this phone call, asking him not to go to the agreed gathering place — some hotel, wasn't it?'

Maxwell nodded. 'The Graveney.'

'Well, this call apparently asked him to go directly to the school.'

'On the Friday night?'

'Presumably,' Vandeleur said. 'You'd need to check it with Paulo.'

'Paulo?'

Vandeleur looked at his man. 'I'd have thought Roger would've been on to that. Paulo is – or rather was – George's lover.'

Maxwell's face must have said it all.

'Come, come, Inspector. This is the twenty-first century; half the bloody government are left-footers these days. It can't come as that much of a surprise to you.'

'Sorry,' Maxwell flustered. 'I haven't been well.'

'Mind you, I think it was the making of George. Being bent gave him an edge. He had to prove himself, I think. And keep proving himself. That's important in our line. No room for sentiment in the money game, you know.'

Maxwell nodded. 'Indeed not. Look, these multi-force things are always a little delicate. You know Roger well, I take it?'

'He's done the odd little favour for us,' Vandeleur said.

'Well, there you are.' Maxwell became confidential. 'And I don't want to do the guy down – I've only met him once. You couldn't give me an address, could you? For Paulo, I mean? I'm afraid Roger's been a little remiss.'

'Sure.' Vandeleur turned to a computer screen and exercised his mouse. 'Lived with George. Yes, I thought so.' Letters flickered on to the screen. 'Grange Road. Acton. I never could understand what led George to live there. It was up and coming a few years back, I suppose. By the way . . .'

'Yes?'

'Don't get me wrong. I'm no bigot. Far from it. But when you talk to Paulo, you might want one or two beefy blokes with you.'

'Really?'

'Psychotic,' Vandeleur confided. 'I've little experience of that whole milieu, Inspector, but I know a malevolent young queen when I see one.'

103

Peter Maxwell saw himself out and, as he did so, slipping out of a side door, he heard a voice he thought he knew.

'Hall,' the voice was saying to the Tower that was Vandeleur Negus's security guard. 'Do I have to spell it for you?'

Chapter Eight

Grange Road, Acton had up and come all right. A modest semi that in Leighford might make a hundred grand was Monopoly money here. Maxwell rang the bell and a swarthy young man answered it, wearing an expensive silk shirt nearly open to the waist and hand-made jeans.

'Henry Hall, West Sussex CID.' Maxwell believed in consistency in his lying. 'I'm investigating the murder of George Quentin.' He was flashing his NUT card again.

'From West Sussex?' The dark young man frowned. 'I don't understand.'

'It's a double killing,' Maxwell explained. 'But I'd rather not discuss it on the doorstep.'

The young man let him in. There were tea chests and cardboard boxes everywhere, with piles of books and ranks of CDs.

'You are . . . ?'

'Paulo Escobar. I live here. With Georgie.' He leaned against a door frame in the hall, folding his arms. 'I already talk to the police. My papers are in order.'

'You're moving.' The West Sussex CID would be proud of Maxwell's powers of deduction.

'There is nothing to stay for. I go back to Bilbao.'

'How long have you known Mr Quentin?'

Escobar pushed himself away from the door frame and threw himself down in a spare armchair. He lit a cigarette. 'Five years.'

'How did you meet him?'

Escobar grinned. 'On the Heath,' he said. 'He pick me up.'

'For sex?'

'For company.'

'So he was lonely?'

Escobar shrugged.

'Was he ever married?' Maxwell asked, still trying to make sense of the man who was the boy he knew.

Escobar shook his head. 'He never said. He liked boys.'

'Boys?'

'People of my age.'

'When did you see him last?'

'Friday. He left for work at seven-thirty.'

'And where was he going after that?'

'To some old friends. His school.'

'Did he mention any names of these friends?'

'One or two.' Escobar blew smoke down his nostrils.

'Could you tell me what they are?' It was like pulling teeth.

'Er . . . sure. There was Asheton. Er . . . Maxwall . . .'

'Maxwell,' Maxwell corrected him.

'That is what I say,' Escobar insisted. 'Why you not write this down?'

'Write it down?' Maxwell didn't follow.

'When I have been arrested, the police they always write things down.'

'Been arrested often, have you?' Maxwell asked.

'*Sí.*' Escobar shrugged. 'Soliciting. GBH. That sort of thing.'

'We know these names already,' Maxwell said. 'This is just confirmation. Tell me, Paulo, was George . . . was Mr Quentin excited about the weekend? I mean, he didn't seem in any way upset or worried?'

Escobar shook his head. 'No,' he said. 'I don't remember that. He have a telephone call on Thursday night.'

'Call?' Maxwell frowned. 'Do you know who it was from?'

'A woman.' It was all coming back to Escobar now.

'Did she give a name?'

'No.' Escobar shook his head. 'I took the call. She say, "Is that Mr George Quentin's residence?" I say, "Who is it wants to know?" She say, "An old friend." I give the phone to Georgie. You know who killed him?'

Maxwell shook his head. 'Not yet, Mr Escobar,' he said. 'We're still working on it. Did Mr Quentin say anything when he put the phone down? Or do you remember any of the conversation from this end?'

Escobar thought for a moment, idling with the thick gold chain around his neck and considering his answer. 'Georgie say, "Excellent idea. Very good. That will get the party going. Halliards it is, not the gravy."'

'What do you think he meant?'

Escobar shrugged. 'I don't know. Afterwards he just went to have a shower. He didn't talk about the call.'

'This woman's voice. Would you know it again?'

'No.' Escobar was sure. 'But it was a foreign voice.'

'Foreign?' Maxwell repeated.

'*Sí*. Irish or Scottish. Something like that.'

Peter Maxwell couldn't really see what all Vandeleur's fuss had been about. Escobar was a little on the Iberian side, but he didn't seem remotely aggressive; perhaps Keith Vandeleur had been confusing him with a whole other body of homosexual. Back in Sussex Gardens that night, Maxwell took stock. George Quentin had been looking forward to the Halliards reunion when a woman, arguably of the Celtic persuasion, had rung him with what may have been a change of plan. He was to go direct to Halliards and not to the Graveney. But why? And at whose instigation?

Maxwell idly flicked through the television channels.

Celebrity Who Wants to Be a Millionaire flashed on to the screen.

'I don't, thanks, Chris,' he said, and phoned a friend instead.

DCI Nadine Tyler had set up her incident room in the annexe behind Leamington nick, overlooking the leafy expanses of the Jephson Gardens. Her life was on hold at the moment, as it always was when a major enquiry was under way; come to think of it, that's how her life usually was. The coffee in the machine didn't taste any better, but it was Sunday and there'd been a corpse on Dr Nagapon's slab now for eight days. A wise old copper had told her once, when she was a neurotic DS on the climb, that a murder that wasn't solved in forty-eight hours wasn't going to get solved. She'd spent the last fifteen years trying to prove him wrong.

'Good morning,' she addressed the team in front of her. There were the usual muttered responses. Hard-bitten coppers in rolled-sleeved shirts, pissed off because here was another Sunday away from home. Whole generations of kids had grown up without their dads, away in incident rooms. The DCI sat down. 'I've had requests from all and sundry for another press conference,' she said. 'Have we anything new to give them?'

Nothing.

'Ben?'

DI Thomas hated Nadine Tyler with every bone in his body. But then he felt much the same about everyone else. Mrs Thomas had realized that well over fourteen years ago and she had buggered off, taking the Aga, the telly and an insurance salesman with her. Thomas wasn't bitter; he was positively poisonous.

'We've no real leads on the car seen near Halliards on the Friday night,' he told the team. 'Of the old boys meeting for the reunion, Maxwell, Alphedge and Muir came by car; Bingham and Wensley by train. We presume the dead man caught a train too. The City police tell us it was most likely the six-thirty from Paddington, if he arrived in Leamington, but there is no record of a cheque payment or credit card.'

'So he paid by cash?' Tyler wanted it clear in her mind.

'According to the City boys, Quentin left work at five-fifteen – enough time to get to the station, and that was the next available train. If he came in via Coventry, it would have been the five-fifty from Euston. After that we don't know.'

'Nothing on taxis, Dave?'

'Nothing, ma'am.' Dave had been ringing and trudging round all week, showing photographs, jogging memories.

'London tell us there's another little problem.' The DCI had already given up on the coffee. 'Because the Bingham enquiry is linked with this one, West Sussex CID have been following up leads, working, as we are, with the Met and City forces. We're all anxious, of course, that nothing falls between the gaps, so to speak, but there seems to be somebody else nosing around, probably a PI, but nobody's got a handle on him so far. He passed himself off as a West Sussex detective yesterday, inter-viewing Quentin's boss and his lover.'

'Any angle there, ma'am?' DS Vernon wanted to know.

'The City boys are checking the financial situation. We may have to bring in the Fraud Squad, because Quentin was quite a wheeler-dealer. There's always a potential motive on the gay front, and his lover has a record against people who looked at George funny. There doesn't seem to be any history of violence between the pair, though. West Sussex and the Met are keeping us informed. Who's doing the follow-ups?'

'I'm on the Alphedges,' Vernon told her. 'Going up to-morrow morning.'

'I've got Asheton and his bit on the side,' said DS Dempster. 'Start in on that tomorrow.'

'Good. Tim, you're on John Wensley?'

'It's a hotel address in Brum,' Tim Hanlon told his guv'nor. 'I hope he's still there.'

Nadine Tyler laughed her braying laugh. 'You've got a thing about Wensley, haven't you?' she said.

'Let's just say I know an oddball when I see one, ma'am,' Hanlon responded.

'You're on the Muirs, Greg?'

Greg Pines nodded. Ever the conversationalist was Greg.

'Which leaves you, Ben . . .'

'With Maxwell,' DI Thomas said. 'And his copper girl-friend.'

'All right. Remember, everybody. We're looking for inconsistencies, changes of story, however slight. Before you tackle these people again, be totally familiar with every word of their original statements. Any deviations from that, I want to know about it.' The DCI stood up. 'Ben, a word?'

The team sloped off to their VDU screens, past ghastly photographs of a dead man with his eyes bulging and a swollen tongue bursting from his mouth. Every time she passed them, Nadine Tyler tried not to look. But every time she had to, to remind herself why she was there.

'Ma'am?'

'Cut the crap.' She turned to her grey-faced number two. Ben Thomas was overweight, his blue shirt cutting into his crimson neck. Cardiac arrest was likely to be his next collar. 'Do you want to tell me what you've got against this Maxwell?'

'Too clever by half, ma'am,' was the DI's considered opinion. 'I didn't appreciate his sidekick taking over like she did.'

'DC Carpenter, wasn't it?' Nadine Tyler checked her notes. 'What was she supposed to do, Ben? She was on the spot and she was a copper. She seems to have handled things pretty well, pressed the right buttons, kept everybody's size elevens off most of the murder scene. If there's a conflict of interests . . .'

'I'll just do my job,' he all but barked at her. 'You can count on that.'

She let the silence say it all. 'When do you start?'

'Tomorrow.'

'This Maxwell's a teacher, isn't he? Won't it be half-term?'

Thomas shrugged. 'Catch him at home. It'll be nice. A day at the seaside.'

Like everybody else in the world, Ben Thomas had been to Leighford when he was a kid. They'd had donkey rides then, along Willow Bay and the Shingle, before the Save the Unborn Gay Quadruped lobby had gone into action and spoilt it all for ever. He remembered a freak show too, when a five-piece midget band had played requests for a couple of bob. Happy, different days.

There was no reply at number 38 Columbine Avenue, the address that Peter Maxwell had given; but there was always Mrs Troubridge, the neighbour, programmed as she was to appear on her front doorstep at the arrival of a strange car next door.

'He's not in, dear. Mrs B will be in to feed the cat later. Can I help?' The old girl appeared to be some ghastly cross between Barbara Cartland and Barbara Castle.

'CID.' Thomas flashed his warrant card.

'Oh dear, is he in trouble again?'

'Again?' Thomas didn't like the sound of this. He'd more or less promised that stuck-up bitch he worked for that he'd go in open handed, with no baggage as it were. Now he wasn't so sure.

'Oh, like iron filings to a magnet with our Mr Maxwell.' Mrs Troubridge smiled, waving the secateurs which were her flimsy excuse for being in the garden in the first place. 'The police are always here. Are you local?'

'No, madam,' Thomas told her. 'Warwickshire.'

'Oh, that's Shakespeare country, isn't it? How delightful. Still, rather too many darkies these days for my liking, I expect.'

Agree with her though he did, Thomas thought it best to move on. 'Do you know when Mr Maxwell will be back?'

'Well, Mrs B – that's his cleaner, illiterate and unconventional but a heart of gold – she told me he's away for the week. It's half-term, apparently. He's a teacher, you see. Charming man and so very clever.'

'Is he really?' Thomas was unimpressed.

'Oh, enormously. Apparently he was captain of his college's team on the very first *University Challenge*, you know, with that nice Bamber Gascoigne; not that horrible Jeremy Paxton – he brings me out in spots.'

'Tell me, Mrs . . . er . . .'

'Troubridge,' the old lady purred, adjusting her lariat of pearls.

'What's his relationship with DC Carpenter?'

'Jacquie? Oh, you naughty man. What are you implying?' And she caught him a nasty one on the arm with her secateurs, luckily closed.

'I'm not implying anything, madam,' Thomas said. 'I'm merely asking questions. It's my job.'

'Well . . .' Mrs Troubridge became confidential. 'I'm not sure what he's been up to in Warwickshire, but she does call at the oddest hours. Whether they actually sleep together, I don't know. Is that a crime, by the way? I mean, I know it's not for us civilians, but what about you policemen? I mean, you can't vote, can you? Or appear on duty with a partially grown moustache? I merely wondered what the regulations were about sleeping around?'

'Yes, madam, that's an interesting question. I must go away and look it up.'

DI Thomas was the last person Jacquie Carpenter expected to see in the Tottingleigh incident room. All day, she'd been sifting through computer records, until she didn't want to see another set of tyre tracks or a VDU screen again.

'I was looking for Peter Maxwell.' Thomas had been sent through by the desk man.

'He doesn't work here,' Jacquie told him. 'But I do and I'm busy.'

'So am I,' said Thomas loudly, staring the girl down. A couple of colleagues looked up.

'Everything okay, Jacquie?' one of them asked.

'Fine, Tom.' She didn't take her eyes off the inspector. 'I was just about to go and get a cup of coffee. Won't you join me, Mr Thomas?'

He followed her to the drinks machine. 'Is your stuff better than this?' she asked, handing him a plastic cup with dubious brown liquid inside.

He tried it. 'No,' he said, and it seemed to break some ice. The DI actually smiled. Incident rooms were the same the world over.

'How do you want to play this?' she asked. 'Am I a witness, suspect or colleague?'

'At the moment,' he told her, finding a seat in a corner, 'you're all three. Is there somewhere we can talk?'

She scraped back a chair from the wall so she was sitting opposite him. 'Right here,' she said.

Thomas got the message. Jacquie wasn't going to be compromised and she was on her own turf. He'd have to play this one carefully.

'I'm following up on everybody connected with Halliards the weekend before last. You gave two statements, one to me and DS Vernon at the school; a second at Leamington nick. Do you want to see a copy of these statements?' He had his briefcase by his left foot. She shook her head. 'No, thanks.'

'Having had time to think,' he said, 'is there any addition or alteration you wish to make to those statements?'

'No.' She smiled sweetly. 'Is that the witness bit over?'

'More or less.' He nodded and grimaced as he sampled the coffee again. 'Now, to the suspect bit. Did you kill George Quentin?'

Jacquie was aware that there were eyes on her back. She half turned and the heads went down, everybody in the room suddenly intent on their own little piece of the Bingham enquiry. 'No,' she said firmly. 'I did not.'

Thomas leaned forward. 'Do you know a man who did?' he asked.

'I might,' she told him. 'The problem is, I don't know who it is.'

'What is your relationship with Peter Maxwell?'

She felt the eyes again. 'Is that relevant?' she asked.

'It might be,' Thomas told her. 'You see, it took two to lift a dying man on to a balustrade and drop him over at the end of a rope. Now, at school, maths was never really my thing, but even I know that two and two make a killer.'

'*Folie à deux?*' Jacquie snorted. 'Who do you imagine Maxwell and I are, Bonnie and Clyde?'

She suddenly realized she'd been shouting, and now there was someone alongside her, a steadying hand on her shoulder.

'Sir . . .' She half formed the words and half rose. 'This is DI Thomas, Warwickshire CID.'

The inspector was on his feet, his hand held out. It was not taken. 'DCI Hall,' Hall said, looking hard into the man's face. 'The next time you wish to talk to one of my officers, on any topic whatsoever, you will contact me personally with such a request in advance and it will be in writing. Do we understand each other, Inspector?'

'Yes, sir,' Thomas said, looking decidedly sheepish for a moment.

'Good. Now, come into my office. There are some things we need to clear up. Jacquie, got a minute? I could use your input on this.'

'I didn't think you were a mobile person.' She lay in the bath that night, cucumber where her face used to be.

'Jacquie, you sound odd,' he told her.

'I've been talking non-stop today,' she said. 'My jaw's aching.'

'Ah, what an honest confession from a woman. And I'm not a mobile person. You gave it to me, remember? Saying it was time I was dragged screaming into the twenty-first century.'

She did, but not for one moment did she believe Peter Maxwell would ever use the thing. 'Are you still in Sussex Gardens?'

'Yep.' He yawned. 'Heartbreak Hotel. What news on the Rialto?' He'd kicked off his shoes and was lying on the bed, his feet up the wall, more or less where he was going with boredom.

'We're in the frame, Max, you and I,' she told him.

'What? Prime suspects, you mean?'

'I had the misfortune to be grilled by DI Thomas today. You remember Smiler?'

'Indeed I do.' Maxwell had slid his feet down to assume a more conventional position. 'Say on, o fount of info.'

'Warwickshire CID are obviously doing follow-ups on all of us there that weekend. I got the short straw.'

'You poor darling. He's obviously got the hots for you.'

'Scrummy.' She edged a sponge aside with her toe, luxuriating in the warmth of the suds. 'I thought it was you he fancied.'

'Ah, I should be so lucky. Did he give anything away?'

'Not until the DCI turned up. Then he was sweetness and light. Mind you, the DCI was the firmest I've known him.'

'Well, well.' Maxwell clicked his tongue. 'Old Henry's just gone up in my estimation.'

'He had a hard weekend,' Jacquie told him. 'Following up the Quentin thing in the City. Seems he was pipped to the post by someone passing themselves off as him.'

'No!' Maxwell was outraged. 'Must be very difficult to play Henry Hall. Not the most animated of people.'

'Max, you wouldn't know anything about that, would you?'

He feigned ignorance and hurt. 'I, dear heart? I am cut to the quick. No, I've been trying to get hold of Stenhouse and his missus. No luck yet. I'll give it another shot tomorrow and then I'll try Alphie. This place is beginning to get me down.'

'Do you want to know the common ground?' she asked him. 'Quentin and Bingham?'

He paused. 'Jacquie?' He was sitting up. 'A few days ago you told me I was on my own. Something about your pretty little neck.'

He heard her snort some bubbles. 'A few days ago I wasn't top of some thick shit's murder suspect list. Suddenly I see things in a rather different light.'

He chuckled. 'Come on now, Jacquie. Come off the fence. What do you *really* think of DI Thomas?'

She laughed with him. 'Right,' she said. 'Similarities. Both Quentin and Bingham were battered over the head with a blunt, wooden instrument, made of willow.'

'Cricket bat,' Maxwell said.

There was a silence. 'Do you know that?'

'Not for a fact, no,' he told her. 'But neither of them died by random selection. Whatever this is all about, Halliards is at the heart of it. A cricket bat would be poetic, don't you think?'

'Who was the poet in the Magnificent Seven?' she asked.

'That would be me,' he told her. 'Similarity on.'

'Both attacks came from behind.'

'Of course. Quent was no slouch. He used to be fast and strong. There are not many people would be able to get one over on him face to face. Did you know he was gay?'

'The DCI interviewed his lover, um . . . Paulo somebody.'

'Escobar,' Maxwell told her. 'That's just a lucky guess, by the way.'

She blew bubbles again. 'Max, was he that way at school?'

'Quent? Never! Well . . . God, I don't know.'

'Would you have known?'

'Not necessarily. Oh, it went on, of course. It does in all single-sex places. There were stories about the Preacher and the school cat. Not to mention the chaplain . . .'

'The chaplain?'

'I said,' he shouted, 'you weren't to mention the chaplain! Ah, the old ones are the best.'

'And there,' she said, 'the similarities end. A dark-coloured car was seen in or near the Halliards grounds on Friday night, Thomas told us.'

'When all of us were whooping it up at the Graveney.'

'All except George Quentin,' she reminded him.

'And the Preacher, who was late.'

'Even so' – she was staring at the swirling patterns of the steam – 'that doesn't tally. The pathologist estimated Quentin's time of death at about two, two-thirty Saturday morning. Where were you then?'

'Policewoman Carpenter,' he said, appalled. 'Are you inter-rogating me?'

She laughed. 'It wouldn't be the first time. Just because you're paranoid, Max, it doesn't mean everyone's not after you.'

'How right you are,' he said.

'There are actually more differences in the two killings than similarities.' She was talking to herself really. 'Quentin found indoors, hanged. Bingham in the open, bludgeoned. There was a clumsy attempt to cover that up.'

'How?'

'He was hidden under an old settee.'

'That's because' – Maxwell was thinking aloud too – 'the deaths served different purposes.'

'How?' she asked.

'Quent was deliberate, public, a set piece, based on the legend.'

'Legend?' She sat up and a couple of her cucumber slices fell off. 'What legend?'

'Well, the hanged boy . . . oh, for Christ's sake, Jacquie, didn't I tell you about that? Yes, I did.'

'No you bloody didn't, Peter Maxwell,' and she was out of the bath, cucumber slices flying in all directions. She grabbed a towel and padded along the landing, rummaging furiously in her bedroom for a notepad. 'What, tell me, what?'

'Well, it's nothing, really,' he told her. 'Just one of those silly old school stories the boarders used to scare themselves shitless with in the dorm after lights out. I will confess, I had forgotten about it entirely. Even seeing poor Quent dangling there didn't jog my memory.'

'Go on, go on. Oh, shit!' She couldn't find a pen that worked and her towel refused to stay up.

'The legend of Halliards is that a lad hanged himself. He was supposed to be so miserable at the place – and God knows I can understand that – that he hanged himself from the bell rope one night. That was back in, oh, God knows, 1840 something. All schools over a century old have stories like that.'

'And who'd have known about that?' she asked.

'Any of us,' Maxwell said. 'All of us.'

'And who'd have known more than anyone else, Max?' she asked, already knowing the answer. 'Who was the historian of the Magnificent Seven?'

'Um, that would be me too,' he said.

Chapter Nine

The cab dropped him at the gate and he walked the rest of the way. The sun threw short, sharp shadows through the gaps in the privet and the dew was still bubbling on the grass. Kept an immaculate lawn, did Richard Alphedge. Maxwell rounded the pampas, rather past its best now that winter was coming on, and he was quietly impressed. If the house wasn't Lutyens, it was his smarter younger brother, with the unmistakable mock-Tudor elegance of those pre-Great War years, before life got so drab and grubby.

He rang the bell, an elaborate, ornate, wrought-iron thing that appeared to have genuine verdigris, not the type you can buy by the yard in Past Times. He heard the echo dying away in the hall beyond the heavy studded oak of the door. A gargoyle letterbox yawned at him from the frame.

'Who is it?' a disembodied voice, like something out of Oz, called out to him.

Maxwell stepped back, trying to find life, perhaps in an upstairs window. 'I'm looking for Richard Alphedge,' he said. 'The actor.'

There was a click to his left and he spun round to stare down the double barrels of a shotgun. A decidedly nervous Richard Alphedge stood at the other end, one eye shut, with Maxwell in his sights.

'For Christ's sake, Alphie. Is that thing loaded?'

'Max!' Alphedge lowered the barrels. 'You scared me to death.'

'*I* scared *you*?' Maxwell crossed to him. 'I'm just glad I'm wearing my brown trousers. Have you got a licence for that?'

'What? Oh, no, don't need one. Sorry, Max, it's a film prop. The most I could have done was nip your fingers in the firing mechanism. What are you doing here?'

Maxwell shook his head. 'I'm sorry. I should have called first.'

'No, no, don't be daft. It's good to see a friendly face. Come in, will you? Cissie won't be long.'

He showed his old oppo into a low vaulted entrance hall that led into a sitting room with glowing oak floors and sheepskin rugs. Alphedge propped the shotgun in the corner and threw back the doors of his drinks cabinet. 'You'll have a snorter?' the actor asked.

'Well . . .' Maxwell sank into the coach-hide furniture. 'It's a *little* early for me.'

'Nonsense. Scotch?'

'You haven't got a Southern Comfort, I suppose?'

'Er . . . no, sorry.'

'Scotch it is, then.'

Alphedge poured for them both. Maxwell noticed how unsteady the man's hands were, how he jumped at every sound, every rustle of the leaves on the windowpane.

'Well . . .' The actor sat down opposite Maxwell and raised his glass. 'Here's to who's left of us.'

Maxwell drank with him. 'You know about Cret, of course.'

'Of course.' Alphedge swallowed hard. 'It's all over the bloody papers. On the telly. Funny how everybody takes it seriously, because he was a High Court bloody judge. The likes of you and me . . .'

'Come off it, Alphie. We're not in the same category, you and I.' Maxwell waved at the trophies around the room and the photographs that plastered the wall. 'Look at that lot – you and John Gielgud, you and Larry Olivier, you and Michael Caine . . . well, look at you and Gielgud and Olivier anyway. My walls are covered in group photos of 7F at Chessington World of Adventure.'

Alphedge chuckled. 'And I can't help thinking you're better off for it. Right now, I'd trade all this in for a bit of peace. It's not much fun being high profile when there's a maniac on the loose. Have the police been to see you?'

'They tried, apparently,' Maxwell said. 'I wasn't there. Half-term.'

'Oh, of course.'

'You?'

Alphedge nodded, taking another swig to steady himself. 'Some pushy sergeant called Vernon. He brought a WPC with him, for Cissie presumably. She was fine, of course; played more cop shows than I've had walk-on parts. I don't know what I'd do without Cissie; a tower of strength, an absolute tower.'

'They want to see if our stories are still the same,' Maxwell said. 'Whether we've remembered anything.'

'Have you?'

Maxwell sighed. 'I wish I could. Alphie, had you met up with any of the Seven – recently, I mean?'

'Recently? God, no. You know how it is. I thought some of them would be dead. Oh, Christ, now they are. The awful thing is not knowing who'll be next.'

'You really think there'll be a next?'

'Don't you?'

'That depends.'

'Don't be such a cryptic bastard, Max; what are you talking about?'

'Whether all of us have pissed the murderer off to the extent that he wants to kill us all or whether there's something else I haven't got my head round yet. What did you do after Halliards? RADA, wasn't it?'

Alphedge nodded. 'Then a spot of rep. I got my first West End break in '68 – *Hadrian VII*. I understudied Alan Bennett in *Forty Years On*. My first film was *Where Eagles Dare* . . . for fuck's sake, Max, what do you want my CV for?'

'Clutching at straws, I suppose,' Maxwell said. 'Think back, Alphie. At any time, did any of us try to contact you? After all, you're undoubtedly the most famous of us.'

'Jesus, Max, I don't know. In my line you get fan mail, groupies, people writing to you asking for parts, auditions. I could fill a bloody pantechnicon with the mail I've received. Can I put my hand on my heart and say one of those letters wasn't from Stenhouse or Cret or Ash or you? No, I can't. Ash came to see me once in the West End – I think I told you; but that was years ago. What does your policewoman make of all this?'

'My policewoman?' Maxwell smiled. 'Well, it's difficult for her, Alphie. Professional ethics and all that.'

'Ah, yes.' Alphedge nodded, staring into the bottomless amber of his glass. 'The sanctity of the confessional or whatever. Talking of which . . . the Preacher.'

'What about him?'

'What ab . . . ?' Alphedge's eyebrows rose in search of his vanished hairline. 'Max, am I the only one to pick up the subtle nuance that the man is as mad as a wagonload of monkeys? What the hell is the Church of God's Children, for Christ's sake?'

'Takes all sorts, Alphie.' Maxwell sipped his Scotch.

'Don't come that politically correct mumbo-jumbo with me, Peter Maxwell. This is me, Alphie, remember? We'd have crossed the road to avoid a chap like Wensley in the old days.'

Maxwell nodded. 'Or given him a good smacking.'

'You must admit, he's odd. Oddly enough, I don't remember him being as odd as that.'

'Nor I,' Maxwell agreed. 'Perhaps that's what I'm looking for, Alphie. While you were bearing the third spear and rounding out your vowels at RADA and I was wrestling with the

History Tripos at Cambridge, what, I wonder, was the Preacher doing? What's he done since?'

The doorbell provided an answer, ricocheting around the enormity of Alphedge's living room. The actor visibly jumped and reached for the gun. No one had used the word 'culture'.

'Just me, darling,' Cissie's voice called from the hall.

Alphedge just as visibly relaxed. 'It's our little arrangement,' he told Maxwell. 'We usually go out together, but if we don't, we use the doorbell rather than coming in quietly.'

'Mr Maxwell.' Cissie had joined them, wearing a sheepskin coat and old trousers.

'Max.' He was on his feet and she hugged him.

'This is a pleasant surprise.'

'I was passing . . .' Maxwell began, then he laughed. 'No, I wasn't. I'm trying to make sense of all this, Cissie.'

'You're sleuthing, aren't you?' she said, throwing her coat on to a chair. She sat on the settee and patted it for Maxwell to join her. 'At Halliards, we girlies spent a little time together. Jacquie told me you had a propensity for it.'

'Did she, now?' Maxwell raised an eyebrow.

'Don't be hard on her, Max. We were all a bit stressed, you know. Oh, nothing like you boys, of course, finding poor George Quentin like that. And now, Anthony Bingham. What was he doing there, Max?'

'Cret? He'd come to see me.'

'To see you?' Alphedge asked.

Maxwell nodded. 'Ryker Hill is a stone's throw from my place. Perhaps he'd tried my home first and had no luck. Anyway, he left a message on the school answerphone. There's only one high school in Leighford, so it didn't take a High Court judge to fathom that one out. Said he'd be along to see me at five-thirty – that was a week last Monday.'

'What did he want?' Cissie asked.

Maxwell shrugged. 'I don't know. It's my guess he was doing what I'm doing now, – sleuthing as you put it, dear lady.'

Cissie smiled.

'He didn't come here, presumably? We all swapped addresses.'

'Richard would have shot him,' Cissie whispered to Maxwell, then smiled understandingly at her husband. 'This is really all *so* bizarre.'

'How would Inspector Morse solve this one?' Maxwell asked her.

She chuckled. 'Well, for a start, there'd be three more bodies than we've got by now. He'd have a few pints in the local, snarl at poor Lewis and bore us all to death with Wagner. Can you beat that?'

Maxwell laughed. 'Not at the moment,' he said.

'Have you been to see anybody else, Max?' Alphedge asked.

'I've followed up on Cret and Quent,' Maxwell told him. 'Did you know Quent was gay?'

The Alphedges looked at one another.

'Quent?' the actor repeated. 'Gay? You mean, as in homosexual?'

'I do,' Maxwell said. 'Do you remember anything like that at Halliards?'

'Well' – Alphedge worked his memory – 'there was the chaplain . . .'

'No, Alphie,' Maxwell said. 'I'm talking about Quent.'

'Good God, no. RADA, now, there's a different kettle of fish. I tell you, if I ever decide to hang up my five-and-nine and write my memoirs, there'll be a few people suddenly off to South America. For instance . . .'

'Richard,' Cissie cut in. 'This isn't exactly helpful, dear.'

'No, you're right.' Alphedge sighed. 'Sorry. Max, do you *really* think it's one of us?'

Maxwell's eyes wandered to the shotgun. 'You clearly do. You did at the Graveney.'

'We're just careful, Max,' Cissie said, and crossed to her husband's chair. She placed her hands on his shoulders. 'I've got the dearest, sweetest man in the world here,' she said. 'I don't want to lose him.'

Maxwell smiled. 'Well, we'll just have to see that that doesn't happen, won't we?'

Maxwell caught the train south and alighted at Haslemere shortly after teatime. He'd had lunch with the Alphedges and had never seen a man whose nerve had so far gone. On the way to the gate, where the cab he'd called was waiting, Cissie had held his arm and had looked up into his eyes. 'You'll keep him safe, won't you, Max?' she'd asked. 'It'll be all right, won't it?'

By the time he'd reached Haslemere, Maxwell wasn't sure that it would. He'd smiled and kissed Cissie's forehead. He was warm and strong and good, as he was to Jacquie, as he was to anyone who really needed him; Don Quixote without the horse.

The windmill that was Andrew Muir sat huddled over a PC at the top of a tasteful town house. He was wreathed in smoke, the wisps snaking around his white beard.

'Max, you bastard,' and he scrabbled to his feet and shook the man's hand. He'd let him in on the front door buzzer and left it to Maxwell's sense of direction thereafter. The attic room in which he worked was very like Maxwell's own but, say it himself as shouldn't, with far less character. For a start, there was no Light Brigade forming up for the Charge in the centre; neither was there a piebald beast prowling the shadows.

'I didn't see you smoking last weekend, Stenhouse,' Maxwell said, noting the pile of fag-ends in the ashtray.

'That's because I wasn't facing a bloody deadline then, dear boy.'

'Ah.' Maxwell found a seat amid a litter of paper. '*Spectator? Economist?*'

'*Horse and Hound*,' Muir confessed. 'The vanishing countryside is big at the moment. BSE, CJD, foot-and-mouth; we've had the lot. When did you last see a field?'

'Er . . . about ten minutes ago,' Maxwell said. 'Surrey and Sussex are full of 'em, you know.'

'Where's your poetry, Max?' Muir asked. 'I'm the last in a long line of hyperbolists. The end of civilization as we know it is good copy. It keeps Janet in booze.'

'Janet not in?'

'Fuck knows. What time is it?'

'Half four.'

'Tuesday, isn't it?'

Maxwell nodded. It had been the last time he'd looked.

'Bad hair day. She'll be popping from Pompadour's in the High Street to Jennifer Poulter's about now for their daily gin-and-aren't-men-bastards bash.'

'That's daily?' Maxwell asked.

'Twice on Thursdays.'

'Well, I'm glad to see you so chipper, Stenhouse,' Maxwell told him, leaning his back against an upright. 'I've just come from Alphie's.'

'Oh, yes. Is he under par?'

'You might say that. Ever seen a nervous breakdown?'

'God, really?' Muir groaned, and leaned back from his computer screen.

'Oh, he's rational enough at the moment,' Maxwell told him. 'Logical, keeps focused on a conversation and so on. But he's terrifed, Stenhouse, absolutely shitten. He and Cissie only go out when they have to and if that has to be separately they have an elaborate ritual of doorbell-ringing and calling. He keeps a shotgun up his trouser-leg.'

'Jesus!'

'But the laughable thing is, it doesn't work. It's a film prop.'

'Jesus!'

'Have you heard from anybody?'

'The law were round yesterday.'

'Who?'

'Er . . . a DC Pines. Surly bastard from the Warwickshire CID. He had some WPC in tow.'

'To talk to Janet.' Maxwell nodded.

'Yes, well.' Muir scowled. 'I don't know how much help she was. Look, Max, it's great to see you again and all, but . . .'

'I know.' Maxwell held up his hands, as Muir settled himself back in front of the screen. 'You've got a deadline and I'm in the way. The thing of it is, Stenhouse, it was bad enough when it was just poor old Quent. But now it's Cret too, well . . .'

'You're right.' Muir pushed his swivel chair away from the keyboard and lit another cigarette. 'For the last ten days, I've been trying to pretend everything's normal. All hunky-dory. But it's not, is it?'

Maxwell shook his head. 'Talk me through it again, Stenhouse,' he said. 'From the beginning. How did you find us all?'

Muir ran the fingers of his non-smoking hand through his hair. 'The beginning was right here in Haslemere, funnily enough,' he said. 'There's a firm called Swinton's, property developers. I was interested in buying some land on the edge of town. Janet's daughter by her first marriage breeds horses and is looking for new pasture. I got chatting to the fellow at Swinton's and in the course of the conversation it turned out they were handling the sale of a school in Warwickshire. Our school, Max.'

'To turn it into a conference centre?'

'Yeah, they had various clients interested. The place shut down as a school over a year ago. I saw it in the press then, property papers. So I contacted the local papers, *Leamington Courier* and so on, and got the gen. I hadn't seen any of you buggers for years . . .'

'Let me stop you there,' Maxwell broke in, 'because I can't help thinking this may be important. Who did you last see of the Seven, after we left Halliards, I mean?'

'Oh, God, now you've asked me. Ash, I think.'

'Ash? When? Where?'

'Bloody hell, Max.' Muir got to his feet, pacing the room. 'You're pushier than any copper.'

'Maybe that's because Alphie might be right,' Maxwell told him. 'Any one of us may be next in some macabre reworking of an Agatha Christie classic.'

'Come on,' Muir scoffed. 'This is the real world.'

'Yes, it is.' Maxwell was grimly serious. 'And the Seven are dying, Stenhouse. Quent and Cret have gone. Who's next? Alphie? Me? You? When did you see Ash?'

Muir stopped pacing and stretched. All morning he'd been huddled over that bloody PC, trying to be rational, trying to get on with his life. 'It would have been three, three and a half years ago.'

'Where?' Maxwell asked.

Muir looked at him, then stubbed out the cigarette and pulled a curtain aside. He handed Maxwell an exquisite bronze statuette of a goat-footed satyr, kneeling over a naked girl, his long bronze tongue snaking away between her legs.

Maxwell nodded. 'Elegant. Not perhaps the perfect centre-piece for the table when the vicar comes to tea.'

'No, it's not to Janet's taste either. That's why it's up here. It's eighteenth-century Italian, Max. Cost me a pretty penny, I can assure you. I came across it in a little art shop in St Christopher's Place, all rather Bohemian, if you know what I mean. And who should be behind the counter but Ash! You could have knocked me down with 3D porn, but it was him all right. The oily bastard hadn't changed a scrap.'

'And this is what he does?' Maxwell passed the object back.

'Quaint, isn't it? Oh, the window's full of art deco and nouveau and ghastly Clarice Cliff et cetera, but Ash makes his real money with under-the-counter stuff like this. You wouldn't think, would you, in this age of video nasties, there'd still be a market for Victorian smut? More your sort of thing, I suppose, you being a historian and all.'

'Thanks,' said Maxwell.

'Anyway, we kept in touch on and off. As soon as I heard about the Halliards closure, I rang him, suggested the reunion. Finding the others wasn't too hard. Cret we knew via the press. His chambers in the Temple were a matter of public record. Alphie, of course, I reached via his agent, a particularly reptilian mid-Atlantic type. Oddly, it was Cret who knew about the Preacher – or at least his church.'

'He did?'

'The Church of the Children of God,' Muir said. 'It's all on the Net. I'll give you a print-out if you like.'

'Just the facts, ma'am.' Maxwell's Joe Friday was legendary and words like print-out scared him.

'Well . . .' Muir was lighting up again. 'It's an American sect thing. They believe in self-denial. Did you notice how little Wensley ate at the Graveney? I didn't see him drink at all. Mind you, I was fairly pissed that Friday night. It's typical of your West Coast pseudo-psychobabble. They were investigated back in '93 over allegations of child abuse, but the charges were dropped. They specialize in waifs and strays – hence the concern.'

'So the Preacher lives in the States now?'

'That's where I reached him. The Church's headquarters are in Sacramento. It was probably the paedophile thing that explains Cret's knowing his whereabouts.'

'So you phoned him?'

'E-mailed.' Muir inhaled sharply. 'Essentially the same letter I sent you, sent everybody. It was a helluva long shot. I was as surprised as the next man when he showed up.'

'Late.'

'Christ, Max, the guy had just flown six thousand miles. I wasn't expecting miracles. He must have been jet-lagged to buggery. You, you bastard, you were the hardest to track down. Quent was a City slicker, but Leighford, Max? Could you be any more down-market?'

Maxwell shrugged. 'Just lucky, I guess.'

'Oh, God, I didn't mean that.' Muir was running his fingers through his sandy-grey hair again. 'It's just that . . . Max, you were the best of us. Oh, you didn't win the cups and the colours, not like Quent, but brain-wise . . . Jesus, you left us standing. And now what are you doing? Casting pearls before swine? God, what a waste!'

Maxwell smiled. 'It's a dirty job, but somebody's got to do it. Where'd you get the key?'

'What?'

'The key to the school. Where did you get it?'

'From Swinton's, of course.'

'And when did you get there – to the Graveney, I mean?'

'All right.' Muir laughed. It was short and brittle. 'I confess. I got to the Graveney on the Thursday and, yes, I did sneak into Halliards that night.'

'That night? That's odd.'

'Why?' Muir wanted to know.

'There was no electricity in the place. Why did you go at night?'

Muir looked at his man. 'You'll find this pathetic,' he said.

Maxwell shrugged. 'Try me.'

'You remember I was a boarder?'

Maxwell clicked his fingers. 'Of course you were. Upper Fourths, wasn't it?'

'Lower Fifths. Pater was out in Aden that year. Took Mater with him. So boarding it had to be. We'd scare seven kinds of shit out of ourselves with ghost stories.'

Maxwell nodded. 'Le Pendu. The hanged boy.'

'I just wanted to relive it, Max, to stand there in that hall with that bell rope reaching to the canopy and Old Harry above and feel the hairs stand up on the back of my neck.'

'And did they?'

'Oh, yes.' Muir chuckled. 'Somehow, standing in that place, the years fell away. All the rationalism and cynicism of age just left me. I had to do it, Max, but I wasn't sorry to leave.'

'Seven kinds of shit?' Maxwell asked.

Muir's laugh was punctuated by the slamming of a door floors below them. 'Ah,' he said. 'Make that eight kinds.'

'Nothing personal,' Maxwell said, looking at the time. 'I've got places to be.' He was on his feet. 'Tell me, Stenhouse, this little pre-visit to Halliards, did you tell the police about it?'

'No,' said Muir. 'Should I have?'

Maxwell shrugged. 'Not for me to say,' he said.

Muir led him down the stairs to the lounge, where Janet was pouring herself something large from the drinks cabinet.

She beamed. 'Max, how nice. Andrew has so few friends to play with.'

'Janet.' Maxwell smiled. 'Good to see you.'

'Absolutely.' The woman gurgled back the ice-filled drink. 'Has my bore of a husband offered you anything alcoholic? He's such an oaf.'

'No, thanks,' Maxwell said. 'I'm afraid I must be going.'

'Must you?' Janet Muir's face was a picture of frozen apathy. 'How sad. Andrew, what the fuck is this?' and she held up a cricket bat, worn and old. It had a new piece of tape around the middle.

'It's a man thing, Janet,' he said. 'You wouldn't understand.'

She threw it towards him and he caught it expertly, cradling the polished rubber handle in both hands for a moment, for all the world like Mel Gibson swinging into action at Falkirk. 'Well, please don't leave it cluttering up my hall, there's a dear. I can do without your endless schoolboy paraphernalia.'

'Stenhouse.' Maxwell shook the man's hand now that his host had leaned the bat against the wall. 'We'll meet again.'

'How very Vera Lynn,' Janet said, freshening her glass.

Maxwell stopped at the door. 'Janet, I've been trying ever since the Halliards weekend to place your accent. It's *very* slight, but it's there.'

'Edinburgh,' she said tartly, 'which pisses Andrew off more than a little, doesn't it, dear? He dresses up like Plum Duff, but

I—' – and the accent became noticeably stronger, – 'am the real McCoy; the crème de la crème.'

Maxwell smiled. 'I'll see myself out,' he told the loving couple. It was time he indulged in a little erotic art. He was a funny age.

Chapter Ten

There is a little shop in St Christopher's Place called Under Two Flags. Maxwell knew it well, having indulged his little Inner Sanctum attic hobby there for some time. A mini Roman legion marched across the shelf in the window, just below Edward the Black Prince, whose charger munched the grass by his steel-shod hoofs. Models to die for. But not today. Today, Mad Max Maxwell was after other objects of virtue. He'd walked past the Amber Centre and thrown a few coppers to the guy selling the *Big Issue*, though he had a big issue of his own. The sun that morning was dazzling. It was Balaclava Day, 25 October. At home, he'd have put on the cherry-coloured overalls he'd bought in the Portobello Road all those years ago, in honour of the men of his beloved Light Brigade who had ridden so well into the jaws of death.

'It's the Mouth of Hell,' a pleasant voice said behind him in the shop. He turned away from the marble carving with the gargoyle lips and flaring nostrils.

'Veronica?' The woman looked different. He'd first seen her in a shimmering ballgown under the lights of the Graveney's chandeliers. He'd last seen her in a green catsuit that showed off her well-positioned curves, on the Sunday they'd all gone their separate ways, numb with the shock of George Quentin.

'Max. This is a surprise.'

Indeed it was. On her own turf, the almost silent Veronica seemed to have a brain. 'I was looking for Ash,' he said.

'Not here, I'm afraid. But, look, I'll tell you what. I'm going home soon after eleven. I'll take you back to the flat.'

'Is he there?'

'He has a lie-in on Wednesdays, poor love. You know, he works so hard.' And she rolled her eyes heavenward.

'I'll call back, then,' he said. 'What? An hour?'

'Fine. Leave your bag if you like.'

'Thanks, I will.'

And Maxwell tipped his hat and stepped into the sunshine. Then he succumbed and ducked into Under Two Flags.

She drove them both through the hustle and bustle of London streets, the sun dazzling on vehicles and shopfronts. The Audi was sleek and silver and Maxwell found himself lying back in its sporty interior. Veronica oozed a certain something. She handled the gearstick as if it were a stage prop in a porn film, and it was difficult to see how her skirt could be any shorter.

'Are you investigating?' she asked him, her beautiful face a mask behind her shades.

'In a manner of speaking,' Maxwell said. 'Have the police been to see Ash?'

'Yes, on Monday. This is really *so* tiresome.'

'I don't suppose Quent and Cret see it that way.'

'Oh, I'm sorry,' she purred. 'That was callous. What must you think of me? The point is, though, Max, we all have lives to get on with.'

He nodded. 'At the moment.'

'What?' Perhaps Veronica wasn't very bright after all.

'Two of the old gang are dead, Veronica,' he said. 'What if Ash is the third?'

She crunched the gears as they drove south-west, snarling

round Marble Arch where the hanging tree of Tyburn once stood. In Maxwell's imagination, George Quentin hung from the gnarled old bough, swaying in the wind and calling his name. He shook himself free of it.

'How long have you known Ash?' he asked her.

'We've been living together for four years,' she said. 'I don't flatter myself I've been unique in that time.'

'Ah, so Ash . . .'

'Sleeps around?' She snorted, and the laugh that followed was hollow. 'He does his best, poor lamb.'

'I saw Stenhouse – Andrew Muir – yesterday. He showed me the little trinket he'd bought in the shop.'

Veronica smiled. 'For a moment, I thought that's what you'd come for. *The Rape of the Sabine Women* is causing quite a stir at the moment. Most of our business is over the Net, of course. It's really thriving. Have you visited our website?'

He looked at her. 'Madam, I wouldn't know a website from a campsite. How's Ash bearing up?'

'Oh, you know Ash,' she said. 'Nothing ruffles him, does it? Do you want to know his theory?'

'He has a theory?'

'Yes,' Veronica said, knowingly. 'They are rather like arse-holes, aren't they? Everybody's got one.'

'Perhaps Ash's make more sense than most,' Maxwell said. 'I'd welcome any ideas about now.'

'Stenhouse,' she said.

Maxwell nodded. 'Ah, yes. I remember Ash's little outburst. Not very kind of him, I thought.'

'He's got a point, you know, Max,' she said. 'Muir *did* organize the whole thing *and* he had a key to the place.'

'Isn't that all just a tad obvious, then?' Maxwell felt it his duty to point out.

'The police didn't seem to think so,' Veronica said. 'Oh, this fucking traffic. Come on!' and she bounced on her horn.

'Ash put this theory to them?'

'Of course. They were very keen. Wanted to know all about Muir and that lush of his.'

'Yes,' said Maxwell, usually the most chivalrous of men. 'Not a particularly pleasant woman. How does Ash think Stenhouse worked it?'

'Somehow, he got Quentin to go to the school. From what we gathered, he was actually killed there. There'd be some story, some pressing reason why he should go there rather than to the hotel. According to the police, Quentin died in the early hours. That gave Muir plenty of time to nip up to Halliards – what is it, ten minutes by car? Less?'

It was plausible so far.

'Muir met up with Quentin at some prearranged rendezvous – school gates, swimming pool, that stupid place you call the Altar or whatever – and went into the building with him. He was either carrying a club or had it stashed inside waiting, and he bashed in Quentin's skull with it. Then he put the bell rope round his neck and . . . bingo.'

'Not exactly,' Maxwell concluded.

'No? Why?' Veronica suddenly swerved to the right and changed lanes without signalling. Maxwell felt his shoulder click in and out of place, but it may have been the seat- belt.

'If it was Stenhouse, he couldn't have acted alone. From what I saw of George Quentin, he must have weighed fifteen stone. Muir is, what, ten, eleven? And dead weights don't help you. Stenhouse must have had an accomplice.'

'Janet,' Veronica said. 'Wouldn't surprise me at all.'

'I got the impression Janet wouldn't train a fire extinguisher on Stenhouse if he spontaneously combusted. Helping him to kill somebody is way beyond that. Anyway, it doesn't explain Cret.'

'All Ash and I know about that is what the papers said.' She paused. 'You didn't do that, did you, Max? Mind you' – she smiled briefly, glancing at him out of the corner of her eye – 'I find that sort of thing quite sexy.'

Maxwell frowned. 'Murder?'

'The sheer animalism of it all,' she purred. 'Muscle and sinew. Did you stove in Bingham's head?'

'Sorry to disappoint you, Veronica,' he said. 'Not guilty. Cret was on his way to see me, certainly, but he never showed up. Somebody else met him first.'

She swung left into an underground carpark and snatched up the handbrake. Unflicking her seat belt, she turned to face him, unzipping her catsuit so that her breasts bounced free. 'Max,' she almost growled, 'before we go up to the flat, we've time . . .'

'I'm not sure Ash would approve,' he told her, trying to look anywhere but at her breasts.

'Ash hasn't been able to get it up for the last two years,' she said. 'He keeps trying with various nubile lovelies, but no joy. Not even Viagra does him any good. Now, I'm not talking about Ash.' She nuzzled closer to him. 'I'm talking about you. And I'm talking about me.'

He reached out, tentatively at first, his right hand hovering near her cleavage. Then he took the zip and whipped it upward. She gasped as her breasts disappeared whence they came and looked at him in astonishment. 'Are you gay?' she asked.

'No,' he told her. 'I'm an old friend of Ash's. You're a beautiful woman, Veronica, but when you've hugged a man's buttocks in the rugger scrum and dragged through some foreign field with him on cross-country runs, well, you owe him more than that. Shall we?' And he was out of the car, grateful for the tarmac under his feet.

Veronica leaned over and glowered at him through the now-open window. 'It's flat six,' she said. 'I've got places to be.' And the Audi's tyres screamed across the carpark, Veronica vanishing in a blaze of brake lights and a puff of exhaust and the righteous indignation of a woman scorned.

★　　★　　★

'I've worked it all out.' Asheton handed Maxwell a king-size Southern Comfort. 'Why it has to be Stenhouse.'

The pornographer's apartment was furnished with a taste Maxwell never remembered Ash having when they were at Halliards. A gigantic nude posed provocatively over the low fireplace and Maxwell's bum disappeared into the soft, sensuous leather of the furniture. Looking around him, Maxwell guessed it had probably set Asheton back a sum not far short of the national debt of Angola.

'Go on,' he said.

'He had the key to Halliards, which meant he could come and go as he pleased. And the reunion idea came from him.'

'That's what Veronica said.'

Asheton looked up at his old oppo. 'Well, there you are.'

'Tell me about Veronica.' Maxwell rolled the exquisite cut glass between his fingers.

'What's to tell?' Asheton shrugged. 'We've been together now for . . . oh, four years.'

'Does it seem a day too much?'

Asheton frowned. 'What are you getting at, Max?'

'I'm not sure,' Maxwell told him. 'At the Graveney, Veronica was . . . what can I say? Monosyllabic. She giggled in all the right places, but her contribution to discussion over dinner was, if I remember rightly, zip.'

'So?' Asheton stretched out his feet on the fur rug before the hearth.

'So, just now, as she drove me over, she's clearly a bright cookie.'

'Oh, yes.' Asheton nodded. 'She is that.'

'What's she like at accents?'

'Accents?' Asheton was lost. 'What the fuck are you talking about, Max?'

'Oh, nothing.' Maxwell let it go.

'Tell me.' Asheton got up. 'Did she offer to suck you off? Or was it something more exotic this time?'

'Ash . . .'

The pornographer smiled. 'It's not the first time,' he said. 'Veronica and I play little games. It relieves the monotony. You're familiar with *Who's Afraid of Virginia Woolf?*'

Maxwell was.

'Veronica would leave Liz Taylor standing.'

'So a few minutes ago, she was trying to "get the guest"?'

'And give you a chance to "hump the hostess", yes.'

'I see.'

'Look, Max.' Asheton was facing away from his old friend, staring up at the huge naked girl. 'The last couple of years haven't been easy. I'm impotent. I know Veronica has her flings – I don't begrudge her that. The rest of it is cat and mouse. She flirts. I flirt. At the Graveney, she was going through her dumb brunette routine, for no reason other than it amuses her. In fact, she's Roedean and Merton, Oxford, Anthropology.'

'Well,' said Maxwell, 'I take my hat off to her.'

Asheton turned to him. 'You can take off whatever you like,' he said.

'But she's wrong about Stenhouse. You both are.'

Asheton sat down again. 'Tell me why.'

'It's just too obvious, Ash,' Maxwell explained. 'Stenhouse arranges the weekend. Stenhouse has the key. Bingo! If I remember aright, Stenhouse was always a pretty shrewd operator. Remember the Great Tuck Shop Scam of '59?'

Asheton chuckled. 'He was lucky there,' he said.

Maxwell nodded. 'Admittedly. But it was meticulously planned. It wasn't Stenhouse's fault that there was that iced bun shortage – could've happened to anyone.'

'But couldn't this be double bluff, Maxie?' Asheton persisted. 'It's so obvious that the police would discount it, as you apparently have?'

Maxwell shook his head. 'It's too great a risk,' he said. 'Quent was the risk-taker of the Seven. Remember Cranton '61?'

Asheton laughed. 'That *was* a close call. Who was that one you got off with? What was her name?'

'I didn't get off with anyone, Ash. You pinched mine in case yours was lonely.'

'That's right, I did. Debbie was the redhead, captain of hockey with thighs that could crack walnuts. Lucinda was the blonde – and I mean natural; tongue to die for . . . But you did go off with somebody.'

'All right, I did. Ethel.'

Ash's face said it all. 'Get away. Big girl? Teeth?'

'Right on both counts.'

'Still, good in the sack, though, eh?'

'I really wouldn't know, Ash.' Maxwell sighed. 'We discussed revision all night – remember, it was our O-level year. The only thing conjugal about Cranton '61 was the odd Latin verb. It did get quite interesting later, though, as the sun came up over the cricket pav; we got on to films. Sean Connery had just had his first break in *The Frightened City*, Newman was in *The Hustler* and Audrey Hepburn was having *Breakfast at Tiffany's*.'

'I think I remember the song,' Asheton said. 'And has any of this got anything remotely to do with Quent or Cret?'

Maxwell sighed, shaking his head. 'Buggered if I know, Ash,' he said. 'But what we're missing is motive. Let's assume that Cret died because he knew something. Or had found something out; whatever. He wanted to tell me, get my perspective. Whoever killed him, knew he knew and stopped him.'

'Why you?' Asheton asked. 'I don't remember you and Cret being particularly close.'

'We weren't,' Maxwell agreed. 'No more than the rest of us. The Preacher was always the odd one out.'

Asheton nodded. 'Odd indeed. I've always been very suspicious of these Holy Rollers, Max. Cults and weirdos. God knows what motivates someone like that. Wensley was a little cranky at school, but he's off the bloody wall now.'

'Does this mean Stenhouse is in the clear, in your eyes?'

'What about both of them?'

Maxwell looked the man in the eye. The old charmer had lost none of his sparkle. For a while the Head of Sixth Form toyed with asking whether he could have a look at the portrait in Asheton's attic. 'Both of them?'

'Yes. Look; whoever killed Quent bashed in his skull first. Well, okay, any one of us could probably do that. If I remember old Frisby's physics lessons, it's all to do with force and gravity and whatnot. But hoisting him up in Old Harry's bell rope, well, that's a job for two, isn't it?'

'The police think so.'

'Do they?' Asheton frowned. 'Ah, of course. Jacquie.' He smirked. 'She can handcuff me any time. All right, then. Stenhouse and the Preacher lure Quent to Halliards – that's why the Preacher was late; he had to arrange things. One of them engaged him in conversation on the landing while the other one clobbered him. Then they hoisted him up on the rope and Bob's your uncle.'

Maxwell threw his hands wide. 'Again, Ash, where's your motive?'

Asheton got up and paced the rug for a while. 'Financial,' he said.

'Financial?'

'Quent was a City type, wasn't be?'

Maxwell nodded. 'Vandeleur Negus.'

'Well, there you are, then. What's Stenhouse's situation, Max? Comfortable, would you say? You've been there, haven't you?'

Maxwell had. 'Modest enough town house in Haslemere,' he said. 'I don't think Janet works, though she probably drinks most of what Stenhouse makes.'

'There we are, then. Envy. A deadly sin, isn't it? Quentin's loaded. Stenhouse isn't.'

'And the Preacher?'

'These religious types are always after a buck. If it's not for retiling the church bloody roof, it's for buying that oh-so-essential Roller for getting to open-air rallies. Trust me on this, Maxie. It's Stenhouse and the Preacher.'

Maxwell finished his drink. 'On that basis, I should be the killer, me and my little ol' thirty grand before tax.' He stood up and took one last look at Asheton's apartment. 'And you, Ash, you're my next victim.'

Now Peter Maxwell knew a thing or two about cults. From the Templars to the Wackoes from Waco, he'd been around. He'd even met the odd Mormon, clean-cut young men in dark suits who'd talked to him about the importance of a family. He who didn't have one. He'd never met a Templar, but that was because they'd burned the last of them in 1314.

The taxi dropped him at the Lodge a little after six. The October evening was closing in after a day of dazzling sun, and long shadows stretched across the lawns and the gravel on which his feet crunched. Amesbury was a late Georgian pile, probably some rich man's country house, with its windows reaching to the ground and its shutters latticed with the bones of wistaria. Someone had painted the place pale blue and it looked like a wedding cake, as though the Brighton Pavilion had gone down to the sea and pupped.

A large woman in a scarlet kaftan answered the doorbell's ring.

'I've come to see the Reverend Wensley,' Maxwell said.

'Do you have an appointment?' The woman's accent was West Coast with a hint of Johns Hopkins.

'No, I'm an old friend. Peter Maxwell.'

'Wait here.'

She showed him into a cold vestibule hung with multi-coloured banners with hand-stitched slogans, reassuring the newcomer that Jesus Reigns, that God is Good and that No Man Stands Alone.

'Max.' A voice like thunder reverberated from the top of the stairs and the Preacher stood there, in a long white robe, looking for all the world like the Son of Man. 'I've been expecting you.'

Wensley floated down the sweep of the spiral staircase and led his man into a small anteroom with a single table and two chairs. All that made this different from a police interrogation room was the wall-to-wall books. Maxwell took in their spines – Kant was there, Spinoza, Descartes and Hume; philosophers long dead, ideas played out.

'You know Cret is dead?' Maxwell cut the preamble. He was tired, jolted from one alien lifestyle to the next. He missed his Light Brigade, he missed his cat; God help him, he even missed some of the kids he taught; but most of all, he missed Jacquie.

Wensley scraped back a chair and sat facing the Head of Sixth Form. 'Yes,' he said. 'The police told me.'

'It's all over the papers. High Court judge and so on.'

'We don't get papers here,' Wensley told him. 'The Church of God's Children are not concerned with that.'

'So.' Maxwell slapped his thigh and looked about him. 'This is the Guildford chapter, is it?'

'We're not Hell's Angels, Max,' the Preacher said. 'But we *are* used to being mocked.'

'I'm sorry, Preacher,' Maxwell said earnestly. 'I didn't mean to give that impression. Why were you late at the Graveney that Friday?'

Wensley looked at him, as though the question was a little preposterous. 'My taxi-driver got lost,' he said. 'He was fine in Coventry, but the back doubles threw him rather.'

Maxwell nodded. 'What did the police ask you? The second time, I mean.'

'Whether there was anything else I could remember, anything I wanted to change in my statement, that sort of thing.'

'And was there?'

'I saw a car in my wanderings.'

'A car?' Maxwell frowned.

'It had slipped my mind.' Wensley shrugged. 'After the dinner, I couldn't sleep.'

'The dinner on the Friday night?'

'Yes. I walked to Halliards.'

'You told the police this, the first time, I mean?'

'Of course. What I didn't remember was the car.'

'Where was this?'

'On the road near the main gates.'

'Whose was it?'

Wensley shrugged. 'I'm not good on cars, Max,' he said. 'Like you, I never use them. It was a dark colour, that's all I know.'

Maxwell was racking what passed for his brain. Wensley was right. He wasn't a car man, either. Other than Veronica's silver Audi and Jacquie's primrose Ka, he didn't have a clue who drove what. 'You didn't see anybody? Anything?'

'A rat,' Wensley remembered solemnly, 'scampering over the rubbish in the pool.'

'What made you go to Halliards, Preacher?' Maxwell asked him. 'It must be five or six miles from the Graveney.'

'I wanted to see it again,' he said. 'On my own. Without the rest of you.'

'Why?'

The Preacher looked at him. 'I told you – I wander; it's what I do. I have my reasons, Max,' he said. 'Let's leave it at that, shall we?'

'Is that what you told the law?' Maxwell asked. 'And were they happy with that?'

'Only the Lord brings happiness, Max,' the Preacher told him. 'He works through us all from time to time. But to answer your question, no, I don't think they liked it at all.'

Maxwell looked at the robed apparition in front of him. 'You know you've put yourself in the frame, don't you?' he asked.

'I have?' The Preacher frowned.

'Think, man. You get there later than anyone, except Quent. Why?'

'I told you . . .'

'Yes, you did. And can your taxi-driver vouch for you? Would you know him again? Did you get the number of his cab?'

Wensley was shaking his head to all three questions.

'So we only have your word for that.'

'We?' Wensley frowned.

'I'm playing devil's advocate here, Preacher. I have to. David Asheton thinks you did it. So does Richard Alphedge. So, unless they're myopic, must the police. Why did you go to Halliards?'

'Let it go, Max,' the Preacher warned.

'You've told the police you walked through a wet, miserable night, a walk that took you . . . what? A couple of hours? Not exactly a constitutional, is it; it was peeing down and windy. You must have been soaked. For what?'

The Preacher was on his feet. 'Thank you for coming, Max,' he said. 'Now, I really have to go.'

Maxwell stood up too. 'Preacher.' He put his hand on the man's arm and gazed steadily into his eyes. 'I'm on your side, believe me.'

Wensley patted Maxwell's hand and removed it firmly from the kaftan sleeve. 'There's been enough blood, Max,' he said. 'I don't ever want to see any more.' And he was gone, the door clicking softly behind him.

Maxwell stood to his full height. He'd talked to them all now – Alphedge, Muir, Asheton, Wensley; the men who were boys when he was a boy. He swung his scarf across his shoulder and hauled up the overnight bag he'd left in the hallway. The building was silent, cold. The Preacher had vanished on his sandalled feet and there was no sign of the lady in red. He crossed the polished floor, catching sight of himself fleetingly in the mirror next to the front door, then he was out into the long shadows and the evening air.

The stars were bright above him, promising a bitch of a frost. And he was still looking at them when they went out, as in one of the more weird sci-fi films of his boyhood. He heard the thud, but didn't connect it with the sickening, deadening pain in the back of his head, the ricochet of vision as his eyes rolled upward and his face hit the grass.

The rest was silence.

Chapter Eleven

Where the hell do you park in London? Jacquie Carpenter hadn't often had to face the question, but now she did. It was all of half an hour before an obliging Renault swung out into the traffic and she was in. It hadn't been very convenient, DCI Hall had told her, for her to take a couple of days now. Yes, it was her right and, yes, the leave was overdue, but they were in the middle of a murder enquiry and nothing was breaking. Jacquie knew all that. And ordinarily Jacquie would not have dreamed of asking, but something odd had happened. Peter Maxwell had disappeared.

This was Friday, the day of a teacher's half-term when he realizes that the blessed week has all but gone. But the sun was still shining on the multicoloured bark of the plane trees as DC Carpenter went in search of the man in her life.

'Yeah.' The crone who ran the hotel in Sussex Gardens had suddenly cooled when she saw the warrant card. 'He was here all right. Bit of a weirdo, if you ask me.'

'I didn't ask you,' Jacquie reminded her. 'Did Mr Maxwell have any visitors?'

'Dunno. I don't bother my guests, they don't bother me. Better all round.'

The crone sucked feverishly on a ciggie as if her life depended on it. 'What is he? Child molester, I'll bet. One of

147

them paedophiles. I knew it as soon as I clapped eyes on him. That's why I told him, I said, we had no Net facilities. I won't have no downloading of that filth in my place. No electronic how's your father here.'

'Glad to hear it,' Jacquie told her. 'When did Mr Maxwell leave?'

The crone padded in her fluffy mules to the desk and flicked through a ledger. 'Wednesday,' she said. 'Quite early. He had toast.'

'Did he say where he was going?'

The crone became confidential. 'Look, dearie, if he's not a child molester, you'll have to admit he's off his rocker. I didn't understand most of what he was talking about. I'll tell you what, though, I was within half an ace of getting Alf to check his bags, wasn't I, Alf?'

Jacquie hadn't seen Alf before. He was like a chameleon, blending in with the ghastly wallpaper and the lurid carpet. Only when he moved did Alf show signs of life at all. With half a mile of fag ash dangling from his chin, he grunted something incomprehensible to the crone, his wife.

'I thought you didn't bother your guests,' Jacquie said.

'Not unless they bother me,' the crone countered. 'And this one was beginning to bother me. 'Ere, he's not an international terrorist, is he? Working for that Saddam Hussein or them Arab Filamentalists?'

'No.' Jacquie couldn't help but smile. 'Nothing like that. Did he say he intended to come back here?'

'I wouldn't have had him,' the crone ranted. 'I'd have got my Alf to chuck him out, wouldn't I, Alf?'

Alf grunted again, passing back the way he had come. Bearing in mind he reached Jacquie's shoulder – and that in a good light – she would really have enjoyed seeing that.

She knew from Maxwell's phone calls that he'd gone first to see Richard Alphedge, and that was on Tuesday. She had the addresses of them all, all six of the Seven who had gone to the Halliards weekend. She put the information to good use now.

'I'm afraid poor old Richard isn't up to interviews today,' Cissie Alphedge told her, in the kitchen of the Lutyens house, passing the cup of coffee.

Jacquie was patience itself. 'Mrs Alphedge, I'm not from a fan club, I am a police officer.'

'I know, my dear, but even so . . . Can't I help?'

Jacquie looked at her. It's odd to come face to face with a face you've seen so often in your own living room. She was a murderess in *Morse*, Jacquie remembered, a mindless old bag lady David Jason felt sorry for in *Frost*, the vicar's wife in *Midsomer Murders*. Cissie probably knew more about police procedure than Jacquie did. 'Peter Maxwell,' she said. 'I'm trying to find him.'

'Max?' Cissie paused in mid-sip. 'Why? What's happened?'

Jacquie's cool grey eyes faltered for the first time. 'Nothing, I hope. He hasn't checked in.'

'Checked in?'

'Been in touch. He was in a London hotel . . . well, bed and breakfast, really, on Tuesday night.'

'He was here on . . . let me see . . . Tuesday? Yes, Tuesday morning.'

'That's what I thought,' Jacquie said. 'Where was he going then?'

'To the Muirs, I think. Yes, he was. He's a good man, your Mad Max; takes things on himself.'

Jacquie smiled. 'He has that tendency.'

'How long have you known him?' Cissie asked.

'Max? Nearly six years.'

'And he still hasn't made a decent woman of you.' Cissie tapped the girl's ring finger.

Jacquie laughed. 'I thought I was pretty decent already.'

'Jacquie . . .' Cissie didn't know how to begin. 'Look, we don't know each other very well, but . . . oh, this sounds just awful. It . . . it couldn't *be* Max, could it? The murders, I mean?'

Jacquie's face said it all. She looked Cissie squarely in the face. 'No, it couldn't. What about Richard?'

Cissie's handsome face folded into a smile. 'Touché, my dear.' She laughed. 'And again, an emphatic "no". Richard is a darling, but he's not the strongest of men. This whole thing has rattled him. I've lost track of the medication he's on at the moment. And even when you catch the killer, I'm not sure he'll ever be quite the same again. Are you making any progress?'

Jacquie sighed. 'It's a complex case,' she said. 'There are three forces working on it now.'

'Well, that's good, isn't it?' Cissie asked.

Jacquie looked at her. Perhaps the old girl wasn't quite as clued up as she thought. 'Yes and no,' she said. 'Three times the input, brainpower and shoe leather, three times the risk of mistakes. That, as Max would say, is the way the cookie crumbles.'

'Yes, I see. Are you able to tell me anything?'

'Very little, I'm afraid, Cissie. Goes with the territory – you know.'

'Yes, of course. You know, it's funny, I've done countless telly involving cops and robbers. Murders by the score. But the real thing is different, isn't it? Quite horrible, in fact.'

'Nobody wins,' Jacquie told her. 'That's the really depressing part. Nobody's life gets back to normal. It's not only your husband who won't be the same again. What time did Max leave?'

'Ooh, let me see. It must have been shortly after lunch. I'd been shopping and Max had a bite with us and then left soon afterwards. I'd have driven him to the station, but I'd already left Richard alone for long enough that day. He'd have had the ab-dabs if I'd slipped out again.'

Jacquie finished her coffee. Then she saw the shotgun propped by the fireplace. 'You *do* have a licence for that, Cissie?'

'Oh, it's a replica, my dear. Richard used it in *The Eagle Has Landed*. It wouldn't do any good, of course, if push came to shove, but it comforts him.'

Jacquie got up and walked to the hallway. 'He's taking it badly, then?' she asked.

Cissie glanced up the stairs and led her to the door. Under the arch of the veranda she held her arm. 'He cries,' she said, 'in the small hours. You know the time, my dear, that terrible time between three and four . . .'

Jacquie nodded. 'The dead of night.'

'Exactly. The time when the teeniest problems seem huge. He's as scared for me as he is for himself. We've talked to our GP, of course. The man's useless. Wall-to-wall Valium isn't the answer. Catching the killer is.'

Jacquie smiled. 'I'm not sure your GP's the right man for that job,' she said. 'Let us have a go.'

'Us the police? Or us, you and Maxwell?' Cissie asked.

Jacquie nodded, her face solemn now. 'Perhaps a bit of both.'

It was late afternoon by the time Jacquie Carpenter got to Haslemere. Peter Maxwell could have told her that the town was mentioned in the Domesday Book and between 1582 and 1832 sent two members to Parliament. Alfred, Lord Tennyson, had died at Adworth House beyond the town's fringes. Jacquie knew none of this. All she knew, as she crawled through the sluggish traffic in the High Street, was that Peter Maxwell had vanished.

'Drinkie?' It was an offer that Janet Muir made several times a day, if not to others, then at least to herself, via those scampering little demons in her brain. She looked rather a fright in her housecoat and turban.

'It's a bit early for me,' Jacquie said, taking the proffered armchair.

'Nonsense, my dear,' Janet slurred. 'There's no such thing as too early. We've already talked to the police, you know.' She was creating a very large gin and tonic in the open-plan kitchen. 'I assume you *are* here in a professional capacity?'

Jacquie nodded. 'Always. I'm looking for Peter Maxwell.'

'Ah, yes. Your better half – or I expect he sees it that way.'

'Not exactly.' Jacquie found it difficult to keep her cool in this woman's presence. What she really wanted to do was to tear her eyes out. 'I understand he was here.'

'Yes, he was.'

'When?'

'Oh, my dear.' Janet winced as the juice of the juniper hit her tonsils. 'Now you've asked me. One day is very like another, really, isn't it?'

'It *is* quite important,' Jacquie insisted.

'What?' Janet, slurred as she was, could pick up another woman's angst at the drop of an olive. 'Afraid he's run off with someone? He does have a certain twinkle, I suppose.' She became wistful. 'If you like that sort of thing.'

'Could it have been Tuesday?' Jacquie persisted.

'It could have been Mardi bloody Gras.' Janet rinsed her tonsils again. 'No doubt Andrew would know.'

'Is he here?'

'Fuck knows. I heard him go out earlier. We lead very separate lives, he and I. He has his articles and what he still nostalgically calls Fleet Street; I have CHOOH. If I'm not stinking by lunch-time, I feel somehow unfulfilled.'

'So you can't tell me when Maxwell was here or when he left?'

'I do remember the bat.' Janet Muir was frowning, pointing at Jacquie with a long-nailed finger jutting out from the glass.

'The bat?'

'Maxwell was just leaving and I fell over it. Andrew had left the bloody thing lying in the hall. If I weren't so rational, I might be tempted to think he was trying to do me in.'

'Are you talking about a cricket bat?'

'Part of Andrew's obsession with yesteryear.' Janet leaned towards her. 'He's made such a dog's bollocks of his adult life, all he's got is memories.'

'Could I . . . see the bat?' Jacquie asked.

'See it?' Janet frowned. 'What the fuck for?'

'Humour me,' was the policewoman's answer.

'I haven't the first idea where it is. I remember telling Andrew to move it.'

'It might be evidence,' Jacquie said.

'Evidence?' Janet hiccoughed. 'How do you mean?'

'Mrs Muir . . . Janet . . . I shouldn't be telling you this, but the pathologists have found fibres in the hair of both dead men – Quentin and Bingham. Those fibres are wood and they come from the willow tree.'

There was a pause while Janet Muir stood swaying. 'So?'

'So, cricket bats are made from willow.'

Jacquie could see realization dawn on the woman's face. Her reaction now could go either way. It would either be loyalty or . . .

'The utter bastard!' Janet spat the words and marched past Jacquie, her heels clacking on the polished parquet floor. She wobbled as she tried to round a tight bend in the hall, then there was a crash, followed by another. 'Shit!' Janet Muir was wrestling, as any woman must at various times in her life, with the contents of her understairs cupboard. Jacquie heard a door slam and a staccato thud as Janet took to the stairs.

'Up here!' she barked at Jacquie, and the policewoman instinctively obeyed, following the furious Janet up the staircase, first to one floor, then to the next. Mrs Muir kicked open a bedroom door and stood there, looking around in contempt. Then she crossed to a louvred wardrobe and wrenched open the door. She rifled through shirts hanging there, throwing trousers and shoes across the room.

'Mrs Muir,' Jacquie shouted above the row, but the woman wasn't listening to the voice of reason. She spun round, an ancient cricket bat in her hand, new tape wound around its centre.

'Here!' she snarled. 'The murder weapon.'

'It seems to have been damaged,' Jacquie noted calmly.

'Doesn't it?' hissed Janet. 'Let's see what's underneath. Splintered wood? Blood? Brains?'

But Jacquie stopped her, easing the bat from her grasp. 'We have people,' she said softly, 'who will do that professionally. Can I take it away with me?'

Janet's eyes were still flashing wildly and she was gnawing her lip. Then she took a deep breath and sat down on her husband's bed. 'He always hated Quentin, you know.'

Jacquie sat down alongside her. 'I didn't know,' she said.

'Oh, yes. You see, Andrew is a competitor, one who likes to win. That's why he hates me. He *never* beats me, you see, not at anything. Quentin was the sporty one, captain of jolly old games and all that crap. I've lost count of the nights I've fallen asleep listening to Andrew's pathetic venom.'

'So you helped him?' Jacquie asked.

'What?' Janet leaned back to get the younger woman into focus. 'Are you mad?'

'What sort of car do you drive, Janet?'

'Car? A Peugeot. Why?'

'What colour is it?'

Janet rose unsteadily. 'What the fuck is this? Twenty bloody questions?'

'As many as I need to ask.' Jacquie's voice was firm.

'Green. Dark green. They used to call it bottle, I believe, but when applied to cars, I understand they call it racing.'

'Is he a strong man, your husband?'

'What are you talking about now?'

'Janet.' Jacquie stood up facing the woman. 'Are you seriously telling me you think your husband killed Quentin and Bingham?'

'You told me about the bat.'

'That's only a potential weapon,' Jacquie said. 'And we don't yet know if it's the one. I'm talking about motive. Did Andrew say he wanted revenge, wanted to call this reunion to get it?'

'I don't remember,' Janet slurred.

'Janet. This is vital.'

'Look.' Janet Muir stepped away from Jacquie, breaking free of her, standing on her own with her hands in the air, trying to hear through the clamouring voices in her head. 'My husband is a bitter, vindictive man. He had a job in Fleet Street which he blew because he wasn't up to it. He could have had the *Mail*, but he didn't have the bottle. Time after time, the glittering prizes went somewhere else. And what does he do now? Turns out trash for small-time magazines at a thousand quid a throw. Yes, he hated George Quentin; Quentin who always outran him, outplayed him, outearned him. George Quentin, who could buy Andrew twenty times over.'

'And you helped him?'

Janet swivelled round, staring at the girl. 'You keep saying that. Why should I have helped him?'

'It took two people,' Jacquie said, 'to hoist Quentin's body on to that bell rope at Halliards. I've danced with your husband, Janet. Arnie Schwarzenegger he ain't. I doubt he could have managed that alone.'

'You're right,' Janet murmured. 'That failure couldn't do anything by himself. Look, do me a favour, will you? Just let me be there when you arrest him. It would make my day. What am I talking about? It would make my bloody year!'

She checked his home number for the umpteenth time as she drove north-east to join the artery of madness that is the M25. Her heart thumped as it always did when she heard his voice.

'You've reached Peter Maxwell. I'm probably buried alive in essay-marking and lesson preparation. There again, I could be

155

down the pub. Leave any message after the Blair and the cat'll get back to you.'

Jacquie would have settled for that – Metternich's rasping purr over the wires, to reassure her that *something* was normal in the world.

'Max, it's me. I've probably used up all your tape by now, judging by the bleeps, but for God's sake, get back if you can. I'm on the mobile.'

His mobile was as dead as a doornail. 'The Vodafone subscriber you are calling is not answering at the moment. Please try again later,' an electronic voice told her. Why was it, in this age of instant communication, you couldn't get hold of the one person you wanted to reach?

The rain set in as she reached the M4 interchange and turned due east, a steady rhythm hammering on the roof of her little car, the wipers humming like bees' wings. So Richard Alphedge was falling apart with fear. That she'd seen before. And Cissie was doing her best to protect, to stay loyal. But what price loyalty in the Muir household? Janet seemed convinced that Stenhouse had done it and Jacquie had the possible murder weapon on the seat behind her to prove it. She'd waited as long as she dared at the Haslemere town house, but there was no sign of Andrew Muir and she couldn't wait any longer. Who knew where Max was, what he was going through? And where was Muir? Would they find a neat pile of clothes on a shingle beach somewhere? Perhaps at Leighford? And would he become the next Lord Lucan, with a row of question marks where a murderer should be?

She rang the bell at the door of Flat 6 and a tall, sultry girl answered it in a long, white towelling robe.

'Veronica?'

'Jacquie? I'm sorry, I didn't recognize you with wet hair. Come in, you're soaked.'

It was the huge nude which Jacquie saw first above the glow of the artificial coals. Uplighters added a dreamy sensuousness to the pastels of the walls and a gentle mood music flooded the apartment. Beyond the rainy tears on the picture window, the lights of west London twinkled in their neon orangeness.

'Get those off.' Veronica handed her a soft white towel. 'You'll catch your death.'

'No, I'm fine,' Jacquie said. 'Can I just drape my coat somewhere?'

'Sure.' Veronica took the jacket and disappeared. When she came back, there were Martinis in her hands. 'Hair of the dog?'

Jacquie could actually have done with a cocoa, but from what she remembered of Veronica at Halliards, and looking at her now, she wasn't sure she knew how to make it. She took the glass and sat on the vast cream settee next to the fire. 'I'm looking for Max,' she said.

'Max?' Veronica sipped her drink.

'Has he been here?'

'Yes . . . er . . . day before yesterday.'

'Wednesday?'

'That's right. He wanted to talk to Ash, but Ash wasn't here.'

'What time was this?'

'He called into the shop in the morning. I brought him back here for lunch.'

'And what time did he leave?'

'Oh, now you're asking. Ten, eleven perhaps.'

'That night?'

Veronica looked confused. 'No, no, the next morning. Yesterday. Oh dear, this is awkward.'

'What is?' It was Jacquie's turn to be confused.

'Well, Max said you wouldn't mind.'

'Mind what?'

Veronica smiled and managed a short, brittle laugh. 'Oh dear . . .' and she glided away.

Jacquie was still turning round when the dark-haired girl came back into the room, carrying a small picture.

'What do you think of this?' Veronica asked.

At first, Jacquie wasn't sure which way up it was. Then it dawned. Two naked women were entwined around each other, padlocks through their genitals and bandages around their eyes.

'It's the latest acquisition for the shop,' Veronica told her. 'A Michele Demison. Paint on gouache. Isn't it exquisite?'

'I can think of a few of my colleagues who would call it filth,' Jacquie said.

'Men!' Veronica snorted. 'Oh, they have their place in the scheme of things. But there are times, Jacquie, when only another woman understands.' She ran a long index finger around the curve of Jacquie's cheek, sliding it down her neck towards the damp collar of her blouse. 'Don't you agree?'

Jacquie kept to the point. 'I am looking for Max.'

Veronica let the painting fall on to the settee, opened her bathrobe and straddled the girl with her naked thighs. 'Have you ever made love to another girl, Jacquie?'

Jacquie *had* moved faster in her life, but she couldn't really remember when. She threw the taller girl aside and stood on the fur rug, quivering with fury. 'No, I haven't. And I don't intend to start now. Where was Max going when he left here?'

Veronica smiled, closing her bathrobe. 'You don't know what you're missing,' she purred. 'Max found it . . . shall we say . . . congenial.'

Jacquie looked hard at the siren on the settee. 'You're saying you slept with Max?'

Veronica nodded. 'Slept with implies a bed, doesn't it? Well then, yes, I slept with him, in the king-size next door. We had our first fuck, though, in my Audi in the carpark.'

'Give it up, Veronica.'

Both girls started at the sound of a male voice. David Asheton stood on the raised area that led to the bedrooms, wearing a towelling robe identical to Veronica's.

'Ah.' Veronica recovered her Martini from the coffee table. 'The green-eyed, limp-dicked monster.'

Asheton stormed across the lounge and poured himself a drink. 'What are you doing here, Jacquie?'

'Looking for Max,' she told him, wondering when it would be *his* turn to open the robe.

'He's not here.'

'Clearly. Where did he go?'

'To see the Preacher, I think. Why?'

'He hasn't been in touch. Where's my coat?'

Asheton glanced across at the lovely girl on the settee. Then he glanced at Jacquie. 'You don't need to go yet, surely?'

Jacquie looked at them both, the sad old lecher and his weird mistress. 'There's nothing to keep me here,' she said.

'Oh, but there is.' Veronica got to her feet and sauntered across to the drinks cabinet, hips swaying provocatively as she moved. 'Something you ought to know about the Preacher.'

'What about him?'

'He came to my room.' She glanced at Asheton. 'Our room, at the Graveney, that Friday night.'

'What for?' Jacquie asked.

Veronica arched an eyebrow, as though to have to say it was beneath contempt.

'Is this relevant?' Jacquie was looking around for signs of her coat.

'We went to Halliards.'

Jacquie's attention was fixed on Veronica now. 'Why?'

Veronica took a sip of the freshened Martini. 'He said he hated the place. He'd always loathed his schooldays. Ash, Bingham, Alphedge, Max – he hated them all. Especially Max. He particularly despised Max. He didn't say why. He told me he wanted to make out – such a quaint, colonial expression that, isn't it? He wanted to make out on the chapel altar. Something to do with showing his disgust at the hypocrisy of the place.'

'Ash.' Jacquie looked at him. 'Is this true?'

Asheton shrugged. 'Am I my concubine's keeper?' he asked.

'I'd had a skinful that night and I sleep the sleep of the dead. It's possible.'

'Possible! You dickweed!' Veronica snarled at him, then crossed to Jacquie. 'Max was good' – she smiled at the girl – 'but the Preacher was better. It gave me the creeps at first, breaking into that place at night. Later on, though, when the Preacher got going, I didn't give it a second thought. I went to a snobby school too. It gave us both a kick to do it there. Almost as if . . . all the old gels from Roedean and the old boys from Halliards were watching us.' She laughed. 'You should try it some time.'

'You broke into the chapel?' Jacquie asked her.

Veronica nodded. 'Mm-hmm.'

'That's odd,' Jacquie said. 'When I passed that way the next morning, when I got Max's call about finding the body, the chapel door was padlocked. I don't remember any sign of a break-in.'

Veronica shrugged. 'Figure of speech. Obviously the Preacher had a key.'

Jacquie stormed across the carpet and turned the corner that led to the stairs. Her coat hung there, still wet, on a hook.

'Jacquie, you can't leave yet,' Asheton was saying. 'It's a filthy night out there.'

Jacquie looked at them both, her Puritan hackles suddenly rising. 'Maybe,' she said. 'But it's not as filthy as the lies in here.'

Chapter Twelve

The rain had set in by the time Jacquie Carpenter had reached the Lodge. It had taken her the best part of an hour to find it – a large, rambling building set back from the road and guarded by ancient rhododendrons whose dark leaves dripped silver droplets in the dark.

She'd asked directions at an all-night service station and had used the opportunity to try Maxwell again. Nothing. Just his warm, comforting voice and the ever-growing number of electronic bleeps.

She stood now on the porch, grateful for the overhang of the gable above her, but not exactly ecstatic about the blinding glare of the security light that bathed her.

'Yes?' a disembodied voice punctuated the steady hiss and drip of the night.

'Police.' Jacquie held up her warrant card to the lens of the security camera.

'Do you know what time it is?' The voice was female. American.

Jacquie tried the Pinkerton approach. 'We never sleep.' It was worthy of Maxwell himself.

There was a whirr and a click and the front door swung wide. Jacquie didn't like dark places. She'd seen too many corpses lying in them for that. But the feeling was older;

something in her childhood she couldn't quite remember, like the moon through curtains and the shining lights of Christmas; indefinable, unfathomable, lurking with a menace of its own. Her eyes acclimatized to take in a sweeping staircase ahead of her and the polished parquet of a large hall with lights, scarlet and gold, twisting slowly in the floor's centre, like moving stained glass.

'It's late.' The female voice came from a black apparition in a scarlet kaftan, floating down the spiral sweep of the staircase.

'I'm sorry,' Jacquie said.

'You gotta name, child?' The black woman was huge, with sparkling eyes and an Afro haircut that had gone out before Jacquie was born.

'DC Carpenter, Leighford CID.'

'Leighford? Hell, honey, where's that?'

'Sussex,' Jacquie told her. 'The South Coast.'

'Well, sugar' – the black woman placed an arm around her damp shoulders – 'I'd love to talk geography with you all night, but it *is* one in the mornin'.'

'I'm sorry,' Jacquie said. 'I need to talk to John Wensley.'

'Reverend John? Why, honey, he's sleeping now.'

Jacquie looked at her hostess. The woman sounded like Dr Quinn, Medicine Woman, and looked like something out of *Green Pastures*. 'Then you'll just have to wake him up,' she said.

'You gotta warrant?' The arm had fallen away and there was an altogether harder tone to the voice.

'I don't need one to talk to somebody,' Jacquie explained.

'You gotta work permit?'

'It's all right, Angel.'

Both women turned. John Wensley came out of the shadows as the Devil might step from Hell. There was no roar of fire, no flash of sulphur, just a tall, lean man with long hair and a long, grey robe. On the other hand, depending on your point of view, he could have been Jesus.

'Jacquie?' Wensley took her hand. 'What's the matter?'

'Max,' she told him. 'I'm looking for Max.'

'Angel, bring us . . . Jacquie, what would you like? Coffee? Tea? We've no liquor here, I'm afraid.'

'Coffee, please.'

'Angel?'

The black lady spun on her heel, muttering.

'Seventh child of a seventh child,' Wensley said by way of explanation. 'She's a bit difficult sometimes. Your clothes are wet. Take them off in here. I'll get you a robe.'

'No thanks.' Jacquie's refusal was perhaps a *little* too prompt, but she was still seething from Veronica's attempts to seduce her. And anyway, if she put on one of John Wensley's robes wouldn't she be one of his, a Child of God?

'We are all children of God,' the Preacher intoned. Jacquie's pulse quickened. Was he reading her mind? Then, as Wensley led her into a small anteroom, she realized it was some sort of mantra. There was an altar at one end and a single row of chairs – hard, wooden, upright. A solitary flame burned from a sconce on the wall.

'You're looking for Max?' He was sitting beside her, peering earnestly into her eyes.

'That's right. Have you seen him?'

'Yes.' Wensley nodded. 'Yes, I have. He was asking questions too.'

'When was this?'

'Er . . . Wednesday, I think. Two days ago. But, as it's already Saturday morning, three.'

'What time was this?'

'Evening. We hadn't long had supper. I . . . oh, Angel.'

The large black woman had arrived carrying a tray with two mugs. 'DC Carpenter is looking for Mr Maxwell, Angel. You remember – you let him in, didn't you?'

'No, Reverend John. That was Gilda. She told me 'bout him, though. Old friend of yours, wasn't he?'

'That's right,' Wensley said. 'Jacquie, I don't understand this. Where is Max?'

'If I knew that' – Jacquie took the coffee mug – 'I wouldn't be here. No one's seen him since Wednesday, Mr Wensley. Not since he came here, in fact.'

'Thank you, Angel.' Wensley smiled at the woman. 'That'll be fine. You get some sleep now. Rough day tomorrow.'

'Yessuh. Good night, Reverend John,' and she was gone.

Wensley smiled. 'She worries about me.'

'When did you see Max last?' Jacquie was persistent. 'And where, exactly?'

'Come with me.' He took her across the dimly lit hall into another anteroom. This one had no altar and was lined with books. It had the air of an interview room. 'Right here,' he said. 'This is where I left him.'

'You left him?'

'I had things to do. I am a guest here, Jacquie, but I have my duties. Think of the Lodge as a sort of youth hostel, if you will.'

'So you don't know that he actually left?'

'Yes, of course. I heard the door go. It's electronic. Buzzes upstairs when it opens and when it closes. I heard it buzz as it closed.'

Jacquie got her bearings from the anteroom, looking across the hall to the front door and the mirror alongside it. 'So he was outside.'

'Jacquie.' Wensley blocked her view. He looked smaller without the broad-brimmed hat and the duster coat. 'You think Max is dead, don't you?'

She looked at him, shaking inside and wanting to cry. Nobody had said that yet. Nobody but her. And she had said it only once, in the tiniest of voices, inside her head. 'He could be the third victim.' Her real voice was stronger than she'd hoped. 'After Quentin and Bingham.'

'God.' The Preacher sat down.

'That leaves Alphedge, Asheton and you in the frame.'

'That's what Max said,' Wensley told her.

'What?' She sat down with him, her coffee discarded, her hand hovering near the can of mace in her bag.

'He said the police had me in the frame.'

'Why?' Jacquie was feeling her way with care. Everything about the Preacher unnerved her. His steel-hard stare, his strained voice; above all his unreadable face.

'Because I went to Halliards on the night Quent was killed.'

Jacquie nodded. 'I know. With Veronica.'

'Veronica?' The Preacher blinked at her.

'You went into the chapel,' Jacquie said. 'Had sex with her there. On the altar.'

Wensley was on his feet. 'Get out!' he said.

Jacquie got up too. 'Is it true?'

'You ask that?' She saw that the ridge in Wensley's jaw was pulsing. 'Of me? Here? In this house? Get out!' And he pushed her roughly so that her head cracked against the door frame.

'Don't do that!' she warned him, trying to stay calm, trying not to retaliate.

'For your own sake,' Wensley growled, 'don't stay here any longer, Jacquie. There are things you don't understand. Don't know. It wouldn't be wise to stay longer.'

Jacquie agreed with the sentiment. She stumbled backwards until she found herself in the hall, then turned and ran.

She wasn't exactly equipped for a night raid. She had a torch, but a torch in the Lodge's grounds was asking for trouble. And her heels would bite into the soft soil near the walls. Above all, she had no clue as to the place's layout and no jurisdiction whatsoever. It wasn't even her patch.

She turned her collar up and tucked the mace into her pocket. The rhododendrons loomed large and monstrous in the early hours' dark, but they gave her shelter and she was grateful for that. She knew that the front door was alarmed, with surveillance cameras and sensitive lights, but what about the rest of it? She felt her shoes squelch on the springy grass and wiped the water dripping from her eyebrows.

It was like those corny old B-features that Max loved – the creaking old house and the driving rain. All that was missing was the thunder lode and thunder light she remembered from Chesterton's poem at school. Pathetic fallacy, Max called it; when old Mrs Danvers stood at the burning window of Manderley or Richard Johnson's ghost-hunting team came unglued in *The Haunting*. But this wasn't celluloid. It was real. And she was scared.

The back of the Lodge had a row of windows that reached to the ground. Here, a gravel patio led to steps, where the ground fell away to landscaped gardens and a circular pond whose fountain had been switched off for the winter. Jacquie edged her way in as close as she dared, but the gravel would betray her and the flagstone path that led to the back door was certain to be alarmed. Her only hope was the single-storey wing that stretched ahead of her, the stables of the old house.

Now she was in the Lodge's shadow, the building rearing up above her at this lower level of ground. Then she saw it; a window half hidden by wistaria giving on to the path. She edged closer, checking to left and right. Then she was on the ledge and putting her weight against the panes. Nothing. It was locked, probably bolted on the inside. She angled the mace can, covering her face with her jacket against flying debris, and smashed the glass.

She knelt there in silence, her heart pounding. There was no alarm. Now that the glass had stopped falling, there was no sound at all. She picked out the remaining shards and found the catch. Then she wriggled forward on her hands and knees and was in. It took a while for the room to reveal its secrets. It was a half-cellar-cum-storage room, with packing cartons and piles of Bibles with lurid dust wrappers. She checked the corners and found the door. Beyond it, a faint glow lit stone steps snaking upward. These, she knew, were the old servants' quarters, where tweenies long dead would scuttle with buckets and brooms and tubs of hot water.

There were doors to both sides and she tried them all. Broom cupboard one. Broom cupboard two. A toilet. All the usual offices. The fourth door wouldn't budge. Locked. She used her shoulder. Nothing. She put her ear to it. 'Max.' Her whisper sounded like a yell. 'Max, are you there?' Nothing. She turned and made for the light.

There was no door at the top of the stairs, just another glow from the candles and the stained glass that created the reflected image in the centre of the hall floor. Two rooms off here she knew – the chapel where she'd drunk coffee with the Preacher and the little library where the Preacher had talked to Max. A third door faced her, and it was this one she tried. She couldn't see any surveillance cameras in the corners, nor in any of the usual vantage points. Anyway, by the time they came to check the loop in the morning, she'd be long gone.

The door opened into an office, wide and spacious, with two computers, banks of filing cabinets and a clutter of phones. Now, and only now, would she risk her torch. The pencil beam darted here and there, flickering over papers, letters and memos without end. There was a visitors' book, but it had not been maintained. The last entry was nearly four months ago. Besides, no one denied that Peter Maxwell had been here; it was just that no one, apparently, had actually seen him leave.

She mechanically checked the filing cabinets, flicking through a battery of names. Angel Kesteven was there and Gilda Schultz, but the name that caught her eye was John Wensley. She was in the act of fishing out the manila when she heard footsteps. She grabbed the file, killing the torch beam as she did so, and ducked behind the cabinet. The light hurt her eyes when it flicked on, and a dark-haired, handsome man stood there, silk shirt open and a belt glinting with studs around his waist. The Preacher followed, no longer in the grey kaftan but booted and hatted, dressed for the road.

The young man was rummaging about, looking for something.

'What are you after, Paulo?' Jacquie heard Wensley ask.

'My keys.' The voice was different, foreign. Jacquie couldn't
quite place it.

There was a jingle. Perhaps the Preacher was holding them
in his hand; perhaps Paulo had found them. 'Come on,' she
heard Wensley say. 'There's a long way to go yet.' And the light
went out and the door closed.

It was already light by the time Jacquie reached Leighford. The
sea was a great silver slab, cold and shifting in the early dawn.
Not that Jacquie saw it. Her mind was racing with the events of
the night and the contents of the file, along with the potential
significance of the cricket bat in the back of her car. She clawed
at the handbrake, killed the ignition and a moment later was
leaning on the doorbell.

'Jacquie?' A large, attractive woman opened the door,
housecoat thrown on in a hurry, no slippers on her feet. 'Jacquie,
may I say you look like shit?'

'Thanks, Mrs Hall.' The detective brushed past her. 'Is your
husband in?'

'In' – Henry Hall was standing in his dressing gown, looking
more than a little bemused – 'and until two minutes ago in bed.
Jacquie, you look like shit.'

Jacquie Carpenter hadn't hear the DCI use the 'sh' word
very often. It wasn't really part of his vocabulary. But then
she'd rarely seen him without his glasses and *never* in his
pyjamas.

'I think you should read this, sir.' She held the file out to him.

'Suppose you paraphrase for me.' It was a little early for
Henry Hall. He led her into the living room. Jacquie had never
been here before, either. She'd always met the guv'nor on
communal turf; the nick, an incident room or among the blood

of some murder scene. 'Margaret, be a love and put some coffee on, would you?'

'Of course, o Master.' But she was calling from the kitchen, with the coffee-maker already in her hand.

Jacquie sat on the settee as Hall opened the large curtains. The brightness of the sky hurt his eyes for a moment, then he turned to face her. 'You know I didn't buy the leave story, don't you?' he said.

She came to the point. 'It's Maxwell, sir. He's missing.'

Hall moved to a chair, sliding aside a pile of newspapers and his kids' homework. 'Men like Maxwell don't go missing, Jacquie, they go ape.'

'I'm serious, sir.'

He knew that. The girl in front of him was tense, pale and worn out. She looked as if she hadn't slept. 'What's the file all about?' he asked.

Jacquie paused, gnawing her lip. Max always told her off for that, said it made her look like Richard III. She usually swiped him around the head with something, and she'd have given anything to have been able to do that this morning. 'Maxwell was carrying out his own enquiries, sir.' She'd taken a deep breath before saying this, only too aware of the DCI's likely reaction. But there wasn't one. He didn't shout, snarl, throw his hands in the air or sob. He just looked at her.

'He went to see all his old mates from the Halliards reunion,' she went on. 'First Alphedge, then Muir, then Asheton, then Wensley.'

'And?' Hall had found his glasses on the coffee table and he put them on. Once more they hid his eyes from the world; exactly the way he liked it.

'I've no proof that he left any of them, other than their word, of course. I began to think . . . well, all sorts of things. What if it's a conspiracy and they're *all* in on it?'

Hall nodded. 'It's been known.'

'Then I got to the Lodge, the place where Wensley is staying until he leaves the country. I think that's what he's going to do now.'

'Doing a runner?'

Jacquie nodded.

'Why?'

'I got this from the office at the Lodge. It's Wensley's file. He's got form.'

Hall shrugged. 'I'm not surprised,' he said. 'Warwickshire CID came up with that. While he was still at that hotel in Birmingham. Various charges against the Church of God's Children . . .'

'No,' Jacquie cut in, 'you don't understand, guv. This has nothing to do with that – or perhaps everything. Wensley did time for murder.'

Hall sat upright. 'Murder?'

'He killed his own family – mother and father.'

'Jesus.' Hall snatched the file, riffled through it, then grabbed the phone, pushing buttons as if his life depended on it. 'Ian? Henry Hall. Look, I want a national alert out, now. A John Wensley, possibly travelling in a priest's get-up. All ports, airports, everywhere. South and east, west. I don't know. He'll probably head for the States, but we can't bet on it. Get in touch with DS Rackham at Leighford. If he's not there, get his home number and wake him up. He's got a detailed description from Warwickshire CID. Then get me Interpol. I need to talk to somebody in Spain, just in case.'

Margaret Hall came in with the coffee, sensing the electricity in the air. 'Three-piece today, Henry?' She sighed. 'I'll take the boys to Mother.'

Hall was waving the file in the air. 'This is good work, Jacquie,' he was saying. 'A breakthrough at last. I'm getting dressed. Margaret, get this girl a bacon sarnie or something.'

He crashed through the large door in front of him and the red-kaftanned woman screamed and leaped back from her desk. The apparition before her was wild eyed, swaying like a wounded bear with dark brown blood in rivulets the length of his face.

'Call the police,' he snarled.

'W . . . what happened to you?' The woman was shouting hysterically, cowering in a corner between desk and filing cabinet.

'Gilda!' a voice thundered, and she froze in mid-shriek. 'Gilda.' It was calmer now. 'It's all right. It's all right. Jesus, Max. What happened to you?' It was John Wensley, standing in the doorway.

Maxwell turned faster than he should have, the room swimming in his vision. He snatched up the phone, the only weapon that came to hand. 'No bat this time, Preacher?' He was edging the man back, out through the door, ripping the phone line from the wall, cradling the plastic in his hand.

'Max?' Wensley was retreating, shaking his head, his hands in the air. 'I don't understand. What's happened to you?'

'Let me make a shrewd guess,' Maxwell hissed, unsteady, sick and shaking. 'When I left you last night, you decided to make me number three on your mad bloody list. Quentin you bashed and hanged. Bingham you just bashed. What's the matter, John, lost your touch, old man?' He raised the phone, about to smash it against Wensley's skull when the Preacher suddenly folded like some outsize marionette. His knees hit the parquet of the hall and his head flopped against Maxwell's groin. He was sobbing uncontrollably. For a moment, Maxwell swayed there, unsure what to do. Then he dropped the phone and fell to his knees, cradling the crying man's head in his hands. He was the Head of Sixth Form again, everybody's daddy, taking away the woes of the world in his strong arms.

They sat together in the light of the mock coals, Maxwell and his Jacquie. Metternich the cat had been as concerned as anybody about his master's disappearance, but he wasn't going to show it.

He just brushed past Maxwell's one good leg and on out into the night – it was a cat thing.

Jacquie looked up at him, her head on his lap, her arms on his arms, warm and soft and safe. She still hadn't slept and it was nearly Sunday morning, the rain pattering down on the dark windows of 38 Columbine.

'You ought to be in hospital,' she told him again as he reached across her for his Southern Comfort. 'You can't fool around with concussion.'

'Concussion, conshmussion,' he murmured. 'And that goes for both of you.'

'Max?' She sat up suddenly. 'Are you still seeing double?'

'No,' he growled, to reassure her. 'Just one and a half.'

She tutted. 'Men!'

He chuckled. 'Now, don't start on that. We'll be here all night.'

She put her arms around his neck, looking at the dark eyes under the white of the bandage. 'I'm just glad it's all over . . . Max?' There was an unusual edge to Jacquie's voice. 'I know that look. Tell me. What?' She arched an eyebrow. 'It isn't over, is it?'

'What does Hall say?'

'I don't know. He seemed pretty convinced by Wensley's file. But then he was also convinced Wensley would run. Wonder why he didn't.'

'All right,' Maxwell said, easing his aching head back gingerly, 'let's put it all together, shall we? I go to the Lodge to talk to the Preacher. He's even curter than usual. Refuses to talk. I leave . . . and wallop. When I wake up, it's in some cellar or other and apparently three days later. I'd lost track of the time – well, you do when you're enjoying yourself, don't you – and assumed it was only one.'

'Which is precisely why you should be in hospital,' she told him again.

He ignored her. 'I managed to get out, don't ask me how, and end up with my attacker blubbering all over me.'

'Max, you haven't read the file. He's a very strange man.'

'Right.' Maxwell tried to focus on the wall lamps around the room. 'Talk me through the file again.'

'When Wensley left school, his family moved, to Spain. Something to do with his father's business.'

'That's right,' Maxwell recalled. 'His old man was in import-export. Sherries. Wines. Something like that.'

'Do you remember him? The old man, I mean?'

Maxwell's cheeks puffed out. 'Yes, I do, actually. I only met him a couple of times, of course. We didn't do the sleepover thing like kids do today. He was a bastard, though, that I do remember. The Preacher was terrified of him.'

'That's right.' Jacquie nodded. 'As he was of somebody at school.'

'Halliards?' Maxwell frowned. 'Who?'

Jacquie shrugged. 'Don't know. The file doesn't say. But he was being bullied simultaneously by kid X at school and by his old man at home.'

'I'm not surprised,' Maxwell said. 'He used to be such a worm, did the Preacher.'

'Well, on 24 September 1963, the worm turned. The file says he loaded up his dad's shotgun early that morning – they were living in Jerez at the time – and blasted both his parents while they were sleeping.'

'Jesus.' Maxwell whistled. He hadn't believed it the first time Jacquie had told him. It seemed no less incredible now.

'There was a lot of extradition talk, wrangling backwards and forwards. In the end, the boy faced trial in Spain, or would have done if the doctors hadn't found him unfit to plead.'

'Why didn't I know about this?' Maxwell asked. 'Christ, Jacquie, he was one of us, one of the Seven.'

'Was he, Max?' she asked. 'You said yourself he never really belonged, never fitted the bill. Who was he afraid of? At Halliards, I mean.'

Maxwell shook his head. 'Quentin?' he guessed. 'Bingham?

Me? I don't know, Jacquie. Maybe . . . well, kids are cruel, aren't they? We all went through it, stupid initiation rites, scaring each other with daft pranks – the hanged boy and so on. It was just part of growing up, just being a kid in the fifties and sixties. But what if it was more than that? What if something was to the rest of us a game and to the Preacher deadly serious? How long was he inside?'

'He was in a secure hospital in Bilbao until five years ago. Then a panel of experts decided it was safe to let him out and he went to the States. Joined the Church of God's Children in Santa Monica in '98. According to the file, he's an ordained minister with powers to baptise, marry and carry out the last rites. It looks as though he took the last bit seriously enough.'

Maxwell was shaking his head. 'Then why am I still alive, Jacquie? Hmm? Tell me that. The Preacher may be a madman, but if he's our boy, he organized Quent's killing like a dream. No forensics other than the bat. No murder weapon linked to him. You tell me Veronica even gave him an alibi, albeit a dodgy one, for the time in question. Bingham wasn't as spectacular, but Bingham had done some homework – probably found the same info you got from the file and was coming to me with it. Even so, the Preacher got there first and stopped him. Again, no forensics. All this action, all this planning, and then he louses up with me. He's got all the time in the world and he messes up.'

'He *has* given you concussion,' she reminded him.

'Yes, but that's well short of "Goodnight, Vienna," isn't it? No, Jacquie, something doesn't add up here.'

She kissed the end of his nose and got up. 'I've got to go,' she said, draining her glass. 'The DCI will want a statement from you tomorrow. Hall's sending a car at ten – is that okay?'

'Sure.' He struggled to get to his feet.

'No.' She held him back, planting her soft lips on his. 'No, you stay there. Now you're not even *thinking* about school on Monday, are you?'

'What? Staff briefing from the Headmaster and possible news of the Ofsted visit? I wouldn't miss it for the world.'

'You stay here,' Jacquie insisted. 'And while you do, I want you to bend that gigantic brain of yours around a name I think you've heard before – Paulo. *Adiós, caro mío.*'

Chapter Thirteen

It's what God made Sunday afternoons for. While some men give their October lawns one last mow before the winter frosts set in and others run up and down football pitches shouting 'Over 'ere, son, on me 'ead', senior policemen sit in darkened interview rooms trying to get some sense out of madmen.

Henry Hall had waited until Nadine Tyler had got to Leighford. He had phoned her during the breakfasting hour and she had hit the road. She'd even toyed with chartering a police chopper, but the Chief Constable was a relative of the Wandering Jew and she knew she'd be wasting her time or the taxpayers' money. Let John Wensley stew for a bit, sweat it out. Hall had e-mailed her the vital passages from the accused's file and she'd used the time while her driver burned rubber to familiarize herself with the information. She didn't know who this sharp-eyed DC was who'd stumbled on it, but Nadine Tyler was secretly pleased that it was a woman and would recommend instant promotion to Henry Hall.

'Tell us about the file.' Hall was slowly turning the pages as the tape whirred like a whisper to his right.

'It's routine.' Wensley looked pale and old, the five-day designer stubble more salt than pepper in the lamplight of the windowless room. 'There's one on every member of the Church of God's Children.'

'Really?' Tyler queried.

'Really.' The Preacher leaned back in his chair. 'It's sent ahead wherever we go. We always inform the local headquarters that we're in their area.'

'And that was the Lodge?' Hall checked.

Wensley nodded. 'Why am I being kept here?'

Nadine Tyler tapped her cigarette on the box before sliding it between her lips. 'Didn't your brief tell you?'

The young man next to Wensley was like something out of a John Grisham novel, all attitude and testosterone. 'My client's brief,' he said, leaning forward, 'is a Legal Aid representative. My name, by the way, since no one's asked, is David Vincent. I have had no time with my client at all, which is unacceptable. As is' – he waited until the DCI had lit up – 'your smoking.'

She looked at him through hooded eyes, then glanced at Hall. She didn't know the man well enough to be sure there'd be no reaction there. 'At the request of Mr Wensley's legal counsel,' she said, 'DCI Tyler putting out her cigarette at . . .' She glanced at the clock. '. . . sixteen-eighteen.' The tape duly logged it all, even to the soft thud as the tobacco hit the ashtray.

'You are being held,' Hall explained, 'on charges of grievous bodily harm and kidnapping of Mr Peter Maxwell.'

The Preacher shook his head.

'Tell us about the murders.' Nadine Tyler was even more likely to go for the jugular now she had been deprived of a smoke.

'Murders?' Vincent looked suitably confused. 'I understood my client was charged with assault and kidnapping.'

'The two are connected,' the Warwickshire woman told him.

'Which murders?' Wensley wanted to know.

'Oh, yes.' Nadine Tyler leaned back in her chair. 'I forgot. You have a choice, don't you? Let's start with your mother and father.'

Wensley's eyes flickered for a moment. The brief looked at

him. It wasn't every day a young man new to the job got himself a real live serial killer, especially one who wore a dog-collar.

'It was all a long time ago,' Wensley said.

'Humour us.' Hall leaned forward. The brief could pick up no rhythm here – it seemed to be nasty policeman and nasty policeman; not the most winning of partnerships.

'I killed them,' Wensley said quietly, 'with a shotgun.'

'Why?' Hall asked. 'Er . . . you don't mind talking about this?'

Wensley shrugged. 'No. I've had a long time to adjust. More counselling than you've had hot dinners. And the Church of God's Children is with me, always. Where would you like me to start?'

'Jerez,' Hall said. 'The summer of 1963.'

'I'd just left school. Perhaps alone of my peers at Halliards, I'd made no plans. I'd toyed with theology at university, but it didn't happen. Father's move had been on the cards for some months. Bingham was off to Oxford, Alphedge to RADA, Maxwell to Cambridge – I don't remember the others. Father was in the wine trade. He imported sherries for his company. They don't exist any more, I understand; went belly-up in the seventies, I believe.'

'But of course you weren't there,' Nadine Tyler said. 'Not in the big wide world, anyway.'

'You know I wasn't,' Wensley said. The woman's archness was enough to test the patience of a saint. 'I suppose it had been building for years. My father was a self-made man, but he set great store by education – he and Mother scrimped to send me to Halliards. I was a fee-payer, you see. Bright types like Max passed their eleven-plus. It broke Father's heart, Mother's too, when I didn't apply to university – I would have been the first of the family to go. The nit-picking started early on.' Wensley lowered his chin on to his chest; the memory still hurt. 'Both of them needling, criticizing. I had no friends in Spain and Father wouldn't let me join the business, start helping him. I tried to apply to the firm direct, but Father blocked it. I drifted into drink, drugs – that scene was just opening up in Spain then. Father found out and made my life hell. So did Mother. One day I just cracked.'

'Premeditated murder,' Nadine Tyler said.

'If you say so.' Wensley sighed. 'I don't actually remember it at all. From the day before until three or four days afterwards, nothing. Short-term memory loss, the psychiatrist called it, brought on by shock. At the trial, they said . . .'

'What trial?' Hall cut in, flicking through the file. 'You didn't stand trial.'

'Mr Hall.' – Wensley was shaking his head slowly – 'I've stood trial a thousand times in here.' And he tapped his temple. 'And each time, the verdict comes out the same: guilty. The judge with his wig and black cap. The hanged boy swinging gently in the wind at the end of his rope. Oh, yes, I've stood trial all right.'

'You're not what?' Hall's face was a mask of disbelief.

'I'm not pressing charges,' Maxwell told him.

It was nearly nine o'clock, that time on a Sunday when teachers and kids alike are thinking to themselves, Christ, no! Monday already. Where did that half-term go? Again!

Henry Hall sat down a little more heavily than he intended on the swivel chair in his office. 'This morning, you . . .'

'This morning I gave a statement to your Sergeant Rackham about what happened. That's all I did.'

'Mr Maxwell' – Hall leaned forward, clasping his hands, making his supplication – 'we have every reason to believe that John Wensley did his best to murder you four days ago. At the very least . . .'

'That's what worries me about your job,' Maxwell interrupted, his eyes dark circles where the bruising to his head was coming out. 'It's largely based on circumstantial evidence, isn't it? On a series of likelihoods and probabilities and calculated risks.'

'I don't follow.' Hall sat back.

'*Somebody* hit me over the head at the Lodge, and somebody locked me in a basement room, but for all I know that somebody was Spring-heeled Jack. I don't have eyes in the back of my head, Chief Inspector. I don't know who did it.'

'We have reason to believe . . .' Hall checked himself, staying calm, staying collected. 'From what we know of Mr Wensley, there is every possibility . . .'

'Uh-huh.' Maxwell wagged an index finger. 'Now what did I just say about that?' Mad Max could patronize for England; he'd been doing it for years. He got to his feet, gingerly, but he did it. 'When you people start dealing in certainties,' he said, 'in absolutes, well, you'll have my full co-operation. Until then' – he winked at the DCI – 'you let the Preacher go, now. Y'hear?' It was a very convincing Clint Eastwood, but it left Hall curiously unmoved.

'You *do* realize' – Jacquie Carpenter was rummaging in the green Scrabble bag – 'I can't tell you anything, don't you, Max?'

Maxwell looked aghast. 'Have I ever, Woman Policeman Carpenter, asked you to compromise your position on my behalf?'

There was a silence, then they both burst out with snorts of laughter.

'Maxwell, you're a shithouse.' She wanted to throw the board at him, but she feared for his still-fragile head.

'That's not how you spell liaison,' he told her.

'But it's a triple!' she squealed.

'I don't care.' He shook his head as heartily as he could. 'That's not how you spell it. There are two "i" s.'

'Bugger.' She tutted. 'I've got three now,' and she slipped the superfluous letter back. 'So you're saying I can't have that?'

Maxwell thought for a moment. 'This is the deal,' he said. 'You fill me in on Wensley and I'll turn a blind "i" to your lamentable spelling skills. Done?' He held out his hand.

'Done.' She laughed and shook it. 'Just remember – you didn't hear any of this from me. Got it?'

He was going to wink, but the movement in Hall's office earlier that evening had cost him dear and he thought better of it.

'Hall's sure he's got his man,' Jacquie said. 'You're not exactly flavour of the month by dropping charges.'

'He'll hold him anyway, presumably?'

'He and Miss Iron Pants . . .'

'Who?' Maxwell's eyes widened as he detected a side to Jacquie Carpenter he hadn't noticed before.

'Nadine Tyler to you,' Jacquie explained.

'Never let a little thing like professional jealousy cloud your judgment, I always say.'

'Hall and Tyler can keep bouncing him backwards and forwards between their patches for a few days yet. He's got a pretty sharp brief, though. He won't let them get away with much for long.'

'So what have they got on the Preacher? What did he say?'

'He doesn't remember anything about killing his parents. All the details have been filled in by other people, so he thinks he's actually remembered it. He even thinks he's stood trial for it. He's spent years in a mental institution, so he's got all kinds of hang-ups. Whenever he enters a room, he recites a stock phrase – "We're all God's Children".'

'That's funny.' Maxwell's half-smile was not one of humour, however.

'What?'

'That's what Alphie said at the Graveney, do you remember? When the Preacher arrived and told us about his church, Alphie camped it up with his Al Jolson rendition.'

'Pissed the Preacher off, do you think?'

Maxwell put down his letters. 'Zircon,' he said blandly. 'God, I'll need a calculator to tot *that* little score up. It's possible; but if so, why didn't the Preacher kill Alphie?'

'Perhaps he intended to.' Jacquie was working out how to capitalise on the 'z'. 'Perhaps, in his strange world, there was an order to it all. It *had* to be Quentin first, then Bingham, then you . . .' She caught his gaze. 'Yes, I know you don't believe it, Max, but look at the facts. On his own admission, Wensley went to Halliards in the small hours of the morning, the time when Quentin died. Whether he was there with Veronica or not doesn't matter.'

'Oh, but it does,' Maxwell disagreed. 'It took two to lift Quent on to that balustrade.'

'Taken a good look at the Preacher's biceps recently? I'd say he could do it by himself. And anyway, I've no aversion to putting Veronica in the frame.'

Maxwell looked at her. 'Didn't exactly gel, you two, did you?'

'Not exactly,' Jacquie said, with that way women have of letting you know how much they loathe other women; it's a nostril thing. 'We know Wensley had the opportunity. If it was Quentin who was bullying him at school, we have the motive. The other bullies in his life were his parents; he killed them back in '63. For the next thirty-five years, he's in a secure unit, going through God knows what sort of private hell. Then he gets out, having found religion – it's a surprisingly common pattern – and plans his chance to finish the job. Muir's invitation comes like a gift from God. And it's so poetic. George Quentin hanging from the bell rope of his old school, the old place that must have had some traumatic memories for Wensley.'

'All right.' Maxwell had a 'q' but no 'u'. 'You've established opportunity and motive. What about the murder weapon?'

Jacquie shrugged. 'He ditched it. My guess is a baseball bat. Courtesy of the Church of God's Children.'

'They're not made of willow, surely?' Maxwell frowned as

far as his bandages would allow. 'What news of Stenhouse's cricket bat, by the way?'

'Clean as a whistle. We don't know why he mended it recently or why it broke, but the lab's established it wasn't against anybody's head, least of all Quentin's, Bingham's or yours.'

'Joy,' muttered Maxwell. 'Got a "b"?'

'Uh-huh.' Jacquie shook her head. 'We're not swapping this late in the game. Especially as you're . . .' She read the score upside down – it was a little trick detectives picked up with time. '. . . nearly a hundred points ahead, you bastard!'

'So all this points us back to the Preacher, does it?'

'Face it, Max. I've been trying to keep an open mind all day, but I've seen the man in the interview room. He's odd, strung out. There are things he's not telling us yet. He's off to Leamington tomorrow where the whole thing starts all over again. The CID there have managed to slap a holding order on the developers at Halliards. They're giving the place another once-over. Tell me about Paulo.'

'Indeed.' Maxwell nodded. 'I thought you'd never raise it. Paulo Escobar is . . . sorry, was . . . the live-in wifey of George Quentin. It's funny, you don't realize at the time that you're at school with Jeffery Dahmer *and* Lizzie Borden. You dashed off the other night, you infuriating hoyden, without filling me in.'

'This Escobar . . .' Jacquie was looking up the list of two-letter words, a sure sign among Scrabble players that the writing is on the wall. 'You met him, right?'

Maxwell nodded. 'Quent's boss at Vandeleur Negus put me on to him.'

'Describe him.'

'Er, let's see . . . about thirty, perhaps a little younger. Dark, curly hair, quite handsome in a Latino sort of way. Your type, I suppose?'

Jacquie pulled a face. 'Let's say I like them a tad more one way.' She smiled. 'He was with John Wensley at the Lodge.'

'What?' Maxwell sat upright. 'When was this?'

'The night I was there. The night I broke in – but don't you dare let that little morsel anywhere near the DCI. They were going somewhere, by car. They came into the office looking for keys.'

Maxwell couldn't get his head, broken as it was, around this. 'So, Escobar, if it *was* Escobar, was with the Preacher. And he was also with Quent. Is he in the file?'

'No.' Jacquie shook her head. 'Which is why I couldn't ask Wensley any questions along those lines. Graham Rackham's off tomorrow grilling the staff at the Lodge – it's my guess Paulo Escobar won't be among them.'

'Mine too. The Preacher moved to Spain and killed his parents before Escobar was born. They let him out five years ago and he went to the States. And that's just a tad longer than Escobar told me he'd been with Quent – four years. What's the tie-up?' Maxwell was talking to himself as much as to Jacquie.

'Quentin and Escobar are lovers.' The professional detective was joining thought processes with the amateur. 'Does that also go for Escobar and the Preacher?'

The Scrabble-players shrugged at each other.

'I wonder,' Maxwell said after claiming yet another score. 'That's all my letters gone there – fifty points plus thirty-one – eight-one, please, Policewoman; I wonder if we aren't talking about the *two* stranglers of Rillington Place?'

'Sorry,' Jacquie said. 'You smug bastard, by the way – you've lost me there.'

'Before your time, my dear.' That was a common enough phrase from Peter Maxwell, God knew. 'John Reginald Halliday Christie, known to his old school chums as "Reggie No-Dick," killed a Mrs Beryl Evans, among others, in the house at Ten Rillington Place. This was back in the fifties, when I was in short trousers and everybody still stood up in the pictures for the National Anthem. Guilty as hell though he clearly was of the other murders, Christie always vehemently denied murdering

Beryl's little baby, claiming that the kid's father, Timothy, did it. Since Timothy Evans had given conflicting testimony and was subsequently already hanged for the murder of his wife and daughter, he could hardly refute it, could he? Everybody assumed that Evans's fourth statement – "Christie done it" – was correct. But was it? There was a niggling doubt in some people's minds – perhaps Christie *and* Evans were killers.'

'So . . .' Jacquie was confused. 'You're saying Wensley and Escobar . . .'

'That's a possible combination.' Maxwell nodded. 'Or Wensley and A.N. Other.'

'You're talking about Muir, Asheton, Alphedge?'

'Or the Man in the Moon.' Maxwell sighed, and put down 'quisling' on the Scrabble board with such a flourish that Jacquie rolled over on the carpet, screaming and beating the floor. 'How very King John of you,' Maxwell felt constrained to comment.

Monday, Monday. Hate that day. The staffroom, that inner sanctum that no child shall enter, was more of a buzz than usual. Was it because there was talk of strike action led by Joe 'Lenin' Hackleton, the NUT rep? Was it the impending snoop-swoop of the Ofsted inspectors? No, it was the speculation as to why Mad Max appeared to have an igloo on his head.

'Obvious,' whispered Ben Holton, the Head of Science. 'Frontal lobotomy gone wrong.'

'I expect he shot his mouth off with his own prejudiced political incorrectness in the wrong place,' said Deirdre Lessing, the Senior Mistress, in a rather shriller tone, designed for Maxwell to hear.

'Stuck it too far up somebody's arse,' Bernard Ryan, the Deputy Head, muttered. He was a man with more chips on his shoulder than Harry Ramsden's.

In the corridors without power, as Maxwell made his way

creakingly to his office, the kids had, as always, a tighter grip on reality.

'Fuckin' 'ell, somebody's bashed Mad Max over the 'ead.'

Eagle-ears Maxwell heard that one. 'There's a Chair at Oxford waiting for you, Sanjit, with logic like that. Don't you let me down, now.'

For the rest of the day, Sanjit wondered why he'd have to go all the way to Oxford, wherever that was, to sit down.

'God, Max.' Helen Maitland held out the cup that cheered. 'Are you sure you should be here?'

'Ask not for whom the bell tolls, Helen dearest' – Max collapsed into the soft chair he'd long ago half-inched from the Sixth Form Common Room – 'it may fall on thee.'

'Sorry I mentioned it.' Maxwell's number two smiled.

He caught her retreating hand. 'Bless you for caring, Helen,' he said, 'but you wouldn't believe it if I told you. How was your half-term?'

'Banal,' she told him. 'Roger and I decorated the bathroom.'

'Crackerjack,' Maxwell enthused.

The phone shattered the moment. Helen Maitland leaned around the door to shoo away a couple of GNVQ students strangely reluctant to get to lessons. Maxwell handled the receiver quite deftly for a man who was, whatever he'd told his light o' love, seeing everything in the plural. 'Stringfellows.'

'Mr Maxwell?' the girl on the switchboard was nonplussed every time.

'Thingee.' Maxwell leaned his aching head back. 'How wonderful to hear your voice. How can we help, Mrs Maitland and I?'

'I have a Mrs Alphedge on the phone. She sounds rather upset.'

Maxwell was sitting up. 'Put her on.'

'Max, is that you?'

'Cissie, what's the matter?'

'Have you seen Richard?'

'Alphie? No, not since I called last week. What's happened?'

'He's gone.' Cissie Alphedge was fighting back tears, trying to keep her hysteria under whatever control she had left.

'When?' Maxwell was used to being an oasis of calm in a wilderness of panic. He knew that repeating the word was pointless and would add to Cissie's terror.

'Er . . . yesterday. I dropped him off at the golf club just before lunch. He said he was tired of being a prisoner in his own house. Said he needed space. Fresh air. He had his mobile in case of emergencies. We'd arranged to meet at one-thirty. I was to pick him up at the club.' There was a pause as Cissie struggled to find the words. 'Only he wasn't at the club. No one had seen him. His clubs were in an outhouse; one of the staff found them there. Max, I'm so worried. This isn't like Richard, is it?'

Maxwell wanted to answer that, but found he didn't have the first clue as to whether it was like Richard or not. He had known the boy, but he didn't know the man. But that wasn't what Cissie wanted to hear.

'No,' he told her, trying to let his voice reach out across the ether. 'But I'm equally sure there's a rational explanation.'

'I'm not feeling very rational just at the moment,' she told him.

'Of course not. Cissie, have you called the police?'

'No. No, I thought . . . Well, I thought he'd be home. I waited up. Rang friends. His sister in Wisbech. Nothing. No one's seen him. Oh, Max, I . . . I hate to ask you. I know you're teaching and so on, but can you help? Can you find him?'

'Cissie.' Maxwell felt helpless. 'I'm a squad of one. You need a team on this. The police . . .'

'No, Max. Richard's been . . . well, odd the last couple of days. I mean, you saw what he was like. When your Jacquie called, he hid upstairs. Actually *hid*. I told her he was resting, but that wasn't actually true. He's falling apart, Max. This business at Halliards, Bingham, it's all got the better of him. The irony is he'd be perfect to play Lear now. Too young, but perfect.'

'What can I do, Cissie?' Maxwell asked.

'Come down, Max, please. I just need . . . another brain on this, a fresh outlook. If then you think we need the police, well, all right . . .'

Maxwell checked his watch. 'I've got to disentangle myself from the chalkface,' he said, mixing his metaphors with the best of them. 'Then I'm on the next train.'

'Bless you, Peter Maxwell,' Cissie said. 'You're a brick.'

'I must be,' said the Head of Sixth Form when he'd put the receiver down.

'Crisis, Max?' Helen Maitland was stirring her coffee with her pen, reading the signs on her boss's face.

'No, no, Helen.' He beamed beneath the bandages. 'Just a catastrophe. Do I look shite enough to have to go home?'

'Does the Pope shit in the woods?' was Helen's rejoinder. It was a question that dissenting churchmen had asked since the Reformation. And it was good enough for Peter Maxwell.

The previous night had been one of those nights at Haslemere police station. The stockbroker belt slipped from time to time and that Sunday had been no exception. There'd been a break-in at Gerard's warehouse on the edge of town and a gang of yobbos had decided to steam through the bus station, relieving startled passengers of their valuables. To cap it all, amid all the mopping-up operations on Monday, a lady named Mrs Janet Muir insisted on seeing the most senior CID officer available.

That was Derek Bishop, a martyr to dyspepsia and a grumbling ulcer that growled like Vesuvius whenever the pressure got to him. It was getting to him now. He was drowning in paperwork and it wasn't even ten o'clock yet.

'How can I help you, madam?' he asked, already aware from his desk sergeant that Janet Muir was related in some way to Godzilla.

Janet Muir took the rather used seat across the desk from the man, slumped as he was in front of a computer screen. 'You can arrest my husband,' she said tartly.

'Oh, really?' Bishop had been caught in the crossfire of domestics before. 'On what grounds, may I ask?'

'First-degree murder,' Janet Muir said. 'Of George Quentin and Anthony Bingham. I shall be your witness for the prosecution.'

Chapter Fourteen

It was a little after two when Maxwell got to the Alphedges'. A grey-haired woman with crying-red eyes answered the door and threw her arms around him. It wasn't a luvvie hug, all hypocrisy and kisses to the air; Cissie Alphedge was terrified and she was letting Maxwell know it.

He held her gently at arms' length. 'You've checked the house?' he asked.

Cissie nodded. 'Three times. It's rambling, Max, but not as rambling as all that. It's so silly. It's like looking for a Jaffa cake one half ate once and put down somewhere. I expect to turn a corridor and see Richard there, smiling or working on his lines. Oh, it's so preposterous.'

Maxwell took charge. 'Relax. First things first. A cup of tea, I think.'

'Tea?' Cissie looked appalled. 'Max, Richard might be . . .'

He held up his hand, the one that stilled whole assemblies on the blast. Sure enough, it silenced this hysterical woman now. 'I need you' – he helped her through the kitchen, feeling how cold her hands were where he held them – 'to be calm, to be clear and to talk me through the sequence of events again.'

Cissie was nodding. He was right, of course. Calm and sensible and soothing. Only then did she notice the bandage under Maxwell's hat. Ordinarily he'd have swept it off in a lady's presence, but he didn't want to alarm her more than she was already alarmed at that moment.

'Max, you look like the last scene of *Cyrano de Bergerac*.'

'Funny you should say that.' He smiled, resting the hat and scarf on a chair-back. 'I seem to have put my panache down somewhere, and can I find it?'

She ran her fingers lightly over the crepe folds, wincing for him, sitting him down. She was Mummy again, taking over, fussing, getting things right. 'What happened?' she asked, and sat down at the table next to him.

'The silliest thing.' He chuckled. 'I tripped over the cat. He's been trying to get me for years, has the Count, lying in wait on the stairs. A couple of days ago, he got lucky.'

'You didn't go to work like this?' Cissie was horrified.

'Madam . . .' Maxwell sat up to his full height. 'Over the years I have gone to work as the Invisible Man, Clint Eastwood, the Mikado, Lord Cardigan and Goldfinger – all for charity, of course. The kids are used to seeing me as a headcase.'

She squeezed his hands. 'I'll make some tea,' she said. And with great difficulty, he winked at her.

Peter Maxwell removed the bandages, feeling increasingly like Boris Karloff. His head ached like buggery, but his thatch of hair disguised the stitches and the bruising was confined to his eyes. He began to think, as he checked in the mirror, that whoever had had a go at him at the Lodge had used a mangle.

'Jacquie?' He was keeping his voice low, prowling the bedroom.

'Max, where are you?'

'The Alphedges', on Cissie's cordless.'

'The Alphedges'? Why'

'Promise you won't tell?' Maxwell gurgled.

'For God's sake, Max,' Jacquie said, 'you are so bloody infuriating. What's happening?'

'Alphie's gone walkabout.'

'What?'

'Missing – since yesterday lunch-time.'

'Have you called the police?'

'Do you guys bother for the first twenty-four hours – when it's an adult, I mean?'

'Not usually,' Jacquie conceded. 'But it's been longer than that now. When did Cissie see him last?'

'At the golf club, Sunday, about eleven-thirty. They'd arranged for her to pick him up two hours later. Except he wasn't there. She's racked with guilt, of course. Her fault and so on.'

'Did she call you?'

'Yes. I haven't been much help, I'm afraid. We drove to the club and asked around, but Cissie's torn between making a complete idiot of her husband and finding out what happened. Nobody I spoke to had seen him at all, but of course the Monday crowd aren't necessarily the Sunday crowd and vice versa. Cissie did find his golf clubs, though.'

'Oh? Where were they?'

'In an outhouse. She showed me where.'

'Where are they now?'

'Here. Why?'

'Don't touch them, Max. There may be forensics.'

'That's a cheery thought, Woman Policeman Carpenter.'

'We've got to face facts, Max,' Jacquie told him. 'Two members of a circle of friends are dead, a third is hit over the head, and a fourth vanishes. It's all getting pretty weird. How's Cissie coping?'

'Asked me to stay over,' Maxwell said. 'Can't stand the waiting and so on. I can understand that. They've got plenty of space here. What's your view on the local law, Jacquie?'

'Call them in,' was the expert advice. 'Given the circumstances, you've waited long enough, Max.'

★   ★   ★

He sat out the night. For an hour or so, he wrestled with it. Should he tell Cissie that Jacquie advised calling in the police now? Should he tell her that Jacquie thought that her husband was probably dead? Not that Jacquie had said so; it was just that Maxwell knew her so well. After that, he'd dozed fitfully. At one point, he thought he heard Cissie's voice on her mobile, shrilly shouting, as she had at John Thaw when he'd arrested her on the telly a few weeks back. But the Alphedges' house was big and it may have been the television; Cissie, unable to sleep, catching some domestic programme they relegated to the small hours – crap for insomniacs.

In the morning, they went to the police station.

'Would you like to tell us' – DCI Henry Hall looked at the sandy-haired man with the silver beard across the desk from him – 'where you were on the day Anthony Bingham was killed?'

'How is my client supposed to know that?' the grey-suited brief wanted to know.

'Let's get one thing straight, Chief Inspector.' Andrew Muir ignored his lawyer. 'Whatever my wife says, I know nothing at all about the death of Bingham, or for that matter George Quentin.'

'Do you know the Leighford area, sir?' Hall asked.

'The first time I came to this godforsaken part of the world was when your boys in blue came to collect me from Haslemere nick. I would not, ordinarily, pass water over a seaside town in England, in or out of season.'

Hall looked at DS Rackham to his right. 'I see,' he said.

They were, all four of them, sitting in Interview Room 2 at Leighford police station. It was Tuesday morning, Day Fifteen of a murder enquiry.

'Chief Inspector,' the brief tried again.

'Clifford, will you please shut up?' Muir snapped. 'The sole reason I have you here is so that I say nothing that may incriminate me.'

'Andrew . . .' Clifford didn't like the way this was going.

'Do you have reason to believe you may incriminate yourself, Mr Muir?' Hall had seen the loophole and leaped through it.

'Look . . .' Muir spread his hands on the interview-room desk like a man at the end of his tether. 'For reasons best known to herself, my wife has put me in the frame for murder. Well, she's like that.'

'You mean she does it habitually, sir?' Rackham asked.

'Of course not!' Muir thundered. 'It's hardly every day one's old buddies shuffle off the mortal coil. What I mean is that Janet takes a delight in watching me squirm; she's not a nice woman, Chief Inspector.'

'She says you have no alibi for the night of George Quentin's death,' Hall told him.

Muir sighed, leaning back in his chair. 'Well, in the words of the great Mandy Rice-Davies, she would, wouldn't she?'

'Are you saying she's lying?' Hall queried.

'Lying and my wife, Chief Inspector, are the greatest double act since Laurel and Hardy. If you are asking me can I *prove* that I spent all night in my hotel room at the Graveney, sleeping like a baby, feet away from the Blood Beast I married, I would have to answer "No". If she is saying I wasn't there, then the troublemaking bitch is lying through her teeth. Have I made myself clear, Chief Inspector?'

'Clear, Mr Muir.' Hall nodded solemnly. 'But not, I regret, *in* the clear.'

'So, Mr Wensley.' DCI Nadine Tyler looked up at the man from the notes on him that lay strewn across her desk. 'You didn't kill George Quentin?'

The Preacher shook his head.

'You didn't go to Halliards school that night, having arranged to meet him there? You didn't half demolish his skull and then finish the job by attaching him to the bell rope?'

'My client has already denied this.' A tired David Vincent sighed, tapping the table with his pen-top. 'On several occasions.'

Nadine Tyler ignored him. 'You didn't arrange to meet Anthony Bingham on Ryker Hill, stove in his head and stash the body under an old settee?'

'Oh, come on, Chief Inspector.' Vincent sat up, bored rigid by the whole endless experience. 'We've been through this with you. We've been through this with DCI Hall in Leighford. My client has rights, you know. I think he's been through enough.'

'He's been through mental institutions,' the DCI continued, turning on Vincent for the first time, 'for murdering his own parents. And he'll keep going through whatever I choose to put him through until I get some answers.'

'You mean until you get a result?' Vincent was shouting back.

'People, people.' Wensley's hands were in the air, his voice calm, his smile almost serene. 'I didn't kill anybody. Yes, I was at Halliards on the night Quent died, but I couldn't get into the building. I didn't have a key.'

'And while you were at the school, while . . . in the grounds, what did you see?'

'A rat, in the swimming pool,' Wensley remembered. 'It was scurrying over the debris. It caught my eye.'

'What else?'

'A car. Parked under the bushes, near the front gate.'

'What sort of car?'

Vincent had had enough. 'Chief Inspector, my client has answered these questions repeatedly. He doesn't know one car from another. Can I suggest the Warwickshire CID get cracking on tyre tracks in the area? Can I also suggest that your time for holding my client is up. Are you going to charge him or release him?'

Tyler twisted the simple gold band on her middle finger. It was displacement activity. Really, she wanted to hit the interfering little shit, but if she did that, she could kiss her career goodbye.

'Why did you hit Peter Maxwell over the head?' she asked.

Wensley faltered, for the first time in this interview. Nadine Tyler hadn't seen that before. Not even when she and Hall had asked about the killing of his parents. The Preacher's face had stayed calm, emotionless. Now the jawline was a hard ridge and she saw him swallow. 'I didn't,' he said.

'Who did, then?' The DCI was a shark, smelling blood.

'That file,' Vincent cut in, like Richard Dreyfus to the rescue. 'Where did you get it?'

Nadine Tyler's eyes flickered across to him. 'Leighford CID. Why?'

'And where did they get it?'

Nothing.

'John?' Vincent turned to his client.

'The file was kept at the lodge.'

'Under lock and key?'

'In an open filing cabinet.'

Vincent's face said it all. He was crowing, delighting in the moment. 'Under what precise circumstances did Leighford CID come by this file, DCI Tyler?'

'It's not a secret . . .' Wensley began, but Vincent stepped in.

'Was it obtained legally, with an authorized warrant?' The brief was in full flight. 'If so, I want the name of the applying office and the magistrate who issued the warrant. If not' – he leaned forward, staring into Nadine Tyler's eyes – 'I want the balls of the bastard in blue who took it nailed to the wall by lunch-time.' He stood up sharply, scraping back his chair, checking his watch. 'John Wensley and his counsel leaving the interview room – assuming, of course, there are no objections – at ten-forty-two.'

Vincent led Wensley out. Neither of them heard the expletives that followed, but then neither of them would have believed they'd come from the lips of DCI Nadine Tyler. The tape was already switched off.

'John Wensley's lawyer, David Vincent, wants your balls nailed to a wall, DC Carpenter.' Hall was standing looking out of his incident room window, a cup of rapidly cooling coffee in his hand. 'What do I tell him? Sorry, I can't oblige. The officer in question is suffering from penis envy!'

'Sir?' Jacquie was frowning as the DCI turned to face her.

'Did you help yourself to the file on Wensley?' Hall asked.

'In a manner of speaking,' Jacquie said. 'You were pleased a couple of days ago. "Well done," you said. "Good work."'

'I don't need the action replay,' Hall said coldly. The only way you knew that Henry Hall was angry was that he turned a whiter shade of pale. 'Two days is a long time in a murder enquiry. That was then. Wensley's walked because you obtained evidence illegally. He might be some airhead who doesn't know what time of day it is, but his lawyer is the pushy type – wants to make a name for himself. And if he can do that at the cost of the odd copper's career, then believe me, he will. Where's Maxwell?'

'Maxwell?' Jacquie faltered.

Hall's face said it all. 'Jacquie, I am not going to repeat every word and phrase to give you time to think. Where is he?'

'Do you want my resignation, sir?' Jacquie felt her heart thumping. This wasn't the first time she'd walked this line. It was a lonely one.

Hall sighed. 'No, Jacquie,' he said quietly. 'This murder enquiry is two weeks old. I want some results. Now, for the last time, where's Maxwell?'

'At the Alphedges',' she told him. 'Richard Alphedge is missing.'

Hall sat down quickly, his eyes locked on hers. 'When?'

'Sunday, lunch-time. Vanished at his golf club. Cissie Alphedge and Maxwell have reported it to the police.'

'Right. Get up there. Find out what's happening. Find out what Maxwell knows. We may well be looking for a third body.'

'Yes, sir.'

'Oh, and Jacquie . . .' Hall stopped her as she reached the door. 'Next time you offer to resign, I might just take you up on it.'

They put out fliers on Richard Alphedge later that day. Passers-by were asked if they had seen this man. Most of them hadn't. As the rain set in from the west by early evening, disheartened PCs in dripping helmets and capes gave up the door-to-door. One old dear felt sure she'd seen him in *Coriolanus* at Chichester recently. Yet another remembered him from *Crossroads* the first time around. But no one had seen the real Richard Alphedge, not on the street, not anywhere.

His car was in the double garage, his shotgun prop still resting in the hall. That night, Jacquie and Maxwell sat in Cissie's lounge in the Lutyens house, while Cissie curled up with a sedative and a good book. She couldn't read a line and sobbed quietly to herself, turning fitfully on the damp pillow until the sleeping tablet kicked in and darkness overtook her.

'This is so bizarre, Max.' Jacquie was curled up on Maxwell's lap, cradled by his arms. 'I don't get it at all.'

'We're not talking about kidnapping.' Maxwell was trying to make sense of the thing. 'Are we? I mean, wouldn't we have heard by now?'

Jacquie nodded. 'Usually,' she said. 'It's been three days. Having said that, there's no rhyme or reason. Some kidnappers make contact straight away. Others after up to a week.'

'God,' Maxwell moaned. 'I don't know how Cissie will hold up under that.'

'She's strong,' Jacquie said. 'Women are, you know. It's the survival thing.'

'Isn't it also true that in most kidnappings the victim's already dead by the time the call comes through?'

Jacquie was quiet for a moment. 'There is that pattern, too,' she said. 'There's a much more likely scenario, Max.'

'Go on.' He looked down at her clear grey eyes gazing up at him.

'Alphedge's fears were correct. He was next, after all. Whether you were meant to be the third and it went pear shaped, I don't know. But if Alphedge was the fourth, then that's it. The killer met him on the golf course and either killed him there or took him away and did it somewhere else.'

'So we're looking for a body?' Maxwell was essentially a man who liked his 't's crossed and his 'i's dotted.

Jacquie pulled his arms more tightly around her. 'I don't like being so matter-of-fact when Cissie's upstairs,' she said, her voice imperceptibly lower. 'But yes.'

Maxwell sighed. 'Well, at least that rules out John Wensley. He was in police custody at the time.'

Jacquie nodded. 'He was. But there's one name I haven't been able to throw into the equation yet,' she said.

'Indeed,' Maxwell agreed. 'Paulo Escobar, spinster of this parish. Tomorrow, young lady, how about you and I find the Don?'

Jacquie frowned up at him. Old sherry adverts like that were before her time.

They drove first to George Quentin's place in up-and-coming, down-and-going Acton. Jacquie's mobile was switched on and she'd written the number down clearly for Cissie. Any news, anything at all, and the actress was to ring. 'We're not far,' Jacquie had said, 'just at the end of a phone line.'

But George Quentin's place was locked and barred. Peering in through the windows, Maxwell could see that the place was devoid of furniture, Escobar's packing cases gone, dust where the Persian carpets used to be. Junk mail addressed to 'the occupier' lay scattered over the hall floor like the random fall of the Tarot pack and the Hanged Man.

So they drove to the Lodge.

A black, shiny face peered around the door, the pearly smile fading as its owner realized who'd arrived.

'Hello, Angel,' said Maxwell. 'Remember me? I was the guest who nobody wanted to leave a few days ago.' He pushed past her into the hall, looking around the airy space.

'The Reverend John ain't here,' she told them.

'We're not looking for the Reverend John, Angel,' Jacquie said. 'We're looking for Paulo. Where is he?'

'Paulo?' A look of confusion crossed the woman's face; or was it panic?

'You don't want us to ransack the place, do you?' Maxwell asked. Just being in the Lodge, with its sanctimonious smell, brought back the headaches.

'You ain't got no rights,' Angel asserted.

'Angel' – Jacquie turned to face her, flashing her warrant card for the first time – 'this is a murder enquiry. Two men, perhaps three, are dead. We want . . . we need some answers.'

'I don't know nothin'.' Angel was waddling away.

'Is that what Jesus would say?' Maxwell stopped her in her tracks. The black woman turned to face him.

'You takin' the Lord's name in vain, mister?' she growled.

Maxwell crossed the parquet floor to her. 'What did Jesus say about murder, Angel?' He looked down at her. 'What did the Lord say?'

'Thou shalt not kill,' Angel intoned.

Maxwell nodded. 'Well, somebody has, Angel,' he said quietly. 'Somebody has killed twice.'

'You sayin' it was the Reverend John?' Angel was swaying, her eyes fixed on Maxwell's.

'No,' he told her. 'It's not John. Any more than it was John who hit me over the head. Why did you do that, Angel? Why did you hit me over the head?'

Jacquie's eyes flashed from one to the other. What was Max talking about? Was this trauma, some sort of delayed shock?

'You was goin' to take the Reverend John away,' Angel snarled, scowling at her man. 'You think he's a killer. Well, he ain't. No, suh. I couldn't let you take him away. The Reverend John, he's a good man.'

'Max . . .' Jacquie began, but the Head of Sixth Form raised his hand. He was on a roll.

'Yes, he is, Angel,' he said. 'He's a very good man. But Paulo, now, he's not, is he? We think Paulo is a bad man, Angel. And we need to talk to him.'

A door creaked behind the two and they all jumped a mile. At the top of the stairs, a dark-haired young man in designer jeans stood, one hand resting lightly on the rail, the other slowly tossing and catching a clasp knife.

'I used too have one of those.' Maxwell smiled. 'Made in Saragossa. Mine had a beautiful tortoiseshell handle. Of course, they're illegal now in this country.' He'd reached the foot of the curving steps.

'You wanna see?' the young man said in his fractured English. 'You wanna see the tortoiseshell up close, uh? Uh?' He darted forward, the blade out, slicing through air.

'Max!' Jacquie was at his elbow.

Maxwell held out his right arm to keep the girl back. He knew she wasn't armed, and for all her police training she would be no match for the knife-wielding Spaniard.

'Do you know *The Gun*?' Maxwell was climbing the stairs, riser by riser. 'It's an excellent little tale from the pen of the late C.S. Forester. All about this huge cannon lumbering across Spain in the Napoleonic Wars. There's a first-rate knife fight in that.'

'What the fuck you say?' the Spaniard asked.

'*The Gun*, Paulo,' Maxwell explained, his arms outspread by way of explanation. 'Do try and keep up.'

Below him, Jacquie was on the first stair, her heart in her mouth.

'They made it into a film called *The Pride and the Passion*. Dear Ol' Blue Eyes, ol' Francis Sinatra, was a guerrilla leader, pretty handy with one of those. Then, of course, there was Paul Newman in *Butch Cassidy and the Sundance Kid*.' He was sufficiently close to his man now that if Escobar lunged he'd reach his target. 'Where good ol' Paul explains the rules of a knife fight.'

Jacquie's hand was already in her bag, fumbling for the mace can, when it happened. Maxwell's left foot came up and caught the Spaniard hard between the legs, thudding into his groin. His eyes widened and his blade dipped just long enough for Maxwell to grab his arm and throw him sideways, sending him bouncing off the wall and rolling down the stairs until he curled in a broken heap at the bottom.

'Haven't seen that one either?' Maxwell asked, brushing himself down and steadying his spinning head. 'Well, probably just as well.'

Chapter Fifteen

DCI Hall was getting nowhere. It didn't help that he had to liaise with his oppos the length and breadth of the Home Counties. If ever there was a case for a national police force, this was it.

'What did Holmes throw up?' Hall and Rackham were both of the computer generation, although both had kids who could do it better, faster, more instinctively.

'Bugger all, guv, if you'll pardon my French.'

It was a Thursday, wet and wild, with the wind whirling rubbish on the street corners of Leighford. DCI Hall wasn't in much of a mood to pardon anything. He watched the rain bounce on his window; beyond, a sea of umbrellas ebbed and swelled along the High Street, swarming shoppers doing battle with the elements.

'Sorry I'm late, guv.' Jacquie Carpenter crashed in, looking like a drowned rat.

Hall turned to face her. 'I've just come from the incident room,' he told the pair. 'A lot of people working and working hard. But nothing's breaking. Nothing at all. So . . .' He loosened his tie and took his glasses off to wipe them. Jacquie thought he looked tired, tetchy. 'Graham, talk me through Anthony Bingham. Where exactly are we on that one?'

The DS riffled through his notes. 'SOCO turned up a lot of

stuff,' he said. 'Tissues, condoms. Most of it you'd need to carry at arm's length at the end of a pair of tongs. Old copy of *Meccano World*, so there's obviously some real perverts out there.'

Hall's frozen scowl said it all. If ever Graham Rackham had thought of going into the stand-up comic business, this morning was not a good time to start.

'Nothing concrete on tyre tracks. We've identified thirty-eight different vehicles from the mud at the bottom of the hill where the body was found. Apart from dog-walkers and courting couples, it's used as a turning place for people who've overshot the A280. Even using Holmes, they reckon it'll be three to four weeks before we get matches on even half of these.'

'Jesus.' Hall sucked air through his teeth. 'And we're no further forward on how Bingham got there?'

Rackham shook his head. 'By train paying cash is still the best guess, guv. He'd have come to Leighford from Waterloo; that's all we can say. There's no record of a credit card and his car is still in his garage.'

'What about the chauffeur? As a judge he presumably had one?'

'The Met have interviewed him,' the DS said. 'He'd had flu at the time of the killing and was home in bed. That's watertight.'

'But he wasn't killed here, was he?' Jacquie spoke up for the first time.

'No.' Hall sighed, wiping his hand on his face. 'Not according to Dr Astley. Jim reckons Bingham's body was dumped in the woods. There is a *slight* glimmer there.' Hall put his glasses back on and rummaged through the paperwork on his desk. 'Here we are. Fibres. Astley's report mentions fibres on the clothing. Bingham was wearing a suit when he died. There are pale blue fibres matted into the material at the front.'

'Which means . . .' Jacquie was frowning, working out the angles.

'Which means he was hit from behind, and fell forward. Astley also found carpet burns on his left cheek and nose.'

Rackham joined in. 'Head wound, guv. There must have been a lot of blood.'

Hall nodded. 'And brain tissue. Who do we know who's bought a new carpet recently?' He closed Astley's file. 'All right, Jacquie, what's Mr Maxwell up to?'

She looked at the clock. 'I would think it's Oliver Cromwell by now, sir – 8 C 4.'

Hall looked at her. Rackham wanted to snigger, but he also wanted promotion, so he thought better of it. Jacquie cleared her throat. 'Sorry,' she said. 'I accompanied Mr Maxwell to the Lodge yesterday. We now know who hit him over the head and locked him in the basement.'

'Oh?' Hall looked at her over his glasses. 'Who?'

'Angel Kesteven.'

Hall and Rackham looked blank.

'She's a receptionist at the Lodge,' Jacquie explained. 'Fully paid-up member of the Church of God's Children. She is also barking.'

'Go on,' said Hall.

'It's a long story, sir,' she said.

Hall leaned back in his chair, cradling his head in his locked hands. 'DS Rackham and I have nothing better to do, have we, Graham?'

'Well, er . . .'

'Does it get us any closer to who killed Quentin and Bingham, Jacquie?' Hall had asked the sixty-four-thousand-dollar question.

'It might,' she said. 'By a process of elimination.'

'Then go,' Hall said.

'You know Maxwell didn't believe his kidnapping was Wensley's work?'

Hall did.

'At the Lodge, he asked Angel outright why *she'd* done it.'

'And?'

'Well the conversation was sort of . . . interrupted.'

'By what?'

'Paulo Escobar.'

'Escobar?' Hall frowned, riffling through his papers. 'Isn't that . . . ?'

'The lover of George Quentin. Yes.'

'He was at the Lodge?'

'Not another bloody Jesus freak?' Graham enquired.

'We were talking to Angel when Escobar appeared, pulled a knife.'

'Jacquie.' Hall looked at his DC. 'Are you all right?'

'*I* am, sir,' she said. 'But I didn't tackle him. Maxwell did.'

'Did he, now?'

'Did you talk to Escobar, sir?' Jacquie asked. 'When you were following up on George Quentin?'

'No, not personally. After that nonsensical mix-up at Vandeleur Negus . . .' He was looking straight at Jacquie.

'Mix-up, guv?' Rackham wasn't one to let his boss's discomfiture disappear so easily.

'When someone impersonated me,' Hall said slowly, patiently, looking his man in the face.

'Oh, yeah.' Rackham's reply was ingenous. 'I'd forgotten that.'

'Quentin's MD told me about Escobar, and I went to the house, but there was no one there. As I was on a tight schedule, the Met followed it up.'

'Well,' Jacquie went on, 'we're talking about one nasty piece of work.'

'And Maxwell coped with that?' Hall asked. He'd always taken the man for a couch potato.

'Straight out of the manual, sir,' Jacquie said. 'Well, the judo throw over his shoulder was. I'm not sure about the boot in the balls first.'

Rackham guffawed and clapped. 'Nice one.'

'Mr Escobar fell down the stairs, guv,' Jacquie said. It wasn't an unusual line to hear from a police officer. 'When he came round, he wasn't talking much. I arrested him for causing an affray and he's now in the local nick. Godalming. Surrey CID are on to it.'

Hall shook his head. '*Another* constabulary.' He sighed.

'It was bound to happen, guv,' Rackham told him. 'If there was going to be any activity at the Lodge, I mean.'

'Before the local law arrived, though,' Jacquie said, 'Wensley turned up.'

'Wensley?' Rackham started.

Hall nodded. 'Warwickshire CID let him go. I had a call from Nadine Tyler. Something to do with illegal acquisition of evidence.' He was looking at Jacquie.

'It's as well he arrived when he did.' Jacquie ignored the jibe. 'At last I think we had the truth from the Reverend Wensley.'

'Oh?' Hall shifted in his chair. 'That's nice.'

'He and Escobar go way back. To the institution in Bilbao. Escobar was just a kid when he was sent there, for knifing a teacher, funnily enough.' Jacquie could be casual about it now; when she'd heard it first, she'd clung to Maxwell for dear life. 'Wensley took him under his wing, looked after the lad, taught him to cope. Wensley, of course, was an old hand. An old lag, doing porridge.'

'It was a hospital,' Hall corrected her.

'That's not how Wensley and Escobar see it, sir. Oh, the Preacher still didn't tell us everything. There are some wounds that run too deep. But he can rationalize it now, handle his own past. They had a long time to talk, Escobar and Wensley. The Preacher told him all about England and his old friends – one in particular, George Quentin. What Wensley didn't know, or so he said, was that Quentin was queer as a wagonload of monkeys. The hospital let Escobar out six years ago – a year before Wensley – and he came over here with a work permit. Still don't know how he got that.'

'Bloody asylum-seeker.' Rackham grunted. 'We give away British citizenship with litres of petrol. Didn't you know?'

'Escobar found Quentin,' Jacquie went on, 'told him about Wensley, struck up a relationship and moved in.'

'And this Angel Kesteven,' Hall said. 'Why did she clobber Maxwell?'

'To protect Wensley. To protect the Church. I read her file, too, guv . . .' Jacquie waited for the bombshell. There wasn't one. So she went on. 'It makes Wensley look like Mr Average. She was born in Watts . . .'

'That's downtown LA, guv,' Rackham cut in. 'Black ghetto.'

'Thanks for the sociology lesson.' Hall's face had not flickered.

'Abuse,' Jacquie went on, 'racial, sexual, physical – you name it. She was on the streets at twelve, a hooker.'

'So the Church of God's Children specializes in misfits.' Hall nodded.

'One of their people found her off her face on heroin. Saved her life.'

'And now she wants to save Wensley's?'

'That's about it.'

'Where is she now?'

'Godalming, next cell to Escobar.'

Rackham grunted. 'Bloody place will be full of 'em.'

'Why was she over here in the first place?' Hall asked.

'The Church moves them around, apparently. It's her stint in the UK, and, of course, her file follows her everywhere.'

'Well, it'll be a bit thicker now, won't it?' Rackham said. 'What did she hope to achieve?'

Jacquie shrugged. 'Angel's not very bright, Graham,' she said, 'and I suppose she's just been scarred too much by what life has thrown at her. She listens at keyholes – just another little trait in her less-than-endearing personality. She got the idea that Maxwell was out to get Wensley, cause trouble for the Church. We might take out writs; she hit him with a crucifix.'

'Apt,' Hall said.

'Heavy,' Jacquie told him. 'She showed us the very one. Then, of course, she had a problem. Maxwell was out like a light, lying on the gravel by the front door. Angel didn't know what to do. She just knew she had to hide him. If she couldn't see him, he wasn't there. So she dragged him inside and down the cellar steps. She found a room and locked him in it.'

'You arrested her?' Hall queried.

Jacquie nodded.

'On what charge?'

'At the moment, GBH, guv. I wanted to talk to you first before we decide on kidnapping, attempted murder. There's a DI Jacobs from Surrey CID waiting for a call from one of us.'

Hall tapped the table with his Biro top. 'What are your feelings, Jacquie?' he asked.

'Close the bloody place down,' was Rackham's informed comment.

'Jacquie?' Hall had been ignoring detective sergeants for years.

She looked at him. 'Maxwell doesn't want to press charges,' she said.

Rackham threw his hands in the air. 'Does he ever?' he asked.

'He feels – as do I – that the woman's been through enough. Kidnapping, attempted murder – it's all getting a bit heavy.'

'I'll talk to this Jacobs,' Hall said. 'In the meantime, why did Escobar pull a knife on Maxwell?'

'Same thing,' Jacquie said. 'Angel sees the Church as her saviour; Escobar feels he owes Wensley. Anything that might harm that – Maxwell snooping, me snooping – they see as a threat. Then, of course, there's Richard Alphedge . . .'

Peter Maxwell crossed his last 't' a little after half past five. 'There, Count,' he said. 'That's the last of the UCAS references for this year. Cheltenham HQ will be delighted to learn that Jason Lee Crump has an IQ off the wall, is already working for NASA at weekends, has to keep fending off calls from Sven Goran Eriksson, who's desperate for him in the English squad, and he's also this year's runner-up for the Booker Prize. And if they believe that lot, they'll believe anything!' He slammed the file shut. 'Thingee Two can work her wonders getting all that on her WPPC or whatever tomorrow. Now, to serious matters.' He hauled himself over to the drinks cabinet and poured himself a large one. 'Murder.'

The cat yawned. Why didn't the old idiot stick his tongue in a bucket of rainwater if he was thirsty? And anyway, the colour on that stuff he did drink . . .

'So . . .' Maxwell wiggled his backside down on to the settee, crossing his legs at the ankles on the pouffe like the effigy on some latter-day crusader's tomb. 'We now know that I was not the third on some maniac's hit list, I just turned my back on the wrong woman, that's all. Which means' – and his face darkened at the thought of it – 'that poor old Alphie might well be.' He looked at the phone, thinking of Cissie. He'd left her with every assurance, with Jacquie's mobile number and that of his own landline. He checked his watch. No, he wouldn't ring her just yet.

'Person or persons unknown.' He closed his eyes, partly to focus, partly to ease the pounding in his head that Angel's crucifix still gave him. 'Lure George Quentin to Halliards, smash his skull and hang him. Let's analyse that one first.' He sipped the amber liquid, rolling it around his tongue, teasing his tonsils. 'Ritual,' he said, opening his eyes again, staring at the single cobweb on the ceiling that had clearly eluded the eagle gaze of Mrs B, who did for him on Wednesdays. 'The legend of the Halliards boy who hanged himself. Poor little bastard probably failed a SAT test or just couldn't grasp the enormous subtleties of Hitler's Lebensraum. Why am I being flippant, Count?' Maxwell reiterated a question everybody seemed to ask him these days. He let his eyes roll sideways towards the feline bastard. 'Because it's the only way to get through the day. So' – he shut his eyes again – 'this was a killing with a message. *Sic semper tyrannis.* Was that it?' He was sitting up now. 'Come, come, Count, you remember your Latin GCSE, surely? No, you'd have taken Classical Civilisation, wouldn't you? The non-thinking man's classics. Endless reruns of *Gladiator* and *Spartacus* videos. *Sic semper tyrannis,* Count – so it always is with tyrants. John Wilkes Booth, the bit player, yelled it to the audience in Ford's Theatre, after he'd put a derringer ball through President Lincoln's brain. Booth was a Southerner, y'see; didn't like Mr Lincoln, who had just trounced the South in a little war thing they had over there. So, is that why Quent died? To avenge a wrong?'

Maxwell got off the settee and started to pace the floor. Metternich the cat couldn't take much more of this. He'd have to start retaliating by licking his bum any minute.

'So what had Quentin done?' Maxwell was asking himself. 'And to whom? He swiped my cigarette cards that time in the Lower Fourths, certainly, but I wouldn't have hanged him for it. Oh, I know, Count, quite. You never said a truer word. Here I am, reasonable, rational, balanced, pinko-liberal . . . Well, all right, I exaggerate. But that's the whole problem in a nutshell, isn't it? A rational person trying to catch an irrational one. Shouldn't that mean I've got the upper hand here? No.' He flopped back on to the settee again. 'No, it just means I'm out of my depth.'

There was a silence. Metternich couldn't bear it and purred, just for the hell of it. No rhyme. No reason.

'All right.' Maxwell was back in the fray again, forcing the grey matter through its paces. 'Assuming we're right that Quent wasn't the random victim of a maniac – and the whole scenario precludes that, really – what about opportunity? Quent hadn't checked in at the Graveney and gone out again; he'd never arrived. Somebody arranged to meet him at Halliards, at an

appointed time, and they killed him. Now, apart from me . . .'
Maxwell caught Metternich's head coming up, the feline
equivalent of a raised eyebrow. 'Oh, ha,' his master snarled,
'that leaves . . . Stenhouse and Janet. He arranged the whole
thing, had a key and owns a damaged cricket bat which *could* be a
murder weapon, although apparently the lab says not. The two
of them together could have lifted Quent on to the balcony with
the noose round his neck. Then there's Ash and Veronica.
According to her' – he got up for a Southern Comfort refill –
'she went to Halliards that night with the Preacher and they had
it away in the chapel. God, the old chaplain would've died. I'm
not sure he realized what women were for. Sorry, that's a rather
politically incorrect comment, isn't it? But, man to man, Count,
as we are . . . Yet, Veronica didn't see or hear a thing. Still, she
was busy and the chapel is a fair way from the entrance hall and
the bell rope. Now, the Preacher, of course, denies all this. Yes,
he was there, wandering the grounds for reasons he can't or
won't explain, but there's no mention of Veronica in his version.
And the chapel was locked the next morning – Stenhouse told
the Preacher he hadn't got a key. So either the Preacher or
Veronica had keys or Veronica is telling porkies.'

Maxwell weighed the situation. 'I think we have to accept,
Count, distress you though it will, that our Veronica is a rather
kinky lady. If she's not doing it, she's talking about doing it –
rather like Year Ten, in fact. Then there's Alphie and Cissie.
They alibi each other, of course. Neither of them mentions
going out again after they went to bed. The Graveney doesn't
have security cameras, apparently, so we can't check that.
Anyway, Alphie's gone. Done a runner?' Maxwell shook his
head. 'If he has, he hasn't let Cissie in on it. Of course' – he took
another sip – 'there is a possibility we're overlooking in all this.
Yes, well, just be patient, will you? I'm getting to it. What if
Cret did it? What if Cret killed Quent? He's a big bloke, could
probably lift Quent by himself if push came to shove. And then
somebody else killed him. Tit for tat. That would explain the

good old blunt instrument – nothing poetic like the Halliards bell rope. Which brings us . . .'

'. . . to motive, Jacquie.' Maxwell was getting his face around a full English. 'You know it's very good of you to do this.'

'I didn't like the look of you yesterday,' she said, 'when I dropped you at school. Thought you needed some looking after.'

'Sorry,' he said. 'Bad hair day?'

'Bad head day.' She sipped her coffee. 'You're right. This whole thing is about motive. Once we've got that, we've cracked it. Sorry, is that obvious?'

He was shaking his head. 'There's nothing obvious about this one, darling,' he said. 'It's been a real eye-opener for me. I had no idea what a bunch of oddballs I was at school with.'

She shrugged. 'They're just people, Max. It's the same all over.'

He nodded. 'Maybe. But they're so damned unhappy. Look at Stenhouse. Dead-end job, wife who hates him. The Preacher – so strung out I don't want to think about it. And as for Ash and Veronica . . . Well . . .'

'Did you sleep with her?' Jacquie didn't want to look him in the face. Not then.

'What?' Maxwell swallowed a corner of his fried bread. It hurt like hell.

'She said you did.'

He chuckled. 'Sorry. That whole experience must have been so distasteful I blinked and missed it.'

She looked at him now and her lips curled into a smile. 'Well, good,' she said.

There was a relative silence while Maxwell chewed his bacon. 'You'd been worrying about that, hadn't you?' he asked.

'I'd no right . . .' she said.

Maxwell shrugged. 'Oh, I don't know,' he said.

'If it's any consolation' – Jacquie was cradling her coffee in both hands – 'I didn't either.'

'What? Sleep with Ash?'

'Either.' She looked at him, wide eyed. 'Both.'

'Ah.' Maxwell paused with the thick Irish sausage inches from his lips. 'Well, *chacq'un à son goût*, as the French have it.'

'It was how the Ashetons have it that bothered me,' Jacquie told him. 'Ash is impotent.'

Maxwell nodded. 'I know. Still, after a hard day at the chalkface I know how he feels.'

'I'm talking about motive, Max,' Jacquie said.

'Say on, Woman Policeman.' Maxwell poured himself another cup. It may have been Jacquie's kitchen-diner they were sitting in, but when it came to coffee with which to face the barbarian hordes, it was *su casa mi casa*.

'What if they do this for a hobby, Ash and Veronica?'

'What, swap you mean?'

'Well, keys on the mat is a little before my time. It's your generation.'

'Oh, no.' Maxwell laughed. 'You're not putting that one on me. My generation put a man on the moon.'

'And they put keys on mats,' Jacquie insisted.

'How does all this fit with Quent?'

'Well, he was gay.'

'So?'

'So . . .' Jacquie poured herself a second coffee too. 'What if Veronica tried it on, not with the preacher, but with Quentin?'

'Go on.'

'He doesn't want to know. There's an ugly scene. Rejection is something Veronica doesn't handle well – I know.'

Maxwell bridled. 'As do I.'

Jacquie hit him – gingerly, of course, because of his head. But inside she was glad. 'Veronica loses her cool, lashes out and all but kills him.'

'With a cricket bat?'

'It's plausible,' Jacquie said. 'It was a school, Max. There could have been bits of kit all over the place.'

'All right, why the school in the first place?'

'That I don't know, yet. Some weird game that Ash and Veronica were playing? Except that Ash didn't know that Quent was gay.'

'And Quent didn't know that Ash was impotent.' Maxwell nodded. 'What a pair.'

'Hang-ups,' Jacquie said solemnly. 'That's what this is all about. Hang-ups.'

'Hangs-up I believe you'll find is the correct term, Woman Policeman. Oh, Christ, look at the time.'

'You've got another half an hour yet, Max,' Jacquie said. 'I'll take you.'

'Drop me off at Columbine, there's a love. If I don't get back on White Surrey's saddle soon, he'll rust.'

'It's like falling off a bike, Max.' She smiled. 'You never forget.'

The local boys were out combing outhouses for Richard Alphedge. It had been four days and so far there had been nothing. No phone call. No sightings. No word.

'Publicity stunt, darling,' the actor's agent said to the one person in the entire country who'd bothered to call. 'If I know Richard – and sadly I do – he'll be holed up in a cottage somewhere, waiting for the world to give a fuck. Well, he'll have a rather long wait, won't he? Goodbye.'

DI Ben Thomas was back at Halliards that Friday. It was bitterly cold, but at least the rain had stopped. Holmes was helping the Warwickshire CID with their enquiries, trying, as was Leigh-ford, to sift the dozens of tyre tracks at the main gate. Everybody knew the place was empty. An old mattress leaned against the

hedge that old Gregson, the groundsman, had once lovingly
tended. The ubiquitous supermarket trolley lay upside down to
the left of the drive, rusting in the winter weather. Already, local
kids had used the windows as target practice. But none of them
went too close or crossed the police tape that still flapped there.
A bloke had hung hisself inside – best not get too near.

Thomas was looking up at the staircase to his right and the
great blank mass of the oriel window with its school crest that let
the winter light flood in. The rope had gone now to the labs in
Leamington. He climbed the stairs, feeling the cold brass of the
banisters under his fingers. Clean as a whistle. SOCO had
combed and recombed the place. They'd found plenty of
Quentin's blood and bits of Quentin's skull and brains. They'd
found footprints all over the area – on the stairs, the landing, in
the hall. It didn't help. Contractors, builders, cleaners – God
alone knew how many people had come and gone over the last
few weeks. And all the suspects' prints were there too –
Asheton's, Alphedge's, Muir's, Wensley's and Maxwell's.

The DI thumped the balustrade and it gave off a low,
reverberating hum. His boss had let Wensley walk, the stupid
cow, over a pushy lawyer and a technicality. DI Thomas didn't
object to a little rule-bending himself. Whoever that bloke was
who'd lifted Wensley's file should have been given a bloody
promotion, not the caution he presumably did get. Not that DI
Thomas ever had Wensley in the frame, not really. He pulled
the leather gloves from his pocket and put them on. Then he
produced the carefully folded piece of paper and smeared it in
the dust and grit on the landing floor. Finally, he tucked it under
a skirting board so that just the corner protruded.

Then he put his gloves away and bounced down the stone
staircase.

'Vernon!' he bellowed.

'Yes, guv?' The DS put his head round one of the classroom
doors.

'Give the stairs a final once-over, will you? I'm off for lunch.'

'But, guv . . .'

Thomas came alongside his man and tapped him lightly on the cheek. 'We've been over and over it. Yes, I know. It's a million-to-one shot, certainly. But this case is going nowhere. As' – and he tapped the side of his nose – 'is my career and yours. Have another shufti, there's a good lad.'

Chapter Sixteen

'Stenhouse?'

Maxwell had been in his Inner Sanctum at the top of the house at 38 Columbine. Pouch belts were bastards to paint anyway, especially when they were on the fifty-four-millimetre scale, but it hadn't helped when the doorbell had rung and Maxwell's brush had leapt skyward, daubing gold all over the plastic face of Captain Soames Gambier Jenyns of the 13th Light Dragoons.

'For fuck's sake, Max, it's pouring out here, or hadn't you noticed?'

Maxwell hadn't, if truth were told. He'd been engrossed, while painting the good captain's accoutrements, with the case of Halliards School. It could have been a three-pipe problem if Maxwell smoked a pipe. As it was, it was several Southern Comforts and a cup of cocoa.

The drenched journalist pushed past his old oppo. 'Good God.' Muir looked from left to right. 'You've got no rooms in your house, Maxie. Is that an old Leighford custom?'

'It's a town house, Stenhouse.' The Head of Sixth Form was patience itself. 'Not very different from your own. You go up the stairs – those are those carpet-covered things ahead of you. Want to put that in the downstairs cloakroom?'

'That' – Muir held it out to him – 'is my very heart and

soul. It is a laptop, Maxwell, a personal computer. The very essence of a journalist's being. Old, but precious. Where's your modem?'

Maxwell raised an eyebrow. 'Do I look like a man on whom the twenty-first century has dawned?' he asked. 'I remember the song, though,' and he broke into it, shaking his hands like a possessed Al Jolson. 'Moh, dem golden slippers . . .'

'Max.' Muir frowned before climbing the stairs. 'Have you been drinking?'

'Just a threat,' Maxwell acknowledged. 'Well, it's wonderful to see you, Stenhouse.'

They'd reached the lounge, all soft in its lamp-glow. 'Ah, a room. You got my message?' Muir laid the polythene-wrapped contraption on Maxwell's coffee table.

'Message?' Maxwell repeated.

'Oh, for crying out loud. Have you left any drink?'

'Scotch?'

'Is there any other kind?' Muir unzipped his dripping mac and stood there holding it.

'Kitchen.' Max pointed through to the neon-lit room. 'Should be a hook or two there.'

'No, I rang here first,' Muir called. 'Realized you'd be casting pearls before swine, and talked to your receptionist – what's her name?'

'God knows. Thingee.'

'Right. Well, she said she'd pass it on.'

'Pass what on?' Maxwell held out a towel for his damp visitor.

'Do stay with the conversation, Max.' Muir sighed. He raised his glass. 'Here's to . . . safer times.'

Maxwell had found his Southern Comfort glass and raised that in salute.

'No, I told your Thingee I was on my way and could you put me up for a day or two.'

'I shall doubtless be informed a week on Tuesday.' Maxwell

gestured for his old friend to sit. 'In education, the wheels of communication grind slow. I read the Hadow report yesterday and that came out in 1926. Put you up for a day or two?' The horror of it all was beginning to dawn. 'Doing a story on the South Coast?'

'Well, I might.' Muir loosened his tie. 'To keep the wolf from the door, you know. The long and the short of it, Max, is that Janet's thrown me out.'

'What?'

'I know.' Muir shook his head. 'Bloody outrageous, isn't it? You give a woman the best years of your life, scrimp and save, working your bollocks off in every bar in the land, and sod me, she packs my bags!'

'Good God. Er . . . the house?'

'Hers. Mummy was something big in the ATS and Daddy owned Midlothian. All I've got is that bloody laptop and printer and a liver like a bar of Aero. Same again?' His glass was empty. ' 'Course, you haven't heard the best bit yet.'

Maxwell refilled. It was going to be a long night.

'She tried to fit me up. With Quent's murder. Went to the law about that bloody silly cricket bat of mine. I ask you.'

'But that's in the clear, isn't it? Jacquie put it through forensics.'

'Did she, by God? Well, there you are. Could have saved the taxpayer an awful lot of money there. I didn't use it on Quent, and I didn't use it on Bingham.'

'So how did it break?'

'What? Oh, the tape?' Muir leaned back, cradling his glass. 'Promise you won't laugh? I was reliving the old days, just before the Halliards weekend, as a matter of fact, driving to silly mid-off . . .'

'As you do,' Maxwell murmured.

'Quite. Unfortunately, I was doing it in the kitchen. Dinged the willow, good and proper, I can tell you. Didn't do much for Janet's imported Italian tiles either. God, that woman's a bitch.'

'So, let me get this straight. Janet went to the police to tell them *you* killed Quent and Cret?'

Muir nodded. 'And stole the *Mona Lisa*, and helped myself to the Crown Jewels. According to her, I'm Jack the fucking Ripper!'

'And now you're my guest,' Maxwell mused.

'Do you mind, old man?' Muir looked oddly small in the half-light, defeated and old. 'Just for a day or two?'

'Where did you say you found it, Sergeant?' DCI Nadine Tyler was holding the see-through wallet up to the light.

'Under the skirting board on the landing at Halliards, ma'am. Must have got kicked there in all the kerfuffle.'

'But it's been three weeks.' The DCI looked at him.

'These things happen, ma'am,' was the best DS Vernon could do.

'Yeah, so does shit, but not on my patch, Sergeant.' The DCI assessed him coldly. 'Give DCI Henry Hall a bell at Leighford. Tell him I'm on his doorstep first thing Monday morning.'

'Under the skirting board?' Henry Hall blinked. 'You mean behind it?'

'Protruding from beneath, I understand,' Nadine Tyler said. 'As though kicked.'

'Kicked or placed?'

'Henry, I've had a bitch of a drive down and I'm tired. I would guess from your e-mails that you and I are staring at the same brick wall about now. Well, that' – she pointed to the note held in its polythene wrapper – 'is a chink in the bloody thing. It's the first one I've seen and I'm not letting it get away. Now I only came to you as a matter of courtesy. Do I go and see him myself or are you going to join me?'

Hall handed back the wallet. 'I wouldn't miss this for the world,' he said, reaching for his coat.

'You've got the address?' she asked.

Hall nodded. 'Oh, yes. But he won't be there. He'll be doing his day job.'

Deirdre Lessing was the Senior Mistress at Leighford High. Although she was nominally in charge of girls' welfare, the girls would rather break a nail or suffer the agonies of split ends than go to her with their problems. Everybody in the school knew that, and none of them could quite work out therefore exactly what it was that Deirdre did. Except Peter Maxwell; he knew perfectly well. She made potions in her office, maimed cattle and sank ships in storms. And Deirdre Lessing cast no shadow and no reflection. Spooky or what?

'Why wasn't I told the maths interviews were today?' She watched the pair coming up the steps on the CCTV cameras. Thingee, who crouched over her machinery in reception like an astronaut in a space capsule, all wires and headphones, hunched over with the weight of the abuse she received daily from parents, told her, 'They're not. They're tomorrow, Miss Lessing.'

'Good God,' Jessica Evans, the Head of RE, said rather appropriately, seeing the same thing from her classroom windows. 'I thought we'd stopped having the Gideons in school.'

As always, the kids were wiser, closer to the mark. Amy and Karen watched the pair who had aroused all the comment striding across the quad. 'That's that copper, that Mr Hall,' Amy observed. 'He done my mum last year for possession.'

'Who's that with him? His bit of stuff?' Karen wondered, while transferring the gum around her train tracks.

'Nah, that'll be his DI. They always come in pairs. They're looking for a woman. They have to have a woman copper in case he tries it on.'

'Who? Him?' Karen looked astounded. 'But he's gotta be forty.'

Amy nodded. 'Old perv. Worst sort.'

'Who they after, then? You don't reckon it's that Mrs Lessing, do you?'

'I wish!' Amy said with conviction. ''Ere, did you shift that consignment of nose studs I gave you?'

''Course,' Karen assured her, rather hurt that her friend should somehow impugn her fencing techniques.

'Not you, then,' Amy concluded. 'It'll be that nurse, that Mrs Matthews, selling crack on the seafront.'

'Nah, she's all right, she is, Mrs Matthews. Got any more gum?'

The Gideons slid up the staircase to the mezzanine floor, where their quarry lay. Sticky labels with the school logo clung desperately to their lapels. It was Leighford High's answer to Dunblane. Any mad machine-gunner in the world could wander into Leighford and gun down anybody – but at least he'd do it with a visitor's sticker on his lapel.

The door was open. And their quarry lolled back on his chair, his feet on the desk. He stood up abruptly as the pair walked in.

'Mr Hall, Ms Tyler, Detective Chief Inspectors, this is a pleasant surprise. Any answers?'

They didn't take his offer of seats, but stood inside his doorway. 'We were hoping you'd have some of those, Mr Maxwell,' Nadine Tyler said.

'I'll just close this.' Hall pushed the door to. 'We don't want children hovering, do we?'

'God, no.' Maxwell shuddered. 'Nothing more unsettling than a hovering child, in my experience.'

'Are you always so flippant?' Nadine Tyler wanted to know, along with so many other people.

'It's a defence mechanism,' Maxwell said, emerging from behind his desk. 'I can't help it. Are you sure you won't sit down?'

Nadine Tyler did, hooking one leg over the other so that her skirt rode up just enough to establish the fact that she was a woman before she was a DCI. Hall leaned his bum against Maxwell's window ledge, glancing out briefly at the cars parked below.

'What do you know about this?' Tyler asked, handing the Head of Sixth Form the wallet. 'No, don't take it out. You can read it perfectly clearly through the plastic.'

Maxwell looked closely. He really must get his eyes tested. Years of having them in the back of his head at the chalkface had taken their toll. 'Is this some sort of joke?' he asked.

'Oh, it's no joke, Mr Maxwell,' Tyler said. 'Neither is life imprisonment. Care to tell us about it?'

'You think this was written by me?' he queried.

'It has your name at the bottom,' Nadine Tyler said, 'and your signature.'

'*My* signature? Looks more like Rin Tin Tin's.'

'It's addressed to George Quentin,' the DCI said. 'Asking him to meet you at Halliards at midnight on the night he died.'

'Where did you get this?'

'Where George Quentin dropped it,' she told him, 'or you let it fall. It probably dropped from his pocket as he went down in a pool of blood. Or perhaps when you hoisted him on to the end of the rope. Careless of you, wasn't it?'

'Very.' Maxwell nodded, looking all the time at Henry Hall.

'Can I take that to be an admission?' Nadine Tyler was leaning forward, forcing Maxwell's gaze to focus on her.

'Admission one shilling,' Maxwell said. 'That was what they'd charge schools at Stratford when I was a kid. You'd get in to watch rehearsals. Brave of them, really, those actors, to expose themselves to the potential ridicule of all us kids.'

Nadine Tyler's eyes flickered for a moment. 'You've lost me,' she said.

'Well, this.' Maxwell handed the plastic wallet back to her. 'It's better than a play, isn't it?'

DCI Tyler leaned back, tucking the incriminating evidence

into her handbag. She glanced at Hall. 'On the way over here,' she said, 'Mr Hall and I had a little discussion. Well, a difference of opinion, actually, along the lines of could he turn his back while I shoved lighted matches under your fingernails.'

'Tsk, tsk, Policewoman,' Maxwell scolded. 'Such repressed aggression.'

'You're lucky it *is* repressed, son,' she said, although Maxwell could have given her ten years. 'It is customary in these matters for the local CID to make the arrest. That Mr Hall has flatly refused to do.'

'Good for him.' Maxwell beamed, and winked at Hall. 'You'll go far, Chief Inspector.'

'There's only so far I can go.' Hall pushed himself away from the wall. 'Have you *any* explanation for that letter?'

Maxwell shrugged. 'None. I've never seen it before.'

'Do you have a word-processor round here?' Nadine Tyler asked.

'Helen Maitland, my number two, has one,' Maxwell said. 'In the office next door.'

'Mind if we take a look?'

'No.' Maxwell got up. 'After you, Chief Inspectors.'

Nadine Tyler went ahead; Hall hung back. Maxwell was like the jam in a detective sandwich.

Helen Maitland's office was the reverse of Maxwell's, minus the film memorabilia. In place of the posters and the Oscar that stood on his desk with the legend 'Mad Max' beneath it, fluffy bunnies held pencil-holders and two cute kids with no front teeth beamed up at people from a silvered frame on the desk.

'Would you mind typing for me?' Nadine Tyler turned to Maxwell.

'I think they've got an old Olivetti in Business Studies,' Maxwell said. 'As a reminder of the good old days. Shall we?'

'What are you talking about?'

'A typewriter, dear lady. That I can manage. Put the paper in the top, tap the keys, ping the thing, sheer poetry. But this . . . how do you switch it on?'

'It's on,' Hall told him.

'Is it?' Maxwell was impressed. 'Well I never.'

'Mr Maxwell.' Nadine Tyler was seething. 'Are you obstructing us in the course of our enquiries?'

'*Au contraire*, madam.' Maxwell shook his head. 'I have, it seems, my name to clear. Unfortunately, I haven't the first idea how to begin.'

'Bollocks!' DCI Tyler snorted. 'You've got eleven-year-olds in this school who can operate one of these.'

'Indeed we have,' Maxwell acknowledged. 'My God, you don't think it's one of them, do you?'

'Maxwell' – Nadine Tyler's patience had just snapped – 'I'd like you to get your hat and coat. We're going to your house.'

'Ah, well, that is a *little* tricky, Chief Inspector. You see, Year Thirteen *are* expecting Lenin's War Communism after break. Then there's the Year Ten Holocaust test.'

'I am just about to forget protocol' – Nadine Tyler stood nose to nose with Maxwell – 'and, in spite of Mr Hall's presence, bust your arse. Now, are you going to co-operate?'

Maxwell looked into the woman's dark, flashing eyes. 'Hat and coat, I think you said?' He went back into his own office and picked up the phone. 'Thingee? Be a love and find Tom Hastings, will you? Ask him to cover my lessons for . . .' He looked at the DCI's glaring features. '. . . the rest of the day. Something's come up.'

For a moment, Metternich toyed with some sort of show of strength. The woman would be a doddle. He'd lull her first with the usual slow curl around her ankles, tail erect, spraying happiness in all directions, then, wham! Eight steel-shod claws with twelve pounds of tom behind them and her tights would be a memory. That *always* caused retreat; nay, rout. But the bloke, now; that was different. He was built like an outside lavatory. Unless, of course, he was allergic and would collapse, a sneezing wreck . . . Then Metternich sniffed again. No, he knew this one. He'd been here before. Ah well, discretion it was. And he vanished through the cat-flap.

'That's funny, Mr Maxwell.' Nadine Tyler had paused in the doorway to Maxwell's study. 'All the way over from the school, you've been telling us how computer illiterate you are. And yet . . . looks like Microsoft have stuffed you right up.' She tapped the laptop and its printer with a manicured nail.

'What?' Maxwell glanced at Muir's laptop and printer on his study desk. 'Oh, no, that's not mine . . .'

Nadine Tyler whirled to face him, glaring briefly at Hall before delivering the time-honoured words, 'Peter Maxwell, I am arresting you on suspicion of the murder of George Quentin. You do not have to say anything, but you may harm your defence if you do not mention when questioned something you rely on in court. Anything you do say may be given in evidence.' She spun on her heel. 'Sorry, Henry,' she said, 'but I couldn't wait all day.'

She flew into his arms and they stayed there, locked in a tightness neither of them wanted to break.

'There'll be sniggers.' Maxwell held her at arms' length. 'Your oppos.'

'Fuck them!' Jacquie shouted. 'Max, what happened?'

They sat down on the hard bench of his holding cell, the one in the bowels of the old Leighford nick, holding hands.

'I fell foul of the law,' Maxwell said. 'DCI Tyler's got a bit of a thing about me, I think. Wanted my body. Settled for my freedom.' He toyed with giving Jacquie his Mel Gibson by way of *Braveheart*, but hadn't the energy for it. Anyway, it would have reverberated around his nine-by-five and brought the coppers running. 'One of her people found a letter at Halliards. It was written to Quent and apparently came from me.'

'I don't understand.' Jacquie was wringing his hands along with hers.

'Neither do I.' Maxwell moved a stray strand of hair from her face, kissing her cheek softly. 'It wasn't my signature, but the thing was typed on a computer and they found Stenhouse's computer at Columbine. That was enough for our Nadine. She was like a rat up a drainpipe.'

'*Stenhouse's* computer?'

'He turned up on my doorstep Friday night like an orphan of the storm. Said Janet had kicked him out, having tried to get him arrested for murder. Needless to say, he brought his computer with him, him being a journalist an' all. And dear old Nadine put two and two together and came up with three point nine.'

Jacquie was thinking. 'The trouble is, Max, there's no way of telling them apart; computers, I mean. It all depends on the printer. The old dot matrix ones were quirky, but new ones – no chance. You can't prove this letter wasn't written on Stenhouse's machine.'

'Well, thanks for the heartening vote of confidence,' Maxwell mumbled.

'That's not what I mean, and you know it. When did Stenhouse arrive, exactly?'

'Er . . . nine-thirty, ten. Why?'

'And when was the letter found?'

Maxwell shrugged. 'Pass. I shall just have to go to jail.'

'Don't be so defeatist,' Jacquie scolded. 'There's no evidence against you at all.'

'Just playing mental Monopoly,' Maxwell explained.

'Have they talked to Stenhouse?'

'He wasn't there when the balloon went up. He takes invigorating strolls along the shingle to clear his brain every so often. They may have talked to him by now. Would that help?'

'Circumstantially, yes,' she told him. 'Stenhouse tells them the machine is his and that it wasn't in your possession until ten o'clock last Friday. If they found the letter before that, you're in the clear.'

'No, I'm not.' Maxwell shook his head. 'As you pointed out, heart of my heart, there's no way of telling one from the other. Many's the black-and-white B-feature in which chummie was caught by the clue of a dodgy typewriter key. But I could have typed that letter anywhere, any time – like the old Martini telly ad, funnily enough. The fact that I can't operate the bloody thing has passed them by, of course. They think I'm lying.'

'But the signature, Max,' Jacquie reasoned. 'They'll compare yours with what's on the letter.'

'I disguised my handwriting, I was in a hurry – they'll have thought that one through.'

'So, you've given up?' She sat back from him for the first time. 'Are you Mad Max? Are you the bloke who tilts at windmills? Fights dragons?' She stood up, shouting at him. 'Are you the bloke I fell in love with, though it was against every rational bloody thing to do?' She looked at him, swallowing hard, blinking back the tears. 'Oh, Max. If only I'd slept with you that night.'

'At the Graveney?' He smiled. 'They'd only say you were my accomplice,' he told her. 'That we snuck out to Halliards at the witching hour to meet and beat poor old Quent. No, I'd rather face this one alone, thanks, darling.'

'Bollocks!' Jacquie snorted. She threw her arms around him, burying her burning face in his shoulder. For a moment, she wanted to cry, to let it all out, to feel him kiss away her tears. But she had a job to do. She pulled back, sniffed, held his cheeks in her hands and kissed him hard on the mouth.

'I've got to see the guv'nor,' she said. 'Then Stenhouse. I've got a feeling DCI Tyler has rather overstepped the mark on this one.'

'Attagirl!' Maxwell smiled as the heavy door closed behind her.

'I know.' Hall's hands were in the air already, placating, calming, preparing to ride the whirlwind.

'With respect, sir' — Jacquie was more in control than she'd thought she'd be — 'what the fuck is going on?'

'Procedure, Jacquie,' he assured her.

She slid back a chair and leaned across his desk, staring into his face. 'You know and I know that Peter Maxwell's never killed anybody. Yes, he's a cantankerous old bastard, stubborn and set in his ways. But he's no more a killer than I am. Let him go . . . sir.'

Hall looked at his DC. Anybody else, any other time, and he'd have shown her the door, taken her warrant card, come the heavy. But not with Jacquie. And not now. 'I can't,' he said. 'DCI Tyler . . .'

'. . . is a first-rate bitch with a lot of hang-ups.'

'Jacquie . . .'

'Hang-ups.' Jacquie was nodding, staring into the middle distance. 'That's what Maxwell said. That's what this case is all about. The question is — whose?'

'We'll sort it out, Jacquie,' Hall promised. 'I can only hold Maxwell thirty-six hours, you know that. It's been . . .' He checked his watch. '. . . nine already.'

'You've got nothing on him,' Jacquie said.

'Circumstantial,' Hall corrected her. 'It's sometimes enough.'

Jacquie wanted to hit him. Reach out across that bloody desk he used like a shield, slap him around the head, knock those blind, blank, cold glasses off and crush them and him under her heel. She wanted to do it because she knew that Hall was right. In Maxwell's good old days, which he talked about at the drop of a rope, circumstantial was enough to hang a man. It had hanged George Quentin already.

Instead, Jacquie Carpenter relented. She turned on the heel she imagined was grinding the guv'nor's glasses and left the office. She was halfway down the dimly lit corridor when her mobile hummed in her pocket.

'Jacquie Carpenter.'

'Jacquie? Oh, thank God. This is Cissie, Cissie Alphedge. I've had a call.' The voice was strained, on the edge of hysteria. 'They've got Richard. He's alive. But they want money.'

'How much?'

'Half a million!'

Jacquie sucked in her breath. 'When?'

'Tomorrow night. They want Max to do it. But I can't reach him. He's not answering his phone.'

'No,' said Jacquie, looking down the steps that led to the cells, 'Max can't come to the phone just now.'

'What? Jacquie, what's going on? Somebody's got Richard. They say . . .' For a moment, the line appeared to go dead.

'Cissie?' Jacquie turned corners in a desperate attempt to regain the signal. 'Cissie, you're breaking up.'

'They say they'll . . . Unless Max brings the money, they'll . . . kill him. Oh, Jacquie, what can we do?'

Jacquie Carpenter put the phone to her chest for a moment, sure that Cissie could hear her heart beating. Then it was up to her face again. 'Don't worry, Cissie,' she said. 'This creep's playing a new ball-game now. He's moved the goalposts. But it's a game we know. It's a game we can win.'

Chapter Seventeen

'I'm still trying to work out,' Maxwell said, watching the trees flash by as the darkness gathered, 'whether you've got something on Henry Hall or whether you just blew the side of the jail off.'

He was angling Jacquie's wing mirror so that he could see at least part of the darkening features of DS Rackham in the back seat. If truth were told, Rackham didn't care for the position he found himself in, either as back-seat driver in a two-door car or as gooseberry to Bonnie and Clyde.

'You know the deal, Max,' Jacquie told him. 'That's why Graham is with us.'

'How did Cissie sound?' he asked her.

'Distraught,' she said. 'Who wouldn't be?'

The deal was that Henry Hall had let Maxwell go. He was what the Victorians called a ticket-of-leave man, on parole. The electronic tag they'd otherwise have strapped to his ankle came in the more human shape of Graham Rackham. Not, as Hall had told Jacquie, that he didn't trust her; it was just that, in kidnap situations, a lone officer was never enough. When they got to the Alphedges', Jacquie would be able to call in the whole local team, with phone taps, wires, electronic surveillance, helicopters and dogs; the full monty of dealing with a psychotic bastard.

★   ★   ★

'No.' Cissie was adamant in the lamps' glow, shaking her head like a resolute terrier. 'None of that. He was very specific.'

Jacquie looked across at Maxwell. He took the woman in his arms and sat her down on the settee. He motioned to Rackham, who in turn looked at Jacquie. Her gesture convinced him – for now. Making the tea it was, and he sloped off in search of the kitchen.

'Tell me again.' Maxwell sat with his arm round her. 'Tell me *exactly* what he said.'

Cissie sighed. She knew it, of course. Knew it all off by heart. That voice. So cold, so chilling. It had etched itself on her soul. 'He said if I wanted to see Richard again, I was to get half a million pounds. The person to bring it was Peter Maxwell. He said he'd call back.'

'What time was the call, Cissie?' Jacquie asked.

'Er . . .' She looked at the grandfather clock in the corner, with its shiny brass face and its smiling sun. 'This would have been after six, perhaps half past.'

Jacquie had already checked the phone. It was a digital sort that recorded the calls. The one at 6.23 merely said 'number withheld'. No surprises there.

Jacquie tried again. 'I need to call people in to monitor his calls, Cissie.'

'No!' the woman shrieked. 'I told you, no. Richard's life is at stake. I will not jeopardize that. I won't.'

Maxwell squeezed her to him more tightly, looking up at Jacquie and shaking his head. This would have to be done the old way. 'Can you manage the sort of amount he's asking for?' he asked.

Cissie looked at him, sniffing back the tears. At last, someone was listening. 'I think . . . Yes,' she said. 'Yes, I can. Trusts and so on. But that will take weeks, won't it? Days at best.'

'You'll have to tell them, Cissie.' Jacquie sat down opposite her. 'Which bank are you with?'

'Lloyds TSB. My branch is in the High Street.'

'How do we play that, Jacquie?' Maxwell asked.

She looked at her watch. 'Tomorrow morning, at nine-thirty, Cissie and I will go to the bank and see the manager. I'll get whatever authorization they need.'

'What if he rings?' Cissie asked. 'The bastard who's got Richard?'

'He has to give you time to get the money, Cissie,' Jacquie explained as gently as she could. 'He didn't contact you until after the close of business today. Anyway, Max'll be here.'

'And it's me he wants,' Maxwell told the shaking woman. 'I'll have to talk to him sooner or later.'

DS Rackham was just coming back with a tray of teacups when the phone rang, shattering the tension that filled the house. Maxwell felt Cissie jump. Jacquie was on her feet, motioning for Rackham to keep still. The sergeant froze like a rabbit in the headlights. And it was Jacquie who picked up the phone before motioning Cissie over. The women stood cheek by cheek, like partners in an insane fandango, listening at the earpiece. Jacquie nodded and Cissie spoke. 'Yes?'

'Is he there yet?' a disembodied voice said.

'Where's Richard?' Cissie asked.

'Maxwell.' The voice ignored her, sounding rather peeved to have to repeat itself. 'Is he there?'

Again, Jacquie nodded.

'Yes,' said Cissie, trying to keep her voice strong. 'Yes, he is.'

'Put him on.'

Maxwell was motioned across. Rackham had put his tray down and was timing the call with his electronic watch. 'Peter Maxwell,' Maxwell said.

There was a pause. 'Is that Maxwell?' the voice asked.

'Yes,' Maxwell said. 'Where's Richard?'

Jacquie's cheek was pressed against his now as they played this one together, literally by ear.

'Safe,' the voice snapped back. 'For now. Have you got the money?'

237

'No,' said Maxwell at Jacquie's silent prompting. 'No, the banks are closed. You must give us until tomorrow.'

'Don't waste my time, you shit!' the voice snarled.

'Look . . .' Maxwell didn't find it easy, being conciliatory with a maniac who'd grabbed an old friend and probably killed two more. 'You've got to be reasonable about this. Mrs Alphedge can get the money, but it will take time.'

'Tomorrow,' the voice grated. 'You've got until tomorrow.' And the line went dead.

'Damn!' Maxwell turned away, furious with the world. 'I really fucked that up.'

'No, Max.' It was Cissie's turn to comfort, patting his arm, calming him down. 'What else could you do?'

'Cissie.' Jacquie looked at Graham Rackham, who was already handing out the teas. 'We've got to tap this phone. With a trace, we'll know where he's ringing from.'

'No.' Cissie was shaking her head again. 'I absolutely forbid it.'

'Max.' Jacquie sat down to talk to him. 'Did you recognize the voice? Did it sound familiar?'

Maxwell blew his cheeks out. 'No,' he said. 'Cissie, you've heard it . . . what? Twice now? Did you detect an accent there? A slight Scots, was it? Sort of Robbie Coltrane?'

'I don't know, Max.' Cissie tried to hold her trembling cup. 'I can't really focus on things like that.'

'Any background sounds?' Rackham asked. 'Clock ticking? Dog barking? Anything like that?'

'Nothing.' Maxwell shook his head. 'Just the voice.'

'All right.' Jacquie took charge, despite Rackham's rank. 'I don't reckon we'll hear anything else tonight. Graham, you happy about watches?'

The sergeant shrugged. 'Sure.'

'I'll take one,' Maxwell volunteered.

'You're a civilian,' Rackham reminded him.

'I'm also going to be bagman on this little operation,'

Maxwell reminded *him*. 'I am involved, Sergeant, whether you and your DCI like it or not.'

Rackham beamed. 'Oh, rest assured, Mr Maxwell. We don't.'

'I can't sleep anyway,' Cissie said. 'I'll take a watch.'

'No, Cissie,' Maxwell insisted. 'We need you fresh for the morning. Got any sleeping tablets?'

'I don't know,' she said.

'Jacquie?' Maxwell put his arms around his friend's wife again. 'Cissie,' he said, looking her in the face, 'I know it's a trite and overused phrase, but try not to worry. Alphie will be fine. Trust me, lady, I'm a Head of Sixth Form.'

She buried her face into his neck and sobbed there quietly. He held her for a moment, then eased her gently away. Jacquie took over from there, leading her towards the hall and the stairs beyond. 'I've got something here, Cissie,' she said, 'that'll help you sleep. And don't worry, I'll be with you all night. There's a phone by your bed, isn't there?'

Cissie nodded. 'Yes,' she said, 'there is.'

'Well, that's fine.' Jacquie took her away, glancing at Rackham as she did so. 'We'll sort everything out in the morning – you'll see.'

When he was sure they'd gone, Rackham flicked out his mobile and started punching numbers. 'Buzzword?' he said, down the line. 'DS Rackham, at the Alphedge place. I want a trace put on the line. Landline number . . .' But before he could finish the sentence the phone had been snatched from his hand and Peter Maxwell dropped it heavily on the carpet, before grinding the plastic to pieces under his heel.

'You stupid bastard!' Rackham snapped.

'No,' Maxwell growled. '*You're* the stupid bastard if you think I'm playing games with the life of an old friend.'

'Playing games?' Rackham hissed 'I'm trying to save the bugger's life. We *are* on the same side, Maxwell. When he rings again, if we've tapped the line, we can find out where he's ringing from, close the net.'

'Cissie made it perfectly clear,' Maxwell said. 'She didn't want that kind of interference.'

'Yeah, well.' Rackham was making for the Alphedges' phone. 'If we listened to the wishes of everybody in a kidnap situation, we wouldn't get any of 'em back.' And he picked up the receiver.

Maxwell was about to stop him again, when Jacquie arrived at his elbow. 'Max.' She stopped him in his stride, looking deep into his dark eyes, which were flashing fire. 'Max, we've *got* to do this.'

'Cissie . . .'

'Cissie is in no position to make rational decisions,' Jacquie told him. 'What I've given her would put an elephant out. She won't stir for the next twelve hours and that gives us time to get everything in position.'

'Jacquie,' Maxwell said, holding her shoulders with both hands. 'We're not trying to outwit Cissie, we're trying to outwit the psycho who's got Richard.'

'If he has.'

'What?' Maxwell blinked.

'If he hasn't killed him already. If he ever had him and all this isn't just a bluff.'

Maxwell was shaking his head. 'You've lost me,' he said.

She sat him down. Rackham waited until this particular little domestic was cleared up. 'Max,' she said. 'You're new to this game. We're not. Did Cissie talk to Richard? The first phone call, I mean?'

'No,' Maxwell said. 'She didn't say so.'

'Right. And without that, we have no idea whether he's alive or dead. Or whether this isn't just some kind of con. Richard Alphedge is a celeb, you know.'

'What, you mean some kind of stalker?' Maxwell was incredulous, but Jacquie nodded. 'Come on, Jacquie. This is me, Max. Are you seriously telling me that Quent and Cret were killed, ostensibly by the same hand, and then somebody just ups and kidnaps an old friend of theirs, just for jolly?'

'For half a million quid,' Rackham reminded him.

Maxwell looked at them both. 'All right,' he said. 'Why the change of direction? Our man murders Quent with something poetic in mind, making some kind of statement. He murders Cret because Cret is on to him. Never mind what happened to me; that's a red herring. Now, he's kidnapped Alphie and is demanding ransom money. It doesn't make sense. He's working from another blueprint.'

Jacquie nodded. 'Precisely. And that's exactly why we need the gear and expertise of the local force. He can keep us dangling for days, weeks on this, Max. All we need is approximately one and a half minutes of airtime with a trace and we've got him. We can pin him down to a room in a house.'

'What they call precision bombing?' Maxwell asked.

Jacquie nodded.

'You'd better believe it,' Rackham weighed in.

'Except that I don't,' Maxwell told them. 'Precision bombing is as much bollocks now as it was in the Gulf War. It doesn't work. Are you sure you're not confusing this with friendly fire?'

The lights twinkled out over the Surrey countryside as Jacquie snuggled against her man.

'Was I wrong?' he asked her. It was nearly four o'clock, but the wrong time of year for dawn to creep stealthily over the windowpanes of morning. It remained as black as a witch's hat in the gardens of leafy suburbia.

'Morally, no,' she murmured, her eyes closed, her brain tired. 'Operationally, yes. You owe Graham Rackham for a new phone, by the way.'

'Let him take it out of my threshold payment.' Maxwell stretched and yawned.

'I didn't think you were going for that.' She frowned, her eyes still closed.

Maxwell shrugged. 'Well, there you go.'

She chuckled.

'What's your best guess, Jacquie?' he asked her. 'Chummie, I mean.'

'Do you want the textbook explanation or my own experience?'

'I can give you the textbook stuff,' Maxwell said. 'The term kidnapping originates in 1860s Britain to denote the selling of children to illegal slave markets on West Indian plantations. Ah, the good old days. I can think of a few I would like to shackle and ship out. The sort of situation we have here first occurred as a Mediterranean form of money-making; most spectacularly when Lord Muncaster and three tourist friends were captured by Greek brigands.'

'What happened?' Jacquie asked.

'You don't want to know,' Maxwell told her.

'I expect it ties in with my own experience,' she said.

'Muncaster and his mates were killed, because the ransom demands were not met.'

'That's not going to happen here, though, is it?'

He looked down at her. 'In the sense that Cissie's going to pay up, no. Your experience?'

'Only one,' Jacquie said, her voice suddenly as small as the hours in which they spoke. 'I hoped I'd never have to go through it again.'

'What happened?'

'It was the year before I was transferred to Leighford. A little girl was taken from outside her playschool. Ransom notes were sent, not phone calls. The experts were called in and decided they were forgeries, hoaxes. We never heard from the real kidnappers . . . we found her body on some waste ground two months later. She'd died on the day she was taken. There was no ransom. No point. Every parent's waking nightmare, Max; the passing prowler, the guy in the white van. I don't want to go through that again.'

He held her close, scenting her hair as he kissed her and they watched the dawn creep from the east.

The next call came at a little after midday.

'It's him.' A quivering Cissie was holding her hand over the receiver. Along the wires, the local CID's switchgear clicked into operation. Maxwell knew, as did Jacquie and Rackham. Only Cissie was in the dark, frozen out on a need-not-to-know basis for the sake of her nerves. Rackham was in the kitchen on Jacquie's mobile, liaising with the monitors in the unmarked van beyond the privet that screened the house.

'Have you got it?' a voice wanted to know.

'Yes,' Cissie said. 'As you asked.' She was looking at it now, a plain black suitcase on the coffee table, hers and Richard's life savings and then some. 'Unsequenced bills – hundreds, fifties, twenties, tens.'

'Right. Put Maxwell on.'

She steadied herself, hating every moment when she was on the phone to him. Then she passed the receiver to Maxwell.

'Yes?' he said.

'You take the next train to Leamington. You will be in the phone box on Platform Three at five o'clock sharp. You will have the money with you. Miss that deadline, Maxwell, and Alphedge dies.'

'Wait.' Maxwell delayed the hang-up, playing for time. 'What proof have I got that Alphedge is still alive?' Out of the corner of his eye, Maxwell saw Cissie's hand go to her mouth. He couldn't help that now. He turned his back on her.

'You haven't,' the voice told him.

'Let me speak to him.'

'Go fuck yerself.'

'No Alphedge, no money,' Maxwell snapped. He'd seen *Payback*. Maybe it was time to be Mel Gibson.

There was a pause. For a second, he expected the sound of the receiver being slammed down. In the kitchen, Rackham was pacing backwards and forwards, his palm sticky around the phone, his heart thumping. Jacquie stood with Cissie, holding her upright, stroking her shoulder hypnotically to calm them both down.

Maxwell heard a click and muffled words. Then clearly, 'Max, is that you?'

'Alphie?'

Cissie cried out, but Jacquie held her back.

'Max.' The voice sounded weak, flaky. 'Max, have you got the money?'

'Yes, yes, Alphie,' he said. 'How the hell are you?'

But the receiver was snatched away and chummie was back. 'Five o'clock, Platform Three,' he hissed. 'And Maxwell – I'll be watching. One whiff of a copper and your actor friend will be joining the Hall of Fame.'

The line went dead.

'Jacquie?' DS Rackham emerged from the kitchen a moment later, the mobile tucked away, looking as casual as he could.

Maxwell took over at Cissie's side.

'How did he sound, Max?' The tears trickled down her cheeks, her eyes overflowing.

'Fine, darling,' Maxwell lied. 'He sounded fine.'

In the kitchen, well away from the crying Cissie, Rackham filled Jacquie in. 'He's on a mobile. Warwick.'

'Warwick?'

'Isn't that . . . ?'

Jacquie nodded. 'Not a million miles from Halliards. Is that where he's got him?'

'You've been there,' Rackham said. 'What's it like?'

'Huge,' Jacquie told him. 'You could hide an army in there. Fields to the rear, river near by. You could land a helicopter on the First Eleven Square. Tell them what we think. I've got to get Max up there.'

★   ★   ★

'By train,' he told her again.

'But, Max . . .'

'No buts, Woman Policeman. Chummie said "train" and train it is. If his threat is genuine and he can see me at the platform kiosk in Leamington, he can see me get off the train too. We're not taking any chances on this, are we?'

'No, we're not,' she told him.

He opened the passenger door. 'How will I know the Warwickshire boys in blue?' he asked.

'You won't. They'll be passengers, porters, used-car salesmen. The point is that they'll know you. That's where Rackham was this morning. While I took Cissie to the bank and you manned the phone, he was arranging for a mug shot to be sent from Leighford to the Warwickshire lads.'

'Could Brother be any bigger?' Maxwell wondered, gripping the case tightly.

'Max, you really should have a chain for that,' she said.

'Don't bother me now, Ms Carpenter,' he scolded, and reached in to kiss her. 'Jacquie . . .'

She quickly raised a finger to his lips. 'Get going,' she said. 'I'll see you at the other end.' And she rammed the Ka into gear and was gone, fighting back the tears. In her rear-view mirror, the man she loved got smaller and smaller until, suddenly, he wasn't there at all.

Leamington station. Four fifty-seven. A garbled voice over the intercom had told passengers it was sorry for the delay but there were track-laying problems near Banbury and the train was running approximately sixteen minutes late.

Maxwell hit the platform running. Somewhere among the throng of people standing around, were the team Rackham had sent in; the passengers, porters and used-car salesmen who worked for the Warwickshire constabulary. He could see the phone box, a soulless glass thing which had replaced the red one he remembered as a boy, where an anonymous voice had patiently told him over and over again to push button B. Shit! A large woman was filling it, along with two pampered poodles attached to slender leads and diamante collars.

The Head of Sixth Form wrenched open the door. 'Madam, I'm sorry,' he blurted. 'I'm expecting a vital call on this line any minute.'

'Don't be silly,' the startled woman snorted. 'People don't ring empty call-boxes.'

'They do today,' he assured her. 'Please, madam. It won't take long, but I must have the phone.'

The dogs looked up at him, whining and yapping.

'Go away or I shall call a policeman,' she shrilled.

Maxwell's nose hovered near hers. 'I am a public schoolboy, madam,' he growled, 'and ordinarily, believe me, I would not behave this way, but if you don't put that phone down now and fuck off, I'm going to throw those two posing pooches of yours on to the line. Do I make myself clear?'

'Help! Help! Police!' the woman shrieked, rather stereotypically, Maxwell thought, as she dropped the receiver and fled, dragging the poodles in her wake.

Maxwell replaced the phone. He didn't see the toilet attendant silently whisk the scene-making woman out of harm's way. He looked up and down the platform. The train he'd been on was pulling out, with a thud and rattle of rolling-stock, the engines building momentum as the thing gathered speed. He checked his watch. Shit. It was 5.04. Had he blown it? Had Railtrack and that stupid old besom conspired to make him miss the call? Perhaps to kill Richard Alphedge?

He spun round in the goldfish bowl that was the call-box. If anyone left on the platform was an undercover cop, they showed no sign. Two girls in a uniform he knew came hurtling along the concrete. The hats had gone and the ghastly grey socks, but the blazers were the same. Cranton. He thought that school had closed too, yet here they were, laughing and joking like the ghosts of his boyhood. Cranton, the private girls' school down the road where Ash and who knew how many others had lost their virginity. Cranton – those heady summer balls the joint staffs of their two schools allowed, but always under the most careful supervision. Cranton . . .

The phone shattered the moment and Maxwell snatched it up. 'Hello?'

'The Jephson Gardens close in thirteen minutes. Get to the phone by the lake. Speak to anybody, Alphedge dies. One minute late, Alphedge dies. Do it.'

'But . . .' The line was silent.

Maxwell bashed open the door, nearly colliding with the schoolgirls. 'You know,' he said, raising his hat, 'your mothers probably made some of us very happy,' and he was gone, out of the side gate he remembered as a kid, trotting along the pavement towards the bridges.

He knew this routine well. It was *Dirty Harry*, the first of the Eastwood Callahans. He ran the storyline in his head. The loony who's kidnapped the fourteen-year-old bounces Callahan all over town, just to check he's not being followed. Corny on celluloid, but this was for real. And there were two important differences. Eastwood was a fit forty-year-old at the time, carrying a .44 Magnum and a flick-knife. Maxwell . . . well, the pounding of his heart as he dashed past All Saints said it all.

The Leam swirled dark under the bridge as he hurtled over it, his hat gone, the heavy suitcase bouncing against his thigh. His breath came in sobbing grunts and he felt as if his lungs were going to burst. Then he was in the park, the lights twinkling among the trees as he scurried along paths without end, making for the lake.

Bugger! Memory had gilded his lily and he'd reached a dead end. He'd remembered the path curving to the left, and now he found himself outside a gents'. In the shadows, a rather un-savoury type half turned, flashing at him in the hopeful anon-ymity of gathering dusk.

'Perhaps later,' Maxwell called out, doubling back the way he'd come, 'when I get my Aids test result,' and he scuttled past the aviary with its chattering finches and took the slope to the lake.

The phone was already ringing by the time he got there, and he all but fell on it. 'Yes?' he wheezed.

'Almost didn't make that one,' the chilling voice said. 'But I guess you really are on your own. All right. No more pissing about. Halliards.'

Peter Maxwell leaned against the glass as the line went dead in his hand. His lungs hurt like hell and he was alone. From somewhere a bell tolled to tell the lurking world that the Jephson Gardens were closing. He put the receiver back. Halliards. He kicked open the door and strolled into the darkening night. This was it. Full circle. Where are you, Jacquie? he wondered as he forced his tired legs to run again. Where are you?

Chapter Eighteen

She watched him burning shoe leather past the Pump Rooms, that faded reminder of Georgian times when people still took the waters in this spa town and everyone knew his place. She kept the engine idling as he whistled down a cab – he who had no breath left at all.

The taxi turned left along a street that edged the gardens, swung left again and then right, past another park and out under the giant archways the Victorians had built to carry their trains, the glory of their age when the Queen, God bless her, came to Leamington and made it Royal. Jacquie Carpenter spun the wheel, her mobile clamped between her cheek and shoulder, breaking every rule in and out of the book.

'He's going right, Graham,' she said, 'right,' and she hauled the wheel over to follow him. All she had now, as the night drew in, was taillights. She didn't want to get too close because she didn't know who was watching, or from where. Maxwell had no idea where she was and she had only the vaguest notion of how much back-up she had and didn't know the area at all.

'Bugger!' She hit the steering wheel with both hands. A red light had separated her from the taxi and she'd been forced to stop. Either that or hit the amber gambler screaming out from her right. 'I've lost him, Graham,' she hissed into the phone.

'Where are you?'

'Christ knows.' She looked around. 'I can't see a place name anywhere. There's a garage to my right – oh, and the station beyond. Max has come back the way he went, more or less. Done a circle.'

Rackham grunted. 'That'll be the cabbie building up his fare. Hang on.'

Graham Rackham was in his own vehicle in a lay-by ten minutes away, acting as a go-between for Jacquie and the local force. It wasn't easy. They had the tracking gear; he and Jacquie didn't. Right hand, left hand.

'Jacquie, the local boys tell me he's likely to have gone straight ahead – that'll put him on the road to Halliards.'

'Halliards?' Jacquie had never waited so long in her life for traffic lights to change. 'So that's it.'

'They don't know. They're awaiting instructions.'

She tried to remember the layout of the place, its angles, its views. 'How big's the team?' She waited while Rackham relayed the question down the line, handling his twin mobiles like juggling balls.

'Ten,' he told her. 'Four marksmen.'

'How near are they to Halliards?' She was moving again now, cutting up a dithery dear and slicing past cyclists, crashing through the gears as she left the lights of the town behind and took the gradient that curved to the right.

'They're on their way,' she heard Rackham say. 'As indeed am I. The team's ETA is niner, repeat, niner minutes.'

'Got it,' she said. 'Fuck knows how far away I am. I hope I know it when I see it. Keep in touch, Graham. Graham?' She rattled her phone, looking at it. Graham Rackham had broken up. The connection was dead. As he pulled out into the traffic, Rackham's rear wheel had clipped the kerb and the car had slewed across the road. The DS heard the shuddering of metal and felt the sickening thud as something hit him in the side. The airbag inflated like a giant white mushroom, sending both his mobiles hurtling somewhere in the car's interior. He slammed on the brakes, blind and sliding, twisting the wheel the way he thought it should go. He didn't see the juggernaut behind him, its cab a merry-go-round of fairy lights. He didn't see its driver, wrestling with the wheel, locking the brakes and screaming at him. All he felt was the jolt as his car buckled from behind and the glass blew out with a series of bangs.

Whatever sounds followed – the scream of tyres and the falling of shattered glass and the rip and bounce of twisted metal – Graham Rackham didn't hear them. Graham Rackham had broken up.

Black trees rose like sentinels along the line of hedges as Jacquie drove past them. The white line and the cat's-eyes led her on. To left and right, the occasional outline, the odd lights from a farmhouse and the orange glow of what must have been the M40 to the west. She hadn't caught the cab, though she'd tailgated cars without number to check the plates, only to swerve out past them, hearing the searing siren of their angry horns. She checked her phone again. Nothing from Rackham. And without him, nothing from the team beyond.

What if Halliards was only a guess? Maxwell could be anywhere, anywhere the instructions from this mad bastard took him. Nine minutes to the arrival of the team at Halliards – if Halliards it was. If only Cissie had allowed a proper monitoring. If only Jacquie had been able to organize a wire on Maxwell.

Then, there it was. A black silhouette filling the skyline to her left, empty and sad eyed. She cut her headlights and her speed simultaneously, sliding the Ka under the overhang of the trees, scraping the wild hawthorn of the hedge. It was at moments like these she wished she hadn't bought a yellow car. The engine was off. The lights were out. She tried her mobile one last time. Nothing. Shit! How useless all this technology was after all – Max was right.

She got out, easing the door closed behind her. How long had this taken her? Five minutes? Six? She kept close to the hedge, grateful for the dark and the silence. If there was a team in the area, she couldn't see them. Maybe they were on their way. She could have used some company about then. Most of all, Peter Maxwell's. She saw a dark car parked tight to the hedge. It was empty. No back-up there.

Now Jacquie was touching brickwork. The pillars of the main gates reared up before her, topped with the stone griffons that were the Halliards crest. The great wrought-iron gates were thrown back, as though the property developers had given up the hopeless struggle to keep kids out. But what kids would come here? Jacquie wondered, glancing back along the pale and lonely road. Above her, the clouds covered the stars. There'd be no moon tonight.

She crept towards the arts block, skulking in the shadows of the low-spreading cedars, keeping off the path where her telltale heels would give too much away. The chapel loomed before her like a fortress, solid and black. The stained glass reflected dully the dead light of the leaden sky, threatening rain by morning. She edged around its buttresses, where staff, long dead, had leant their bikes, where town criers without number had rung their passing bells. The archway in front of her was as black as pitch, but she couldn't risk her torch. Acclimatized as her eyes were to the dark of the grounds, she wasn't ready for this. It sucked her in like a black hole, like some magnetic void she was powerless to resist.

Now she was in the cloisters, her right hand clasped around the mace can in the handbag over her shoulder. A chilling wind whipped the corner here, riffling the faded papers that Maxwell had tried to read three weeks before when they'd found the hanged body of George Quentin. She reached to her right, using her left hand, and felt the chiselled iron of the Gothic handle that was bolted to the chapel door. She tried twisting it. Locked. As locked as it was the night Veronica had said she'd made love on the altar with the Preacher.

Jacquie walked on, feeling as though she was treading on eggs. The archway to her right led out to the curve of the drive and the Headmaster's house, shrouded in cedars and guarded by a high privet hedge. Ahead, the door that Stenhouse had unlocked led to the main corridor, Big School and the entrance hall where George Quentin had died. She tried the handle here and this time it worked.

There was no rattling of locks, no scream of hinges long rusted, just the whisper of a draught excluder. She caught the door before it slammed against the wall and stood there, waiting. Ahead, the corridor was long and dark, but there was the faintest of lights halfway along. She'd always seen this place in the daylight, never in the dark, and it frightened her. More than the Lodge with its antiseptic chill and its eternal light twirling on the floor. She felt so cold she thought she'd be sick.

The light, she knew, came from the oriel window beyond where the bell rope that hauled Old Harry from his slumbers and summoned the lost generations of Halliards to their lessons once hung. In her mind, she watched them go, legions of them, laughing and chattering in a dim echo down the years, with their tasselled caps and bright blazers and undying hopes.

She kept to the centre of the corridor, unsure of the class-rooms to her right, the dark little doors to her left. Then she was at the foot of the stairs, rising dark and worn to one side. To the other, the statue of the school's founder, standing proud and erect on his marble plinth; he who had seen so much, and watched George Quentin die.

She was afraid to turn, but she had to turn; to her right, as the hairs on her neck stood on end and the only sound was the creak of her shoe and her own heart thumping.

'Max!'

A body twirled in the darkness, a long scarf trailing almost to the floor. There was a click and Jacquie felt simultaneously the cold muzzle of a gun behind her ear and her handbag being snatched away. A solitary light floodlit the scene; a hurricane lamp to dispel the darkness.

'Sorry to disappoint you.' Richard Alphedge swung forward, his foot in a stirrup at the end of the long, dangling rope. 'It took quite a long time to rig all this up again, after those bastard coppers took it all down.' He hopped to the floor. 'But this' – he looped the cord around its iron housing on the wall – 'this was *my* job. *I* was the Bell Prefect.' He looked at the two women in front of him. 'Thank you, my dear, for looking after Cissie so nicely for me.'

Something heavy and metal sailed through the air and Alphedge caught it expertly. '*This*' – he held the automatic out straight, its muzzle unmistakably locked on to Jacquie's head – 'is not a film prop.'

'Sorry, Jacquie' – Cissie slipped from behind her to stand alongside her husband – 'but you really shouldn't have meddled, should you?'

'Where's Max?' Alphedge growled.

'I thought he was here.' Jacquie's voice echoed in the stillness of that great hall. The hurricane lamp at Alphedge's feet threw huge, bizarre shadows on the walls. The gun in the man's hand looked to be three feet long.

'He is!' It was Maxwell's voice, echoing and re-echoing round the stairwell.

'Max!' Jacquie had never been so glad to hear a voice in her life.

Alphedge's gun swung right and left. He was gripping it with both hands now, probing it into the dark recesses of the lamp's shadows.

'Sorry I'm late.'

'Show yourself, Max,' Alphedge snarled. They all heard the safety catch click. 'Or the girl dies.' He was closing on Jacquie, pointing the gun at her head again.

'Oh dear, Alphie.' Peter Maxwell sauntered into the light from under the stairwell at the far side, where a bank of lockers had hidden him from view. 'Have you stooped so low? That's a B-feature line if ever I heard one.'

'Don't patronize me, you bastard. Is that the money?' He was talking about the large suitcase by Maxwell's feet.

'It might be,' Maxwell hedged. 'There again, it might be your dirty linen.'

'Cissie,' Alphedge ordered.

The silver-haired woman strode across the tiled floor, scattering dust and spiders.

'Uh-huh.' Alphedge had sensed Maxwell about to move. 'You won't outrun this bullet,' he said.

Maxwell sighed. 'Really, Alphie. This is quite appalling. One clumsy cliché after another. Why don't you nip up on to the roof and shout "Top of the world, Ma"? At least the old Cagney number had some class.'

Cissie retrieved the case and lugged it across to her husband.

'What's all this about?' Jacquie asked. 'Why are you doing all this to get your own money back?'

'Do you want to tell her, Max?' Alphedge called over his shoulder, trying to keep an eye on them both. 'I expect you've worked it out by now.'

'I hadn't.' Maxwell sat down, slowly crossing his legs like some unlikely Buddha, folding his hands in his lap. Jacquie hadn't moved, her head still tilted slightly back away from the muzzle of the PPK that was invading her space, threatening to blow that head away. 'Not until I bumped into two little girls on my way here tonight. By the way, Cissie.' He looked at her with genuine admiration. 'Why you've never got a BAFTA is beyond me. Wasn't she good, Jacquie? Played the part of the loving, increasingly frantic wife to perfection. You, Alphie . . .' Maxwell grimaced in the sharpness of the lamp's light. 'Well, I don't want to be a critic . . .'

'Why not?' Alphedge snarled. 'Everybody else is.'

'Yes, I know. Well, you fell apart too soon. All that shaking, nervous-breakdown, I'm-next stuff. It wasn't only the lady, I thought, who doth protest too much. The threatening voice over the phone was good though.'

'We're still waiting, Max,' Alphedge said. 'And my trigger finger's getting tired.'

Maxwell shook his head, tutting. 'There you go again. Well, well, to cases.' He suddenly linked his fingers and cracked them. Alphedge licked his lips and blinked at the sound. Jacquie hadn't taken her eyes off the gunman's face. What game was Max playing? She'd seen faces like that before – faces of men on the edge whose every nerve was concentrated in that trigger finger like a watch spring.

'Quent and Cret were dead, like old Marley. Jacquie and I had dismissed coincidence, random killings, that sort of thing. That left me – and I knew I hadn't done it' – Maxwell looked his cutest, fluttering his eyelashes at Cissie – 'the Preacher, Ash, Stenhouse or you. Now everybody wanted to believe it was the Preacher because he comes across as barking. You, I take it, knew about his parents?'

'Oh, yes.' Alphedge half smiled. 'But I thought bringing it up might be a tad heavy handed of me and lead to other suspicions elsewhere, so I decided to let someone like Miss Plod here dig that one up.'

'Indeed.' Maxwell beamed. 'No, the Preacher was just *too* likely – the weird garb, the spooky sect. Like a male model from the Serial Killers R Us catalogue. I had to check him out, of course, but he was never really in the running.'

'And then?'

'Stenhouse. Now there's a tragedy you could have played one day, Alphie.'

'Meaning?'

'What a sad case. Opportunities wasted, dreams turned to dust. "He could have been a contender" ' – it was pure Brando – but all he had in the end was a bitter, twisted drunk of a wife who tried to turn him in.'

'What?' Alphedge gave a brittle chuckle. 'For the murders?'

'Yep. No, Stenhouse organized the reunion, Stenhouse had the key — it was just too pat. Unless he was operating a double bluff and I knew he wasn't clever enough for that. So that reduced it to two — you or Ash. And that's why I was late getting here tonight, funnily enough. I gave old Ash a ring, on that mobile you gave me, Jacquie. You see, it was those two schoolgirls I bumped into; those two from Cranton . . .'

Jacquie frowned. 'Cranton?'

'The girls' school down the road,' Maxwell reminded her. 'God, we had some times there, didn't we, Alphie, huh?'

'Oh, yes.' Alphedge's eyes were burning into Jacquie's now, his lips twisted in a hideous half-smile.

'You see, I kept thinking whoever killed Cret Bingham was just covering up for the *real* murder — poor old Quent. It must have been the Sunday we all left the Graveney. You or Cissie let something slip, didn't you? And I'm sure it wasn't you, Cissie, my dear — you're far too good an actress. No, it was Mighty Mouth here.'

'That's enough, Max,' Cissie scolded.

'No,' shouted Alphedge. 'Let him go on. Let him have his moment of glory.'

'You knew Cret had sussed you the moment you said it. You must have followed him, hung around, seen what he did. A long shot, of course, because he could simply have rung the boys — and girls — in blue.'

'I knew he wouldn't do that,' Alphedge snarled. 'When you're an actor, dear boy, you know human nature, read it like a book. Bingham may have been a High Court fucking judge, but he always deferred to you, Maxie. You were the brains of the Seven always, weren't you? I knew he'd go to see you, compare notes, test theories. I just got to him first.'

'With that?' Maxwell pointed to the gun.

Alphedge nodded. 'It's a great persuader.'

'Shame about the pale blue carpet, though, Cissie,' Maxwell murmured. 'What with Cret's blood all over it and all. Still, someone who can rustle up a half a mill ransom money can manage a bit of One Thousand and One for the Axminster, eh?' Maxwell was delighted — it didn't hurt to wink any more. 'I presume it *was* a cricket bat you hit them both with?'

'Oh, yes,' Alphedge assured him. 'After Cret, I burned it in the incinerator.'

'Then you thought, "Why not implicate dear old Maxie?" After all, Cret told you, I assume at gunpoint, that he was coming to see me. So you drove with the body to Tottingleigh woods and dumped it under that old settee on Ryker Hill. Inspired choice that — although you couldn't have known I often take constitutionals there. I thought planting the note was a bit of overkill, though.'

'Note?' Jacquie saw Alphedge falter for a split second, but it wasn't long enough.

'The note you stashed round here somewhere that put me in the frame for George Quentin.'

'You're talking bollocks, Max.' Alphedge sneered. 'You know, perhaps Cret was wrong, perhaps we all were. You're not the brains, you're a rank amateur.'

'Which brings us to Cranton. Quent's death had to be something to do with our time at school — everything else was a red herring. Ash confirmed it when I spoke to him a few moments ago. Cranton, '62. We mentioned it, he and I, at the Graveney on the Friday we arrived. But we were talking at cross-purposes. I was referring to the old dog pinching my girl, as he did at the Cranton ball in '62; he was referring to what he'd caught you and Quent up to.'

'Get it over with, Richard,' Cissie snapped, the strain of the last few minutes beginning to tell.

'Oh, no,' Alphedge growled. 'I want Maxwell to know why he's going to die.'

Slowly, keeping his back to the wall, Maxwell got up. Jacquie blinked. How had he done that from a sitting position? 'Cranton '62,' Maxwell remembered. 'A still and tropic night in the grounds of the school. It was magic, wasn't it, Alphie? There were lights in the trees, our joint orchestras belting out the hits of the year interspersed with the odd waltz. I had a gorgeous girl on my arm. So did Ash . . . And you had George Quentin. Modesty forbids me in mixed company to be graphic as to which parts of your bodies you'd linked, but it sure as hell wasn't your arms, was it?'

'Shoot him, Richard!' Cissie screamed.

Maxwell was walking towards his man, his heart thudding. Alphedge's gun was – what? – two feet from the head of the woman he loved. 'It was all so silly, Alphie,' Maxwell said quietly. 'Oh, I know they were different days and the law was the law then, but Christ, you were kids. We all were. Somebody asked me recently if I knew that Quent was gay. I didn't. I'd forgotten all about Cranton '62, because I didn't see it. It was just gossip at the time, just rumours. We'd all forgotten about it, Alphie, so why?' He pointed at the rope, taut on its housings. 'What in God's name was the point?'

'Point, you imbecile?' Cissie screamed at him. She took one stride and slapped him across the face. Jacquie jumped, but Maxwell rolled with it. 'Quentin was a predatory homosexual. He forced Richard. That appalling night at Cranton, he forced him, had him bent over a tree. It's something people never talk about, isn't it? Male rape – the last taboo.'

'Cissie . . .' Alphedge was shaking his head, the tears streaming down his face.

'He's lived with that ever since. The shame. The disgrace. You say they were different days. Yes, they were. But you say that from today's liberal vantage point. Richard went to pieces from that day. His father disowned him. Don't you remember any of this?'

Maxwell shook his head.

'You smug, conceited bastard,' she growled. 'Richard was raped by that . . . that animal and you didn't even know.'

'It's in here, Max,' Alphedge said quietly, pointing to his

head. 'It has been ever since it happened. I swore one day I'd kill George Quentin. I had dreams of it happening – of him dangling from this rope, *my* rope. Perfect, poetic justice. Cissie knew, of course. There are some things you can't keep from your wife. When I heard from Stenhouse, suggesting the reunion, it was like a gift from God. Unlike the rest of you, I knew exactly where George Quentin lived – and worked. I got Cissie to ring him, to set up a joke. Quent would go to Halliards, not the Graveney, and help me rig up a hanged-man scam to scare the shit out of Stenhouse. It tickled him enormously. The poor, stupid bastard didn't know he was going to his death. Cissie and I, of course, had got to the Graveney early and pinched Stenhouse's key. Then we met Quentin and it was pure, bloody joy. Replacing the key in Stenhouse's pocket over breakfast the next morning was the most difficult thing about it.'

'But why all this?' Jacquie asked. 'This whole ransom non-sense?'

'To get me here,' Maxwell said. 'You knew I'd worry at it, didn't you, Alphie?'

The actor nodded. 'Like some bloody terrier,' he said. 'I thought I'd end it here, now. Where, in a way, it all started.'

'That's all fine and dandy, Alphie.' Maxwell's face still stung from Cissie's slap. 'But you won't make it this time. It was all a bit OTT, wasn't it? A little on the luvvie side, all this. Did you seriously think, with Jacquie around, the police wouldn't be called in to look for you? They're outside now, Jacquie, aren't they?'

Jacquie nodded. 'Ten-man team. Plus DS Rackham. Six of them are marksmen, Richard. One of them will get you. You know it.'

'And Cissie,' Maxwell threw in. 'In the dark, they won't take the chance she isn't armed too. Give it up, old son. It's all over.'

'Oh, no,' growled Alphedge, lining up his aim on Jacquie's jaw. 'It ain't over until the fat lady . . .'

Maxwell didn't give him time to finish the cliché. Dragging

from nowhere his distant memories of the ruck and the maul, he drove his shoulder hard into Alphedge's body. The actor's arm came up and the gun barked in the sharp light, sending a bullet ricocheting against the marble statue. Both men hit the wall beyond and Maxwell rolled clear. Alphedge didn't roll at all, but lay in a heap with his head still upright.

Jacquie moved for the first time in what seemed hours. She kicked the gun away from him and snatched it up, holding it with both hands, aimed first at Alphedge and then at Cissie. The actress was wailing as if in a scene from *Electra*, kneeling beside her husband and cradling his head. Her fingers were bloody in the lamplight.

'The ricochet,' Jacquie said, and fumbled in her pocket for her phone, stabbing out 999.

'Cissie.' Maxwell could see that the man was dead as he crouched next to them both. 'Cissie, you can't help him any more.'

'But I have to,' she blurted. 'Can't you see? He can't help himself. He never could.' And she fell on to Maxwell's chest, crying into his shirt.

At the far end of the corridor a door crashed back. There were shouts, torch beams flashing in all directions. 'Armed police!' a voice barked. 'Put your weapon down and lie on the floor. Face down. Now.'

'Police,' Jacquie called back, throwing Alphedge's gun down with a clatter. 'DC Carpenter, Leighford CID.'

'Christ almighty.' Ben Thomas pushed his way through the flak-jacketed marksmen and stared at her. 'Alphedge?'

Maxwell looked up at him.

'I don't get it, guv.' DS Vernon was at his boss's elbow. 'That note I found . . .'

'*You* found?' Jacquie turned to him. 'Where?'

'Just up there,' Vernon told her. 'First landing, under the skirting board.'

Thomas was checking Alphedge for a pulse. There wasn't

one. Jacquie was looking down at him. 'Who suggested, Sergeant,' she asked, 'that you look there?'

'The DI . . .' Vernon stopped in mid-sentence.

Thomas and Maxwell were kneeling together, staring into each other's eyes. They were both surprised by what happened next. Jacquie Carpenter grabbed Thomas's collar and yanked him upright. She spun him round to face her. 'Are you going to DCI Tyler with this or am I?' she asked. His face said it all.

'Anybody seen my sergeant?' Jacquie asked as the marksmen took Cissie away.

'DS Rackham?' Vernon shuffled a little by the stairwell. He looked at her. 'I'm afraid DS Rackham died this evening, DC Carpenter. An accident in his car. I'm sorry.'

Maxwell's hand flew out to catch Jacquie's.

'Somebody switch that bloody lamp off,' he said.

Captain Soames Gambier Jenyns was placed, smoking his cigar, at the head of C Troop, 13th Light Dragoons, in the diorama on the trestle table in Maxwell's attic. Like the case of Halliards' hanged, he was finished.

Maxwell hung the gold-laced forage cap on its hook and padded down the stairs. When he reached the lounge, the doorbell rang, so he kept on walking. Beyond the swirled pattern of the frosted glass was a face he knew, a face he loved. He let her in, kissing her in the lit hallway.

'How was the funeral?' he asked her.

'Oh, you know,' she said, her head on one side. 'As well as can be expected. He was all right, was Graham Rackham.'

'Yeah.' He hugged her. 'Come on.' And he led her up to the lounge.

It was warm and the lamplight was soft as the November evening settled in. Metternich the cat had vibes about this. There was something in the air, a chemistry that he, feline eunuch that he was, couldn't quite fathom. But he felt, in his own tommish way, a bit of a gooseberry. He looked up at Jacquie, lashed her with his tail as if to say 'Just remember who *really* runs this place', and left, off to the world of the chase and the kill.

'Cocoa?' Maxwell asked her.

She smiled. 'Southern Comfort.'

Maxwell frowned. 'Wait a minute. That's the good stuff.' And he poured for them both.

They touched glasses in the firelight. 'Here's to them all,' Maxwell said. 'To Quent, to Cret, to Ash, to Stenhouse, to the Preacher . . . and to Alphie. He was really the saddest of us all, wasn't he?'

She nodded. Then she put her glass down and relieved him of his. 'No sadness tonight,' she said, and took his hand, leading him to the stairs.

'Do this mean,' he asked her, 'what I think it do?'

'It do!' She smiled at him.

'You know,' he said, switching off the lights as he followed her up, their fingers still twined, 'if this were a novel, what is about to follow would have to be shown, even in this permissive age, as a row of dots. Wouldn't you say?'

She would . . .